ACCLAIM FOR [illegible] PREVIOUS NOVEL, *SEDUCED*

"Four-and-a-half stars! Very sensual…great fun….Sharp and often bawdy repartee only adds to the fire and sexual tension that Britton builds so well….Pamela Britton is well on her way to stardom!"

—***Romantic Times***

"*Seduced* has everything readers crave in historical romance and more. This one is headed for your keeper shelf."

—**Amanda Quick, author of *Slightly Shady***

"Britton's plucky characters keep the story fresh….This delightful tale outshines many romances of its ilk, and the protagonists' spry wit and comic antics will have readers on the floor in stitches….A suspenseful finale."

—***Publishers Weekly***

"Seductive….This story line hooks the audience."

—***Midwest Book Review***

"It isn't easy to write a tale that makes the reader laugh and cry, but Britton succeeds, thanks to her great characters… .A romance of self-acceptance, suspense, and humor, this book will be a hit with fans of Amanda Quick, Lisa Kleypas, and Karen Robards."

—***Booklist* (starred review)**

"What a wickedly amusing and sexy narrative Pamela Britton has woven in her spectacular *Seduced*! It is non-stop entertainment from the most unusual first line to the surprising ending….A hilarious…remarkable book….Hats off to Pamela Britton for an irresistible story!"

—**BookLoons.com**

more…

"I raced through *Seduced.* Sexy, quick-paged, and fun...a superlative read with an ending that is as well set up as it is surprising and left me with tears in my eyes. I eagerly look forward to Ms. Britton's next offering."

—ScribesWorld.com

"A terrific, and surprisingly humorous, romance...well-written...a joy to read. Ms. Britton's special blend of sensuality and humor are sure to win her a loyal following."

—RoadtoRomance.dhs.org

"Well-written dialogue....I really enjoyed this story....Ms. Britton is truly a wonderful writer. Do yourself a favor and become *Seduced*!"

—ARomanceReview.com

ALSO BY PAMELA BRITTON

Seduced

Tempted

PAMELA BRITTON

WARNER BOOKS

An AOL Time Warner Company

WARNER BOOKS EDITION

Cover design by Diane Luger
Cover art by Franco Accornero
Hand lettering by David Gatti
Book design by Giorgetta Bell McRee

Warner Books, Inc.
1271 Avenue of the Americas
New York, NY 10020

Visit our Web site at www.twbookmark.com

An AOL Time Warner Company

Printed in the United States of America

First Paperback Printing: January 2004

10 9 8 7 6 5 4 3 2 1

For the one hundred Breyer model horses.
For getting me the real thing when the time came.
For never making me sell my horse when I landed atop a fence instead of on the other side of one.
For letting me drive the Lancia during high school.
For saying all that mattered was that I was OK when I totaled it.
For always being Pam's Pop and P.J.'s Mom.
For the best Christmases in the world.
For making Codi's Christmases just as special.
For all the things you did, all the things you continue to do, and all the things you are to me . . .
this one's for you
Mom and Dad; I love you.

Acknowledgments

I don't think any book I've written hasn't owed some thanks to certain behind-the-scenes individuals. This book owes thanks to Patrick Lynch who helped shed light on English law enforcement and court trials in the shires of England. And to the writers of the *1811 Dictionary of the Vulgar Tongue* which gave color to my heroine's speech.

Thanks also goes to my Ya-Ya sisters: Leanne Banks, for the hours of phone therapy. Cherry Adair, for the *years* of therapy (and the loan of a hotel room so I could finish this book). And Jennifer Skullestad for telling me I couldn't tie the child up (darn). And to the gals at Delphi who are always willing to invoke the HoF on my behalf. You're the best, guys.

My editor, Karen Kosztolnyik, who understands my writing to the point that I'm delirious with joy that we're working together. Your smiley faces make my day.

Lastly, as always, to my husband Michael who never ceases to amaze me with his understanding and patience of a writer's psyche and who loves me to death, even when I'm on a crazy deadline. I <3 U.

Dear Reader:

In 1794 the Marquis of Wellesley married Hyacinthe Roland, his mistress.

In 1871, Richard Jackson was made a baronet, right after he married *his* mistress.

In 1847 the second duke of Cambridge, an heir to the throne of England, married Louisa Fairbrother, an actress, in defiance of the Royal Marriage Act. He remained faithful to his wife until his dying day.

Prologue

It all started in the late sixteenth century . . . or perhaps even before that. History is a fickle creature and facts ofttimes get blurred, but throughout the ages it has always been reported that the dukes of Wainridge were scoundrels. Licentious, disreputable scoundrels.

Wicked Wainridge was what they called the first duke, and not because of a penchant for sinning. Wherever he rode mothers would clutch young daughters to their bosoms, whispering, "Best behave, my sweet, or Wicked Wainridge will ride off with ye." And to be sure, there was a good possibility of exactly that, for the duke's sexual appetite was also rumored to be legendary.

But it was the second duke of Wainridge that truly cemented the family's name. In his lifetime he absconded with three heiresses, two married ladies (one of whom stayed with him after her release) and a woman rumored to have been on her way to becoming a nun, but who . . . um, changed her mind.

"Scandalous," whispered the people of that time.

"Outrageous," murmured others.

And so it began. For generations to come Wainridge men followed in the footsteps of the first and second dukes. Wicked Wainridge was what they were always called. By the end of the fifth duke's life, they were legends. Licentious legends to be sure, but legends nonetheless.

To this wondrous reputation the heir to the eighth duke was born.

George Alexander Essex Drummond didn't want to be a rake. Indeed, from an early age the young Alexander behaved in a manner contrary to that of previous heirs. Instead of playing an imaginary game of chase the maid, he played chase the villain, or pirate, or any other type of miscreant. Never once did he pinch a member of the female staff. Never once did he try to seduce his governess (though the old duke hired the comeliest). Lord, much to his father's dismay, he didn't lose his virginity until he was fifteen.

"Good lord," the duke railed. "You don't like"—horrors—"*males*?" he asked Alex one day.

Alas, no, his son reassured him, for he definitely preferred women, just not . . . so many.

That allayed the duke's fears only marginally, for as his son became older, it became patently obvious that he preferred cutters over copulation.

Alex tried to buy a commission in the Navy. His father forbade it.

He tried to become a privateer. His father caught wind of that, too.

In the end, they settled upon a compromise. The young heir was allowed to work for the Customs Board chasing smugglers, a job the old duke considered harmless since confrontations were rare, but was, for a young lad, fabulously exciting.

The young marquis thrived.

Over the years, he worked his way up to revenue commander, and a damn fine one at that. He had a knack for knowing what night a ship would sail, an instinct for knowing where to place his own Revenue Cutter so that he could catch that smuggler in the act.

Only one thing marred his happiness. No matter what he did, no matter how well he performed, his family's licentious reputation preceded him.

Always.

And so in the winter of 1816, the marquis—who was one and thirty years by now—found himself sent to the small town of Hollowbrook, a quaint coastal community with a not-so-quaint habit of avoiding revenue on imported goods.

Lord Warrick entered town like King David entered Jerusalem: Tall, proud, lacking only the low-toned hum of reverent voices chanting behind him in welcome.

The smugglers should have been impressed. And they might have been, too . . . if Lord Warrick's family history hadn't been recalled. Indeed, they took to calling him Wicked Warrick in honor of his illustrious heritage. There was even a maid or two who tried to see if there was any truth to the rumors, much to Alex's dismay.

And so the marquis had something to prove. Well, he'd always had something to prove, which might explain why he'd become so compulsive about the way he ran his ship—and his life—like a clock maker ran his timepieces: everything in its place, every gear working in perfect order. It fair drove his staff and crew mad.

A week after his lordship began sailing Hollowbrook's coast, the first arrest was made. A few days later, yet another one. And three days after that, another one still.

The townspeople went a little mad. Here was an end to their livelihood. No more fortunes would be made, not that the townspeople were swimming in blunt. No, indeed. They sought only to put food on the table. To clothe their children. To keep a roof over their heads.

For many, all that disappeared the day the marquis of Warrick sailed into Hollowbrook's harbor.

And so we come to the end of our tale, though the beginning of another, for it is said that nothing angers a man more than losing his livelihood. Lord Warrick decimated Hollowbrook. That, it could be reasoned, was why they decided to make him pay.

'Twas Tobias Brown, head smuggler, and a man who'd just barely escaped Lord Warrick, who was put in charge of the project. But though he tried and tried to come up with a satisfactory plan, it all boiled down to one thing: Who had access to his lordship? Well, perhaps two things, for what would they do to his lordship if they *did* have access? Matters weren't helped by the fact that Lord Warrick's duties took him up and down the coast, his reputation such that more than one Custom House requested his aid.

And then one fine spring day someone spied an ad in the *London Gazette,* and wouldn't you know it, the person advertising for a position was the very lord they plotted against?

HEAD NURSE NEEDED.

Must have experience with difficult children.
Good character, etc. etc. Marquis of Warrick, 106,
Manderly Street, London.

Aha, Tobias Brown thought. Here was a chance to infiltrate the enemy lair. Here was an opportunity to find an appropriate means of revenge, to perhaps even start the smuggling ring again; for if they could track his lordship's moves, they would be able to gauge when and where to land contraband.

But who would infiltrate his lordship's home?

Who, indeed . . .

"Oh, mum, so brave, you are," the maid said, her eyes

Part One

Mary, Mary, quite contrary,
How does your garden grow?
With silver bells and cockle shells,
And pretty maids all in a row.

Tommy Thumb's Pretty Song Book,
c. 1744

Chapter One

No red cape.

No pitchfork.

No horns.

All in all Mary Brown Callahan would say that the Devil Marquis of Warrick didn't look a thing like she expected.

Oddly enough, she felt disappointment. Of course, she couldn't see his lordship all that well what with him sitting upon a bleedin' throne of a chair behind his bleedin' monstrosity of a desk.

"Please have a seat," he said without looking up, his eyes firmly fixed upon a document before him, a clock on a mantel behind him *tick-tick-ticking* in an annoyingly sterile way. Somewhere off in the distance another clock chimed the quarter hour, the *bong-ding-dong-dong* finding its way into the room. Muted sunlight from the right reflected off the flawless, polished perfection of his desk. The ink-blotter lay exactly square, almost as if someone had used a measuring tape to place it. Papers were stacked at perfect right angles. A fragrant, rather obnoxious-smelling truss of red roses and rosemary squatted in a fat vase. It made Mary long to reach forward and mess it all up.

Instead, she took a seat, nearly yelping when the plush

blue velvet did its best to swallow her like she were Jonah and the chair a whale. She jerked forward, looking up to see if his lordship had noticed. No. The swell were still engrossed in his work. Hmph.

She waited for him. Then waited some more. Finally, she began to tap her foot impatiently, her toe ticking on the floor in time with the clock . . . quite a merry beat when one got into the tapping of it.

The scratching of his quill abruptly stopped. His head slowly lifted.

Two things hit Mary at once. One, Alexander Drummond, Marquis of Warrick, had the prettiest eyes she'd ever seen, blue they were, the color of a seashell when you turned it upside down.

Two, he was not the ugly ogre she'd been expecting, which just went to show a body shouldn't believe all the things that are said, especially when those words came from her silly baboon of a father, Tobias Brown.

His lordship blinked at her, frowned, then said, "I'll be with you in just a moment," slowly and succinctly—as if she had a whole hide of wool in her ears—before going back to work.

She narrowed her eyes. Would he now? *Well la-de-da.* His high-and-mightiness were right full of himself, wasn't he, in his fitted jacket made of a black wool woven so tight, the fabric looked as shiny and as soft as a well-bred horse's coat. His cravat wasn't tied as intricately as some of those she'd seen—those worn by the dandies who strolled up and down Bond Street with silver-tipped walking sticks that they jabbed into the ground like the very earth offended them. No, his lordship's cravat was simply tied, seeming to cup the chin of what was a very handsome face. No sense in denying it.

Nothing slug-faced about it, which was how most lords looked, to her mind at least. This cull had a chin that was almost square, his nose not at all large and aquiline, but rather narrow and—could it be—a bit crooked? Above the eyes that she'd noted before sprang midnight black hair with strands of gray that peppered the bulk of it, those strands pulled back in a queue, the whole combining to form a face that would make a bold woman stare and a shy woman blush.

"Did your daughter give you that?" she found herself asking, more because she wanted to look into his extraordinary face again, rather than down the edge of it.

And so once again he looked up. His quill stopped its annoying scratch, the black jacket he wore tightening as he straightened. Thick, very masculine brows lowered. "I beg your pardon?"

"The gray hair," she said, pointing with a gloved hand at his hair, and then motioning to her own carrots in case he needed further clarification.

And now those black brows lifted. "As a matter of fact, no. 'Tis a genetic trait inherited from my father. All Drummond men have it."

She pursed her lips, liking the way his voice sounded. Low and deep and perfectly controlled, as if each syllable was measured and weighed before let loose on the world. "Only the men? What would you do if a woman were born with it? Strangle the lass?"

His lips parted. His jaw dropped, but he was only struck all-a-mort for a moment. Too bad.

"No, Mrs. . . ." He looked down, his white cravat all but poking him in the chin as he pulled sheets of papers toward him. She recognized them as the ones John Lasker had forged. John had the best penmanship in

Hollowbrook. "Mrs. Callahan. We do not shoot our children."

Got his ballocks in a press, hadn't she? Hah. She almost smiled.

"And," he continued, "Since it would appear as if you're determined to interrupt me, I suppose we should just begin the interview for the position. That way, you can be on your way, and I can return to my work."

Mary perked up. At last. Two, maybe three minutes and she'd be out of his lordship's home. For one thing Mary Callahan didn't want, and that was to nurse his daughter. No, indeed. She'd sooner let those fancy gents what practiced with their pistols down by the Thames use her for target practice. She'd only come to appease her monkey-brained father, a man who'd gone a wee bit crackers with his plot of revenge against the marquis. (Although now that she'd met the man, she could well understand her father's aversion to the cull.) No, indeed. She'd do everything in her power to thwart that sapskulled fool, that she silently vowed. And then she'd return to her real job, which was a fair way from St. James Square.

"I see you're from Wellburn, Mrs. Callahan."

She leaned forward, placing an arm nonchalantly on his desk as she pretended to look at the papers. He smelled nice, almost like cinnamon, which made her wonder if he'd used the spice in that fancy coffee of his, the one whose smell she could still catch if she inhaled deeply enough, which she did, which he must have heard because his brows lifted again. Next he looked at her arm, up at her, then at the arm again. Pointedly.

"Is that wha' it says?" she asked, not removing her elbow, and not trying to smooth her Cockney accent, something she could do, if she had a mind to. She tilted her head, and Lord knows why, but when their gazes met, she smiled. Mary Callahan had a bonny smile. Truth be told, she had a lot of bonny traits—or so she'd been told. Fine green eyes. Dimples. And an endearing way of looking at a man from beneath her thick lashes, not that there was any reason to look up at his lordship that way.

The marquis, however, didn't appear fazed. "You're not from Wellburn?" he asked, his face blank.

He had the composure of a corpse.

"If that's what it says, then I suppose I am." She leaned back, noticing that his eyes darted down a second. Quickly. As if he'd glanced at her breasts, found them interesting, then looked away again because he couldn't believe he'd done something so common. They were a fine, ripe bushel, though she was surprised his lordship here would be noticing. She'd have thought that kind of thing was beneath his hoity-toity nose.

"You suppose?"

She shrugged, one of the seams in the dress Fanny Goodwin had sewn popping a bit at the shoulder. It was blue with darker blue ribbon trimming the demure, long sleeves, and yet there was nothing demure about it. The bloody thing was sewn in such a way as to lift her breasts and hold them out for his lordship's inspection like they were pudding molds sent up from the kitchen just to suit his taste. And perhaps they did for she could have sworn he glanced down again, though he covered it under the guise of moving his gaze to his papers again.

"Been travelin' a lot," she said. "Hard to keep track."

"I see." And the words were clipped out: I. See. Gritted teeth. Stiff jaw. Bayonet up his backside.

He kept his gaze on the papers. "Do you enjoy being a nurse, Mrs. Callahan?"

"No."

His head snapped up again. He was going to get a bleedin' neck ache if he kept that up. Up. Down. Up. Down.

"No?"

She shook her head. "Can't stand children."

She had the rum-eyed pleasure of seeing his mouth drop open. "But it says here you love them."

"Who said that?" she asked, and she really was curious. Fineas Blackwell, her father's longtime chum, must have made John write that down. He had a wicked sense of humor, and saying she liked children was laughable indeed.

"Mrs. Thistlewillow."

That explained it. "Mrs. Thistlewillow would claim Beelzebub loved children."

His lordship had fine teeth, she noticed. And she had occasion to study them because his mouth hung open again. Not a rotted one in the lot.

"Mrs. Callahan. I get the feeling that you have not read your references."

She snorted. Couldn't help it. She'd no intention of getting hired for the job, so why read forged references? "I make a point not to read what others say about me." And she was bloody proud of that fact. She might be a poor smuggler's daughter. She might be a wee speck on his lordship's boot heel, but Mary Callahan—lately of the Royal Circus—stood on her own two feet . . . literally as the case may be. Damn the rest of the world.

He shook his head, picked up her references, then tapped the edges of the papers on the desk as he said,

"Mrs. Callahan. Thank you for coming, but it appears as if a mistake has been ma—"

"Papa!"

Mary's arse fair puckered to the chair. Blimey, what a screech. The door swung open with a resounding boom that rocked all around it, including her eardrums. She swiveled toward the door. At least, she tried to. The bloody chair held her backside down like a Scottish bog.

"Papa, Simms says you're interviewing another nurse."

A little girl of about eight ran by, her hair streaming behind her. Black it was, and in sore need of a good brushing. She landed in a puppyish jumble of arms and legs in her father's embrace, dust motes circling like buzzards in her wake. "I don't want a nurse. I *told* you that."

Ah. The little termagant herself.

Mary held her breath as she waited for his lordship to look up, to dismiss her, which he'd obviously been about to do before the hellion had come in.

"Gabby," the marquis said. "Be polite and say how do you do to Mrs. Callahan."

Polite? Bugger it. Mary wanted to *leave*.

"No," the little girl snapped.

"Do it, Gabby. Now."

The little girl drew back, her face only inches away from her father's. They were practically nose-to-nose, the marquis' handsome, arrogant face stern and disapproving. Lord, the man could scare kids on All Hallows' Eve with a look like that.

The bantling wiggled on his lap. Then her face turned resigned. She shimmied down, landing with that soft *shush* of leather soles on fine carpet. The gray dress looked stained with juice, Mary noted, her black slippers that peeked out beneath white petticoats smudged with dirt. But she was a cute little moppet with her father's startling blue eyes and dark, curly hair that rustled as she moved.

"How do you do," she said, dropping into a curtsy that somehow seemed, well, *mocking*. And then she rose, looked sideways out of her eyes, and that cute little moppet with the pretty blue eyes stuck out her tongue.

Mary stiffened.

And that seemed to be the reaction wanted for the hellion gave her a smug smile.

Mary's eyes narrowed. Never one to be gotten the best of, especially by some pug-nosed whelp, she stuck her tongue out, too.

"Papa," the little girl breathed without missing a beat. "Did you see that? She stuck her tongue out at me."

Mary looked up at the marquis. What? Wait a bleedin'—

"Gabby," he said. "I know well and good that you stuck your tongue out first. Apologize to Mrs. Callahan immediately."

"No," the little girl snapped, her tiny hands fisting by her sides.

"Do it," he ordered.

"No," she yelled.

Mary covered her ears. "Land's alive, m'lord. Don't argue with her. I'll lose me hearing. 'Tis plain as carriage wheels that she's not going to apologize."

For the second time that day—the first being the time he'd caught his first glimpse of the stunning Mrs. Callahan—Alexander Drummond, marquis of Warrick, felt speechless. It defied belief, the things that kept coming out of the nurse's mouth. Simply *defied*.

"I beg your pardon?"

She arched red brows, and was it his imagination, or did those pretty green eyes of hers narrow?

"She's not going to apologize. What's more, I don't want her bloomin' apology. Fact is, I don't want to be her nurse, either."

Alex thought he'd misheard her again, was even tempted to lift a finger to his ear to clean it out in the event there was something wrong there, but then Gabby said, "Good. Leave," verifying that the unexpected words had, indeed, been correctly deciphered.

"I will," she answered right back, rising from her chair.

"Sit down," Alex ordered. Granted, a minute ago he'd been about to tell the outspoken lady to leave. Now, oddly, he found himself taking her side.

"Please," he added when—good lord—the woman looked ready to defy him.

She slowly sat, but she didn't look too pleased about it.

"Gabby, you may leave. I will speak with you upstairs."

His daughter's lips pressed together, something he knew from experience meant a tantrum. "I'm a bastard," she yelled in a last-ditch attempt to put the nurse off.

Alex winced. He knew the child was inordinately sensitive to the fact that her mother had left her on his doorstep. He could sympathize, still incensed himself that a woman could do such a thing.

He looked at Mrs. Callahan to gauge her reaction, but she merely lifted a brow. "Are you now?"

"I am."

"Is that the excuse you use for your poor manners?"

Gabby sucked in a breath. "Did you hear that, father? She said I have poor manners."

"Well, you do," Mrs. Callahan said.

"Do not."

The nurse snorted, the inelegant sound somehow seeming to fit the redoubtable nurse perfectly. "You don't even know how to curtsy properly."

"Do, too."

"Not by the looks of the one you just gave me."

To Alex's absolute and utter shock, his obstinate daughter took a step back, straightened, and then gave the nurse a curtsy that would have done her mother proud . . . if she'd had one.

"There," she said upon straightening.

Mrs. Callahan wrinkled her tilted nose. "Hmm. I suppose that was a *wee* bit better, but no proper little girl disobeys her elders."

Gabby glared. So did the nurse.

Alex decided he'd had enough.

"Gabby, go to your room."

His daughter opened her mouth to give her standard protest. But an odd thing happened. He saw her stiffen again. Saw her clench her fists. Saw her straighten. "As you wish, Papa."

Alex just about fell off his chair.

She turned, gave him a quick, *perfect* curtsy, nodded to Mrs. Callahan—who, of all things, stuck her tongue out again—then left.

Silence dawned. Alex could only stare.

"If that's the way she behaves, 'tis a wonder someone hasn't given your daughter a basting." Her full lips pressed together. "Fair wanted to do it meself."

He blinked, found himself clearing his throat. "Mrs. Callahan, how long, exactly, have you been a nurse?"

Her face lost some of its composure. She straightened much the way Gabby had straightened a moment ago. "Long enough, m'lord," she answered with a tilt to her lively little chin and a challenging sparkle in her eye.

"How long?" he asked again.

"Long enough to know you must be desperate indeed for someone to fill this post if I'm still sitting here."

He drew back, once again startled by her frankness.

But the way she'd challenged Gabby into behaving . . .

It was a remarkable technique. "Where did you learn to handle children that way?"

"Handle 'em like what?"

"So expertly."

She snorted, her pretty eyes glowing like a wick. And, yes, she was very striking although he was hard pressed to understand why he thought so. He was never very fond of red hair. And this hair looked to be rather unruly what with its ringlets and waves, for all that it was pulled up off her face in a bun. And yet there was something about her that caught his attention. A sort of vivaciousness that made him think she was laughing at him . . . or at the world. She *glowed*, he realized.

"It's the way I raised me younger brothers. Four of them I have, though they're all grown now. I assume what works for the poorer classes works for the nobility, too."

Rather a pert answer, but he was a reasonable enough man to admit there might be some truth to her words. He stared at her for a second longer, a bit disbelieving that he was actually contemplating the idea of hiring her. She disliked children. Well, he knew a blacksmith that didn't like horses, but he was still a fine farrier.

"Let me explain Gabby's unusual circumstances."

Was it his imagination, or did she actually look impatient? No. That couldn't be. And yet he couldn't dismiss the idea for she seemed rather vexed. It was there in the way she flung herself back in her seat, her breasts jiggling in a way that drew his eye. Actually, the whole package drew his eyes—

"Ahem. Yes. She is my daughter, that I do not deny," he said, feeling his skin redden, for he was almost certain she'd caught him staring. Again. "She was left on my doorstep for me to raise when she was only a week old. I've done my best for her, but my duties as a Revenue Commander ofttimes take me away. As such she has grown up rather independent and strong-willed. I try to compensate for her difficult nature by paying her nurses a pound a week."

Her eyes clearly said, *A pound a week?*

He nodded, her reaction making him feel a bit more in control. She was a servant. Driven by money. They all were. "If you take the job, and I am in no way convinced you are right for it yet, you will receive one pound a week for your troubles, a great deal of money as I'm sure you know. It is nearly as much as my butler makes."

"A pound a week," she whispered, her whole expression undergoing a change. "And all I need do is nurse the bantling?"

"Indeed, however, your response to my earlier question puzzles me. If you do not like children, why do you nurse them?"

She stared at him hard, and he had the oddest feeling

she was mulling over something. "I was lying," she said at last.

"I beg your pardon?"

She nodded, her eyes having lost some of their earlier impatience. "I'd decided on my way here that I didn't want the job. I ain't never worked for no nobleman before and I didn't want to start."

He felt his brow wrinkle in surprise. "Then why did you apply for the job?"

She stared at him for a moment. "My father made me do it."

His brows lifted. Well, he could certainly understand one's father's influence on one's life. "I see. So you decided to botch the interview."

"Yes, sir. I mean, m'lord."

"But now you've changed your mind. Because of the money?"

"Mayhap."

"Mayhap. What do you mean mayhap?"

"Convince me."

"Convince you—" He felt words dam up his throat so that he had to cough to dispel them. "Mrs. Callahan, I can hardly hope to convince you if you yourself are uncertain about the job."

"Are you a kind master?"

He jerked in his seat. "Well," he huffed. "I should hope so—"

"Do you chase the maids?"

"I *beg* your pardon."

"Your look of outrage is answer enough."

"Mrs. Callahan—"

She held up a gloved hand. *A gloved hand.* "Now,

now. Don't go all smarmy-faced on me. A body needs to be certain of a few things before they say yes . . . or no."

"And *are* you saying no?"

"No."

"No, you do not want the job? Or no, you are not saying no?"

"No, I'm not saying no. Gracious, you're making me head spin."

"And you mine, for it is *I* who should be asking the questions."

"Then ask."

She shrugged in a dismissive way. Unbelievable.

"I'm waiting," she said when he didn't immediately respond.

He almost told her to leave right then, but something about the way she stood up to him made him hold his tongue. Gabby needed a stern hand and he had a feeling Mrs. Callahan would provide exactly that. Perhaps too firm. "Have you ever struck a child before?" he asked to allay that fear.

"Been tempted to, but no."

He lifted a brow. "I see. And you've worked with difficult children before?"

"Only me father."

The words almost shocked an exclamation from him. Gracious. How common. "That is not the kind of child I had in mind."

"Well then, the answer is no."

"How about difficult people?" He held up his hand quickly. "Aside from your father."

She pursed her lips in thought. "Old man Mathison were a real handful," she finally said. "Used to hit me in the backside with a slingshot whenever he'd catch me crossing his field. Hurt like the dickens, it did, the old cove."

He stared across at her unblinkingly, a part of him unbelievably wanting to laugh.

Still . . .

He looked back down at her résumé, reviewing her qualifications. There could be no doubt that she had the experience necessary for the job. And the way she'd handled Gabby . . .

"And where is Mr. Callahan?"

"Dead."

Marvelous. "My condolences," he said instead.

Sleep. It must be that he needed sleep. But before that, he needed to hire her as his daughter's nurse.

Ah, but was *he about to hire her?*

He thought it over for a few minutes longer. Truly, according to her references, she was the best candidate he'd interviewed so far. Granted, he seemed to be a bit attracted to her.

A bit?

Yes, a bit, but that he could contain. After all, he would never be so common as to seduce a member of his staff. And yet it was still a few more moments before he arrived at a decision, the redoubtable Mrs. Callahan once again tapping her foot as she stared at his bookshelves, her tongue clucking in her mouth.

"I shall give you a trial," he said at last. The clucking stopped.

You're mad, Alex.

"Two weeks, at the end of which we shall evaluate your performance. Of course, that is assuming you are still interested in the position?"

She looked at him again, eyes narrowed. "A pound a week?" she reiterated.

"Nearly fifty pounds per annum."

"And all I have to do is keep an eye on the hellion? Feed her? Dress her?"

"That is, I believe, rather the point of being a nurse."

She still didn't jump at the offer, not that he was surprised given her earlier recalcitrance. Then she did something odd. Rather, something more odd than what she'd done before. She scrunched her face, blinked a few times, then slowly nodded. When she straightened, Alex felt a surprising stab of hope.

"I'll take it," she finally said.

"Very good. When can you start?"

"When do you want me to start?"

"Today."

"*Today*?"

"If your affairs are so in order."

"But I—"

"If not, next week will be just as well."

She blinked, stared at him for a long moment, then said, "I'll start today."

"Good," he said, rising. "I'll have Mrs. Grimes show you to your room."

Chapter Two

She was a feather head. A chaw-bacon. A regular chuckleheaded dummy.

Nurse the child, indeed.

What the devil had she been thinking? She should have told him no, like she'd planned.

"Right this way," said a chicken-breasted housekeeper who'd introduced herself as "Mrs. Grimes," with the unspoken "Queen of the household," and "*La-de-da,* aren't I a special one?" following her words.

Queen of bloody Bedlam, if Mary didn't miss her guess, for as she climbed the stairs she realized not a sound stirred within the house, which was bleedin' odd given the fact that there was a child here somewhere. A house should have sounds. Creak some when you stepped on the floors. Smell a bit. Have stains on the carpet. Only these floors were covered with spotless plush rugs, the kind that cost more than a fisherman made in twenty years and that your feet sank into with a soft sigh. She knew this for a fact because there was a hole in the bottom of her right boot and what she could feel through that hole felt like satin clouds. She lost herself in the feel of it for a moment until the same clock as before suddenly struck the hour, scaring Mary nearly half to death with its *ding-dong-bong-bong* and then loud *Bong. Bong. Bong.*

"The home was built without servants' stairs, which is most troublesome at times," the housekeeper explained, and her voice had that odd quality the elderly sometimes got. It wobbled like she couldn't control the amount of air she expelled through her throat. "If you run into any of his lordship's guests, or his lordship himself, you are to keep your head down. Do not make eye contact."

"Turn me into a pillar of salt if I do?" Mary mumbled under her breath.

Mrs. Grimes paused mid-step. Mary nearly ran *smack* into her iron stiff back. Ach. She'd likely get stuck by brambles.

"His lordship said you were an outspoken miss."

She'd heard her? "Did 'e now?" And why did her heart suddenly begin to pound in a peculiar way as she waited for the woman to expand on the comment?

Mrs. Grimes nodded, her nose pinching together in the oddest way. There was a wee crick in that nose, making Mary wonder if someone might not have lost patience with the lady once and bashed her face in. She wore a gray gown that made her complexion look unhealthy and that turned her blue eyes the color of cheese mold. She wasn't a pretty lady with her angular face and too thin frame. Mary supposed that might account for her sour disposition. It often did.

"And did he not say anything else?" she asked before realizing she shouldn't care what he thought of her.

"No," Mrs. Grimes said firmly. "Only that you will attend your charge at each meal and take her out for air and exercise on a daily basis. And to that I will add that your position in the household will be below that of myself and of Simms, our butler, and, of course, the governess, when one is hired."

Mary lifted a brow; the woman stared down at her like she were a fancy mort come to steal his lordship's virtue . . . as if such a thing were possible. "Don't worry none, Mrs. Grimes. I won't be getting airs above meself." Nor seduce the lord and master.

With an arch look, the lady said, "See that you don't," and it came out sounding *doh-hont.* She turned and led her up another flight of stairs, down a narrow corridor with multiple doors on either side that Mary thought must be the family quarters, then up yet another flight. "Servants' quarters," she explained, stopping on the top floor. "Your room is the last door on the left."

And without another word, the woman turned and shuffled back down the stairs.

"Hmph," Mary said, shifting her satchel into her other hand as she took a deep breath of stale air. "Nice ta meet you, too."

Resisting the urge to stick out her tongue, she headed toward her room, the whole morning sticking in her mind like the sting of a burr's needle. Weren't just his lordship what was full of himself, but the whole bleedin' household.

She'd almost convinced herself to leave, but then she opened the door to her bedroom.

Blimey, she'd died and gone to heaven.

Her very own bed sat near the middle of a wall. A real bed, not a straw-filled bag of barnacles that she'd been sleeping on lately. She went over to it, sitting down upon the edge, sighing at the way her backside sank into it.

Feathers. It were a feather-filled mattress. Lord love a duck (or perhaps not . . . since it was likely a duck's feathers she sat upon), she'd heard about such luxuries, but never expected to actually sleep upon one. That were reserved for the nobility, which she supposed she was, well, not directly, but now that she worked for one, she obviously shared the wealth.

She got up, slowly spinning around. Light, lovely, soft rays of sunshine washed in through a tall, paned window to her right. How she'd wished these past years for a room with windows. Even a tiny one. Alas, she'd never had that luxury. Until now.

Then she saw the brick mantel to her right.

"Coo, me own fireplace, too."

Well, that settled it. No more blue toes in the morning.

Then her eyes caught on a letter on that mantel, the piece of parchment folded up with the words TO THE NEW NURSE scrawled on the outside.

Mary set her satchel down and plucked it from its perch, opening it a second later.

Dear New Nurse, it said.

Leave.

Leave now.

Do not be tempted by the money.

You will end up in Bedlam if you stay and nurse the child.

Leave.

Leave, leave, leave.

The Old Nurse

Mary's brows lifted as she read the words. "Hmph," she mused. "Not very promising."

A scratch at the window interrupted. Mary turned,

brows lifting once again as she said, "Lord above. How the devil did *you* find me here?"

Abu, her pet monkey, stared back at her with wide, monkey eyes, the color of which suddenly reminded her of the color of his lordship's desk downstairs. Black brows set into white fur with a pink-skinned face made him look almost human as he stared inside the room. Once he realized she'd spotted him, his small body suddenly bounced up and down like a rabbit with springs on his feet.

"Silly mite, you'll fall if you don't watch yourself."

He seemed to understand her words, for he stilled, a wide, monkey smile that never failed to amuse Mary spreading across his face. And in a world where smiles were all too rare, she put up with the monkey's temper and mischievous nature.

She went to the window, opening it. "Come here, imp."

The monkey needed no second invitation. Little, almost human hands reached for her, his frog-like legs launching at her. In the blink of an eye, he sat on her left shoulder, question mark tail wrapped around her neck, his little throat *clickity-clickity-clicking* as his furry, white chest expanded and contracted in excitement.

"Really now?" she pretended a conversation. "Oh, I agree. He *is* a pompous windbag, he is. Did you see the way he looked me up and down? I thought myself a bleedin' beggar woman for half a second. Thinks he's royalty, he does. Well, I suppose he is, in a blue-blooded sort of way, for he *is* heir to a dukedom. And I'm going to have to put up with his fussy nonsense, all thanks to me scaly dad." Although truth be told, 'twas her own greed what got her in trouble.

The monkey nodded, his rust-colored eyes blinking into her own. The wee little thing had more brains than the man what sired her, that was for certain.

"How did you find me up here?" she asked him, scratching behind his human ears, a favorite spot. "You were supposed to wait until I could let you in, silly spider, though I don't blame you for not wanting to wait outside. Busy that street is with all those swells rattling up and down the road, their tigers and grooms hanging off the backside like barnacles on a piece of plank. I'm surprised they don't all crash into each other—"

Abu flung himself away.

"Who in heaven's name are you talking to?"

Mary jumped like a squirrel hit by a peanut. Alexander Drummond, his high and mighty marquis-ship. Or lordship. Or what ever they called him, stood in the doorway, looking as pompous and full of himself as that caricature she had seen of *A Dandy* hanging down on Fleet Street.

"What in the blue-blooded blazes do *you* want?"

He jerked as if her words had clapped him across the face. "I *beg* your pardon?"

Only then did Mary realize her welcome could hardly be called cordial, not to mention, very subservient. "Oh my goodness, m'lord, I thought you were someone else," she improvised, glancing around for Abu who cowered behind the door. "Beg your pardon. What can I do for you, m'lord?"

She had a belly-aching feeling that he saw right through her lies for his eyes narrowed, his mouth pressing together before he said, "I came to see how you liked your room," which was accompanied by a suspicious stare.

Came to see how she—

Why, who'd have thought? She almost softened toward him then. Almost, because right at that moment, that very moment, she saw Abu start heading toward her.

Oh, Lord.

The door shielded him from the man's view, but not Mary's. His little simian lips contorted and flexed as he made faces at her, not that the cull could see. Abu's tongue darted out, Mary knowing such a gesture could only mean one thing, and one sound.

"Don't," she cried before he could make the rude noise.

Abu and the marquis froze.

Mary fixed her gaze on the marquis, smiling to cover the sharpness of her tone.

He looked utterly bewildered. "Don't what?"

Good question.

"Don't—" She searched for something to say, scratching at her hair, and the tight bun. "I don't know how to thank you for such fine quarters."

He drew himself up. "Oh." But then he looked perplexed again. "You're quite welcome."

And then Abu leapt toward her nightstand.

"No," she cried, only to look at the marquis. His eyes had gone quite owlish. "N . . . no doubt you say that to all your new servants."

He blinked. So did Abu, her pet still shielded from his lordship's view—thank the lord above. And then Abu's attention caught on the porcelain washbasin laid upon the stand.

"Indeed," the marquis repeated.

Abu moved to pick up the basin.

"No, no, no," she said hurriedly, stamping a foot in

Abu's direction. Her pet stopped. She looked at the marquis. "Is that all, m'lord?"

He looked at her oddly. "Actually, no." He blinked a few more times, shook his head a bit, then said, "My daughter is awaiting you in the nursery. I thought I'd show you the way."

"Excellent." She rushed past the startled Abu and directly at the marquis, who also looked startled. She slammed the door behind her, and then headed down the hall.

"Mrs. Callahan."

She stopped, turned back to him.

"We need to go this way."

"Oh," she said, staring up at him. And if she were honest with herself, which she always tried to be, he had nice eyes. Kind, even. Mary always said a body could tell a lot by a person's eyes. People were like animals in that way. Soft and warm meant you could trust a person. Sharp and narrow meant watch yourself. His lordship here had exceptionally soft blue eyes, eyes with little flecks of silver mixed in, bringing to mind a bottle of mercury she'd once seen crushed in the street—

A screech filled the air.

They both froze.

"What the blazes was that?"

"Was what?"

"That sound. It came from your room."

"What sound?"

He straightened. "Mrs. Callahan, I very distinctly heard a screech come from your room."

"Really?" she breathed in her best feather-headed way.

He narrowed his eyes. "Yes."

And before she could step in front of him, aye, before

she could place a hand against his chest to stop him, he had his hand on the door, was opening it . . .

"No, don't." She grabbed at him.

"Mrs. Callahan—" he tugged. She looked beyond him. The room was . . . empty.

Oh.

She almost let him go, her relief was so great, but suddenly she became aware of his hand. Such large, masculine fingers he had. Elegant, really. Fingers that brought to mind artists and sculptors and a deft touch with reins . . . or perhaps a really top o' the trees manicure.

She dropped the limb. "I'm sorry, m'lord. I feared you were charging into danger. If you did, indeed, hear something, it might be unsafe."

"Don't be ridiculous," he said, his arm dropping back to his side. His fingers clenched and unclenched, just like hers. "*You* just came from your room and nothing happened to you." He stepped into the aforementioned room and paused in the middle of it. Mary realized Abu must have left through the still-open window. Thank the lord for that.

Then she noticed something else. His lordship looked rather tasty from the backside. Aye, he was splendidly shaped what with his wide shoulders that filled out his jacket in such a way that she knew it wasn't padded. Indeed, his forearms looked most healthy, too. Muscular, like a stallion that had covered a lot of mares.

She blushed.

"Hmph," he said, more to himself than to her as he looked around. Next he went to the window, peering out to the alley below. When he turned back to her, his brows had lowered.

Abu jumped onto the ledge behind him.

Mary stiffened. "Let's leave," she said before charging toward him and grabbing his lordship's hand and all but towing him from the room like a barge. As she turned to shut the door, she caught a glimpse of Abu sticking out his tongue.

"Mrs. Callahan, I must insist you stop touching me in such a familiar way. It's very unseemly."

"Indeed, you're absolutely correct." She let go of his hand, but the contact still remained, warm, masculine fingers having left behind the same sort of warmth the shell of a stove left behind long after its fire had been banished. How . . . odd.

He lifted a brow.

She thought she heard a scratch at the door. "Shall we proceed?"

He stared at her for longer than made Mary comfortable, his mouth opening at last to say, "Follow me," in an arrogant tone.

Mary followed, for the sooner they were away from each other, the better. Warm stove, indeed.

And so Mary headed toward her charge with a belly full of optimism, certain that she had only to use a stern hand to keep Miss Gabriella in line. Aye. That letter had to have been left by a weak-kneed ninny. *Leave. Leave now,* she silently mimicked. As if she hadn't raised four brothers. She could handle the lass. She would have her eating out of her hand in no time.

She were a demon-faced fairy, that was for certain.

"Miss Gabriella," Mary called nearly two hours later. She opened the door to what looked like a water closet, only to gawk for a full ten seconds at the marble pedestals apparently made for sitting on. She went to it, pulled the chain above it, amazed when water filled the bowl only to disappear suddenly. She pulled the chain four more times before remembering she needed to find Miss Gabriella. Lord, who would have thought the bleedin' nobility emptied their bowels on fish-shaped pedestals?

Ten minutes later she was still searching. She stood in the middle of a long hall with doors on either side of it, clucking her tongue as was her habit to do when vexed. Next to her, a life-sized portrait of a feather-capped nobleman stared down at her from atop a rearing black stallion with no tail and skinny long legs.

"What you bleedin' starin' at?" she asked it before slowly turning around as she tried to think of another place to look. "I'm not as bog-minded as you think," she added. "I knew this would happen. But the vile brat disappeared quicker than ale at a boxing match."

A tap on her shoulder brought her around sharply.

"Who, might I ask, are you talking to?"

Mary jerked. The marquis faced her. "You're going to make me bleedin' heart fail if you keep sneaking up on me like that."

She waited for the aforementioned organ to settle back to its normal rhythm, but it was a fair way from doing that what with the handsome cove staring down at her. What'd the nobility do, breed for looks like they bred for good noses on hunting dogs?

"I beg your pardon, Mrs. Callahan. I did not mean to frighten you."

Slowly, the buzz of adrenaline faded.

"Who were you talking to?" he asked again.

"Myself," she said, placing a hand against her hips.

"I see," he said, one brow lifting like a string tugged at it from above.

And how he could be so bleedin' controlled and yet so handsome to look at beat the bubbys off of her. He made her heart pitter-patter in the queerest sort of way which just went to prove she'd gone bleedin' crackers starting with the moment she'd agreed to take this toad-faced job.

"And when you were having this conversation with yourself were you, by chance, referring to my daughter as the 'vile brat' and if so, might I ask how she's connected to 'ale disappearing at a boxing match'?"

"I've lost her," she admitted because she was tired of searching for the ankle biter and thought maybe he could help.

"Lost who?"

"Your daughter."

He straightened a bit, the cull seeming to be not at all surprised.

"I see," he said.

"We were playing hide and seek," she felt the need to explain, though why she did so, she couldn't guess. Likely he wouldn't care.

"Ah," he said.

"Indeed," she mimicked his well-cultivated tone.

He lifted his left brow. "Perhaps not the wisest game to play given my charge's propensity for pranks."

"You don't think I didn't think of that? But the little hellion only wanted to play hide and seek. No charades. No shuttlecock, just hide and seek. I should have let her hide in a closet then locked her in it."

He lifted his right brow this time. "You seem a bit agitated."

"Of course I'm bleedin' agitated. I've been looking for her for nigh on an hour."

"Mrs. Callahan, do you always swear?"

She stiffened, having been so upset she hadn't even noticed the slips of her tongue. "Aye, my lord. 'Tis a wee bit of a problem I have. Beg your pardon." She bobbed a curtsy just like a proper servant would.

"See that it doesn't happen around my daughter."

Though she hated to do it, she really did, she curtsied again. "I'll do my best," she said, then muttered under her breath, "If I ever find the whelp."

"As to that, I shall help you."

Oh, lawks, he'd heard that, too*?*

"I am familiar with the *whelp*'s hiding places." He nodded, indicating she should follow, then said, "Come," like she was a retriever with a duck in its mouth.

Come, she silently mouthed, but she followed as ordered. This was why she didn't want to work for the nobility. Treated everyone like they owned them, they did. And yet here she was.

Someone should clout *her* over the head.

Off she went, only to be brought up short by an ear-piercing scream, and not a monkey scream either, but a full-fledged female-type scream, the kind that meant the person was frightened for her life.

She looked at the marquis and the marquis looked at her. They both turned and ran.

"It were a demon," the scullery maid panted. "Little it was, but with big teeth, and a fierce growl that stole ten years off me life."

What it was, Mary realized with a sinking heart, was Abu, though how the little mite had wandered into these chambers, she had no idea.

"Where did you see it?" his lordship asked, Mary's

eyes narrowing at the genuine concern he exhibited for his servant.

"In your room, sir. I was cleaning out the ash when something dropped from the chimney."

Well, that explained that.

"I screamed and it screamed back, pointing at me and bouncing up and down. 'Twas a terrible sight it was, m'lord, one I'll never forget. Ghost white face. Beady black eyes. Sharp teeth."

Mary closed her eyes, tilted her head back, shook her head. Lord, could this day get any worse? First she'd succumbed to greed and agreed to work for the cull and now Abu was running rampant around his lordship's fancy house.

"Go below," the marquis said. "Get yourself a good, strong cup of tea. Mary, you go with her."

Mary's eyes snapped open. "Go with her? I think not, m'lord. I'm staying with you."

"Do not be absurd."

She gave him a look for calling her absurd. "Your daughter is lost in this house, m'lord, or hiding, or playing. But wherever she is, she might need me should she run across A—" she bit back her pet's name just in time. "A big scary thing," she corrected.

"She's right, m'lord. If the thing catches her, she might get carried off."

Carried off? Was the maid sucking opium between chores?

"I'm going with you," Mary said, drawing herself up, just as he did, then narrowing her eyes—just as he did—for good measure.

"Oh, very well," he said.

"Oh, mum, so brave, you are," the maid said, her eyes

going misty. She reached out and clasped Mary's hands. "Bless you for being so brave for Miss Gabriella's sake."

"Brave?" Mary said, feeling unexpectedly guilt-ridden. "I think not."

"Oh, you are. You are. 'Twas a frightening beast he was, for sure."

The only thing frightening about Abu was the talent he had for getting her in trouble.

"Mrs. Callahan," his lordship said, having stopped his trek toward his bedroom. Mary looked up at him just in time to catch a look of impatience in his eyes. "Are you coming, or no?"

Mary squared her shoulders, the feeling she had boding ill for the outcome of their search.

He took her to his bedroom.

Of course, Mary had expected this, but what she didn't expect was the bleedin' size of the place. How silly she felt for being all giddy over her own lodgings when it was a broom closet in comparison. As big as Westminster Hall, his lordship's room was, well, mayhap not *that* big, but near enough. High ceilings. Scalloped moldings. Gilt-trimmed furnishings atop a richly carpeted floor. And the smell of it. Masculine, it was, smelling of snuff and shaving soap and other man-type things.

But what caught her attention, what had her all but gawking, was the four-foot-high bed to her right. At least it looked four feet off the ground, and five feet wide. Maybe six. Lawks, it made her bed look like a hay manger. A bedcover with a matching canopy done in peacock blue hung over it. Matching drapes framed the windows opposite where she stood, right down to the gold tassels that hung off their corners. All it needed was a carved wooden crest at the foot of the bed, and a royal red coverlet with gold trim, and you'd have a replica of King George's room, or so she imagined.

"Are you coming?" he asked again.

Mary jumped. His lordship had stopped, too, and was it her imagination, or had his face reddened a bit when he noticed where her gaze lay?

Nah. She was imagining things.

She nodded, motioning with her hands for him to shoo. She wasn't sure, but she thought she saw his eyes narrow a bit at the gesture. Mayhap even saw him glance past her to the bed again, but she couldn't be sure because the next moment he was turning away. Mary surreptitiously kept an eye out for Abu. The little wretch. Where the devil was he hiding? And what the blazes would she say when they found him?

"Stay back, Mrs. Callahan, for the creature could be dangerous."

Dangerous. Hah.

He opened the door.

A furry body launched itself right at the marquis's face.

"Oh my goodness," Mary cried.

His lordship stumbled back. Abu screeched. Mary tried to reach for him. Abu, not his lordship.

"Get it off of me," he yelled, clawing at his face.

Mary tried, Abu screeching at the top of his lungs. She tugged. His lordship tilted toward her. Abu let go. Their legs tangled.

And in that moment, Mary knew they were going to fall. Abu must have sensed it, too, for the little wretch leapt away at the last moment.

"Demme," she murmured. And then Mary closed her

eyes, closed them because as his lordship fell toward her, she knew it would hurt.

It didn't. Not at all.

She opened her eyes, first one, then the other, her brow scrunched together in an anticipatory wince that she never had to use.

He'd landed with elbows on either side of her. Mary was impressed. And not because of how he landed, but because of the way he felt nestled against her. They were like two spoons that fit perfectly, though she supposed he'd be the silver one and she'd made of tin.

"What the blazes was that?" he asked, craning his neck in the direction Abu had run off. He had a tiny scrape on the right side of his neck, little furrows of red that could only have come from Abu. She should know, she had a perfect view of it. Cords of muscle framed either side. Bronzed by the sun, they were, a testament to his time spent on the high seas.

Lord help her. Were those goose pimples she'd gotten?

"Was what?" she murmured distractedly, because, hell's fires, the feel of his lordship pressed against her made her realize he might not be so stuffy after all.

He looked down at her, likely about to call her blind, only they both froze. Really, she could feel the way his legs hardened against her own, the way his chest flexed, the way his shoulders stiffened.

Her breath caught. His did, too, only to be released in a gush. She could feel it waft against her face, the smell of his air sweet and deliciously masculine. And, no, those eyes weren't the color of seashells at all. They were the exact shade of a bluebird's feather, downy and soft and focused solely on her. And then something drifted around them, something tingly and warm that enveloped Mary in a cloud of surprise and temptation. Maybe it was the look on his face: part disbelief, part aloof chagrin. Maybe it were the devil, for Mary's father used to swear he saw a red-capped fairy dance in her eyes. But something made her soften beneath him, made her lick her lips before saying softly, "Either someone's dropped a sausage down your pocket or a large watch fob's pressin' into me leg."

Chapter Three

Alex thought he'd misheard her. That was the reason why it took him so long to form a retort. Certainly it couldn't be the way his body reacted to the feel of her pressed against him.

"I beg your pardon?" and he was abashed to hear his voice sounded rather hoarse.

"I said—"

"No, no." He coughed. Frog in his throat. "I heard you," he said, pushing himself to his feet.

Get away from her.

"I believe it is my watch fob, Mrs. Callahan."

Not giving her a chance to comment, he straightened his jacket to cover the evidence of his reaction to her, evidence that jutted out . . . like a sausage. Good Lord.

He looked down, first to make sure the evidence was properly concealed. It was. Then at her. He became rooted to the floor.

Control momentarily slipped, fascination fell into place. Lord, she was a sight with strands of her fiery hair loose around her face. Like a painting he'd once seen of a Turkish woman as she reclined amongst pillows, her face peered up at him with that damnable glow in her eyes, her lips slightly tilted as if she fought a smile. Those lips made him long to lean down, to help her up, to . . .

Carry her to the bed?

He jerked, completely taken aback by the notion.

"My lord, did you find it?"

Their gazes had to be wrenched away from each other in order to land on the butler.

"Sarah said she was attacked by a creature. Did you see it?"

"Indeed, I did," Alex admitted to the man. He glanced back down at Mary.

Buff-colored sheets, the kind that glowed in candle-light—those would look stunning against her naked flesh . . .

He jerked his gaze away again, and damned if he didn't feel his manhood bob in his breeches.

"Unbelievable."

"What, sir?"

Alex met his butler's gaze. "The creature attacked me," he said without missing a beat. Lord, he needed to concentrate.

"Gracious, sir, are you all right?"

"I am."

"And did it attack you, too, Mrs. Callahan?" the butler asked.

"No," he heard her grumble. "His lordship did."

"His *lordship*?"

"She jests, Simms. We collided with each other in my attempt to escape the creature."

"Run away in fear is more like it."

"I was *not* afraid."

"*Get it off me,*" she mimicked softly.

"I *beg* your pardon?"

She slowly climbed to her feet, Alex abashed to realize he hadn't even offered her a hand.

"But that's right enough, m'lord. Most men of your rank collapse under pressure." She leaned toward him, brow lifted teasingly. "Too much inbreeding, I says."

Too much—

Collapse under—

He had to all but bite his tongue to avoid saying something rude and ungentleman-like. But then he caught the twinkle in her eyes. Lord, she was funning him. How . . . familiar. But he would not reciprocate. No indeed.

Perhaps maroon satin sheets.

Alex!

Turning his attention to Simms, he said, "Gather the male staff. Arm them with whatever you can. We'll find the creature if we have to tear the walls down."

"No, you can't."

Both men looked at Mary.

"Miss Gabriella is still hiding," she said reasonably. "What if one of your staff finds her and mistakes her for the creature?"

Damnation, but she had a point. And a good one, too.

New respect for her filled him. She had a cool head, Mrs. Callahan did. Even if she did have an outspoken tongue. Sausage, indeed.

"Very well, no weapons, but we'll continue the search."

Did he hear her sigh? Could she be that concerned for his daughter's well-being?

Perhaps she was. Hmm. Perhaps hiring her had not been such a mistake, after all. Granted, he found himself damnably attracted to the lady, and her manners terribly forward, but that he could keep under control.

And then his manhood bobbed again.

* * *

They didn't find the creature. Alex had a hard time deciding what infuriated him more: the fact that their search had proven fruitless, or that he couldn't get the seductive image of Mrs. Callahan out of his mind.

And though he tried for the rest of the afternoon, and for most of a long, restless night, he found himself unable to deny that he'd felt a surprising surge of desire for his daughter's new nurse. He woke the next morning with his manhood as stiff as a board, the ache to bury it between Mrs. Callahan's sweet thighs so urgent that it made him roll over, stuff his face in his pillow, and groan.

Hours later, as he worked in his study, he still felt a stirring every time his mind strayed to thoughts of her, which was altogether too frequently. Every sound grated against his consciousness. *Was it her?* Every nerve seemed attuned for contact with her. *Did she feel it too?* Every thought seemed directed to the memory of what she'd felt like against him yesterday. *Would he see her today?*

Rot and bother.

He didn't like it. Not one little bit.

His butler chose that moment to deliver the morning post.

Alex looked up. "Have my daughter and her nurse begun their daily routine?"

Where the devil had those words come from?

"Mrs. Callahan is still abed, my lord."

Alex stiffened. "Still abed?" he found himself repeating.

"Indeed, sir. Several of us have tried to rouse her, but she refuses to answer the knocks on her door."

Alex rose from his desk abruptly.

"Is there a problem, sir?" his servant asked.

"After yesterday? Indeed, there could be." Visions of his new nurse mauled by the creature entered his mind.

Alex left the room before he knew what he was about. And if he were honest with himself, he would admit that he was merely looking for an excuse to set eyes on her again, for surely if something had happened, someone would have heard a scream. Only he refused to be honest with himself, thus he thought the whole way up the stairs that she might be in serious jeopardy.

"Mrs. Callahan," he called as he found her door.

No answer. A genuine stab of concern jabbed at his gut.

"Mrs. Callahan?" he tried again. He placed his ear on the door, put his hand on the knob. Not a sound.

Reminding himself that this was his home and that he had every right to look in a room that might be vacant or occupied by someone in distress, he swung the door wide.

Mary Callahan lay atop the covers of her bed, naked as a babe.

Good lord—

She was . . .

He swallowed, but it went down wrong, a bubble of air paining his insides. She lay face down, half her body uncovered, a white sheet draped over the small of her back, yet exposing her stunning backside, only to cover the back of her thighs in such a way as to look contrived. Her hair, that glorious hair he'd admired yesterday, lay loose around her head. She hadn't braided it. Hadn't put it in a cap. Didn't do any of the things most matrons would do. Instead it and she lay atop the bed like a lazy cat, content in the world as it moved around her.

Odd's blood. He almost fell to his knees at the lust that hit him square in the groin.

He must have let out a groan. Must have done something that penetrated the edge of her consciousness because she rolled over, exposing her breasts to his view, those plump, white globes shifting off to the side and looking no less stunning as they did so. The urge to go to her, to lie down, to suck on that dusky red nipple . . . Lord, to do any number of things he knew he had no business doing, much less *thinking* of doing, stoked a fire not even willpower could contain.

"Is she awake?"

Alex stepped back and slammed the door so quickly, Mrs. Grimes actually flinched. "No, no," he fumbled for words. "Ah, no. She isn't."

Good lord, was that him sounding like a blithering idiot?

"Well, let me go in and wake her then."

"No," Alex said sharply. "Do not do that. She, ah . . . she might need her rest."

A very ridiculous excuse to be sure, but he simply didn't care. If Mrs. Grimes saw Mary Callahan the way she looked, she'd likely have a fit of the vapors. And then rumors would fly about the household that he'd been caught gawking at the new nurse's naked flesh.

But *what* lovely naked flesh.

Alex!

"Are you certain, m'lord? Miss Gabriella has yet to be dressed. I've never heard of a nurse oversleeping her first day. Why, is it not her job to rise early and see to her charge?"

"Let her sleep," he said firmly. "But send her to me the moment she awakens."

"As you wish, m'lord."

No, no, no. He didn't wish it at all. Not at all.

She'd been naked.

He felt his cheeks heat. Damnation. He felt like he'd come face to face with his first light o' love. He, one of the most feared revenue commanders employed by the Crown. A man who had dispatched more smugglers than most men had teeth. He was afraid to face his daughter's new nurse.

And yet he must. If he didn't reprimand her for her very obvious failure of duty, there would be talk. The staff might speculate that he found Mrs. Callahan attractive. That he was soft on her because of it. It wouldn't do. Even if it was true.

And so he made his way back downstairs, entered his study and prepared to wait.

He didn't cool his heels long.

Not ten minutes went by before he heard the sound of footsteps bounding down the stairs, his manhood having not relaxed one iota as he'd waited. Those footsteps crossed the marble hall with the sharp *rat-tat-tat* of a Naval drummer. There was no knock. No announcement of her name. Nothing. She charged into the room, the door slamming behind her with a *boom* that stirred the hairs on his head and blew his feather quill off his desk with a soft *shiiip* of sound.

"So you're a bleedin' Peepin' Tom, are you?"

And the awakened version of Mary looked downright outraged. Alex actually felt his eyes widen as she came at him.

"I beg your pardon?"

"Don't you give me that," she said, coming to stand before him. She wore the same dress as yesterday, only for some reason today her breasts seemed bigger. Then again, he'd seen those pert, luscious breasts in all their naked glory. Perhaps he had a finer appreciation for them now. They truly were a spectacular set. What was it the lower orders called large-breasted women? Ah, yes, a bushel bubby. Her bushels were very, *very* bubby.

He blinked, realized the direction his thoughts had taken, and groaned silently.

"I know well and good you were in my room," she said, placing her hands on his desk and leaning toward him, bushels all but spilling out. She'd pulled that glorious hair off her face, the bulk of it flowing over her shoulders and down her back. Yet some of the strands escaped from the side to fall down and touch his desk. The color was as bright as copper, yet as soft as autumn grass. It made him long to reach for it, to feel it, to curl a strand of it around his index finger and tug her toward him one tiny inch . . . at . . . a—

"I heard you slam the door then tell Mrs. Grimes that I was still abed. Now how'd he be knowing that, I asked myself, unless he'd seen me?" She leaned even closer. "Naked."

And even though Alex prided himself on control, he felt that one word stab into him.

"I'll not tolerate such behavior," she said. "In fact, I've half a mind to resign right now. How dare you enter my bedroom uninvited?"

He slowly rose. He had the pleasure of seeing her lean back a bit, saw the way her eyes widened when he leaned toward her, too. Thank God he wore a jacket that concealed his damnable reaction to her.

"Mrs. Callahan," he said softly, having to fight another daft-witted urge to glance at her breasts.

Control, Alex. Get control. You're not the type of gentleman to have his head turned by a servant.

"I would have had no reason to invade the inner sanctum of your bedroom had you shown up on time to do the job you were hired for."

Her eyes narrowed. Then she lifted a brow, her full lips pressing together for a second before she tilted her head and gave him a look reminiscent of a dairy maid he'd once seen . . . just before she poured a bucket of milk over some poor sod's head.

"Well, now, if that isn't just like a man. Blame it on the woman, would ya? Sure as ducks fly, it's me own fault *you* walked into my bedroom, looked your fill, then slammed the bleedin' door on your way out."

"I thought you might be injured."

"Injured? And how would I have done that? On me bleedin' pillow?"

"You're swearing again."

"I don't bleedin' care," she said. "I'm angry. You had no right to feast your peepers on me birthday suit."

She was right. He hadn't. He should have backed out of the room immediately. Should have jerked the door closed. Should have done any number of things other than barge into her room himself.

"You are right, Mrs. Callahan. I am entirely at fault. If you wish to leave my employ, I will certainly understand." *Please, oh please, oh please, let her resign.* "I had no business entering your room as I did. I only hope you understand that I was truly concerned about your welfare what with a strange creature running about."

She drew back even further, her hands leaving his desk to be placed on her hips, and of all things, she clucked at him—her tongue flicking against the roof of her mouth like she imitated a trotting horse. How odd. And then those glorious green eyes of hers peered at him intently. The color of hot peppers they were this morning, vivid and vibrant and far too spicy to suit his peace of mind.

"What could you have possibly thought happened?" she finally asked.

"You have to ask that after yesterday?"

He could tell the moment the memory of him lying atop her filled her mind, could tell by the way her lids lowered an instant before her eyes looked away from his own.

"How could I forget that?" he thought he heard her say.

His own composure slipped a bit. "Yes, well. Such is the reason why I thought you might be in distress. At this point, I have no idea if the creature has left the house."

She didn't move.

"I would never have invaded your room otherwise," he reiterated. "And in hindsight I likely should have sent Mrs. Grimes up in my stead. Again, I will understand if you wish to resign."

But lord help him, a part of him didn't want her to do so. He almost closed his eyes and groaned. It didn't help matters that she didn't say anything. Nor did he. And then the awareness returned, that bloody desire that filled his mind and made him want to turn away.

"How much did you see?"

Alex almost swallowed another air bubble. "I beg your pardon?"

She lifted a red brow. "Did you get an eyeful or did you only catch a glimpse?"

Good lord, what a question. And yet he found himself answering despite the fact that he knew he should say nothing, that he should act like he'd seen only a sheet, or perhaps a hint of flesh and nothing else. Instead he found himself saying, "I saw it all."

And, Lord, he would never forget it. Never. Never. Never.

The air filled with a heavy presence Alex recognized as desire.

"I see."

Lust, he admitted. 'Twas lust he felt.

For a servant.

Through sheer force of will, he drew back from her. Sat down, even, though he near broke his shaft in doing so. "Yes, well, again. My apologies. It shall never happen again."

He didn't look up at her. He had a feeling if he did, something might happen. Something he desperately wanted, but that he refused to act upon. *Ever.*

"Thank you for coming by," he said, bending down to pick up his quill from the floor, his words sounding breathless as his movement forced air from his lungs . . . or so he told himself. "I will expect that in the future you will endeavor to wake up in a more timely manner." He straightened, then pulled a piece of paper toward him. "That will be all," he waved dismissively. Only he had to clench the quill more firmly because his bloody hand shook.

Silence reigned again. He chanced a peek up at her. She narrowed her eyes one last time before turning on her heel and heading for the door. Alex felt like clucking, too. Or clutching his face in his hands, or squeezing his cheeks together hard between his palms and puckering his lips like a fish, something he used to do when he was a child. Instead he dipped his quill in ink, putting it to paper, not revealing his inner turmoil by sheer force of will. The door closed. He looked up, his whole body deflating upon realizing she'd left.

What did you want her to do, Alex?

Proposition him, he admitted. Bloody hell, he'd wanted her to proposition him.

When he glanced back down on the paper, he stared in horror at what he'd written.

Tempted, tempted, tempted.

She'd turned into a daft-witted fool. It was the only excuse she had to explain how she could be so bleedin' attracted to the cull. Lord above, what kind of fool gets her head turned by a lord? A bloody marquis, no less?

Mary leaned against the door to her bedroom, Abu emerging from beneath the covers he'd slept under last eve. Thank goodness his lordship hadn't spied the little monkey curled up at her feet.

And if he had, what of it? He had no business being in your room.

But not only had he been in her room, he'd seen her *naked.* Seen her exposed to the elements. For the first time she'd been viewed by a man, and god help her, it made her feel as fiercely alive as when she'd stood upon Beechem's Cliff back in Hollowbrook. Stood there in the rain and lightning with the wind whipping her hair back and yet the whole time not the least bit scared, just curiously, wonderfully *alive.*

She closed her eyes as she recalled the look upon his face down stairs. His gaze had looked empty for a second, then just as quickly filled with something hot and heavy and that made an answering heat build in her woman's mound. Aye. Got it bad, she had. Her lips fair tingled at the thought of smacking his mums, the memory of how it'd felt to lie beneath him yesterday making her thighs sweat. Lust fever. No doubt about it. For a bleedin' lord.

Of all the daft-witted things.

Abu chattered something at her just before he bounded into her arms. She hugged his furry little body next to her, thinking she'd best keep his lordship out of her mind, and out of her room. The man was a clever cull and it might not take him long to realize she was as affected by him as much as *he* was *her*.

And that she was *no* nurse.

Chapter Four

She managed to avoid him for the next few days, though there were times when she thought plucking out her eyelashes would be a less painful job. His lordship's daughter could make a saint turn into the very devil. Their battles were loud and long, Mary wondering how long it would be before their arguments reached his lordship's attention.

Thus, when Mary was summoned to see him not many days later she thought, indeed, that it was about her performance as a nurse. Truth be told, she almost hoped it was. A pound a week wasn't enough blunt to watch the lass. *Two* pounds a week wouldn't be enough. He should be paying her a hundred pounds. A day.

Still, her heart flapped in her chest like a spawning fish as she went downstairs. Ach. The heart palpitations only increased when she knocked on his door a few moments later.

"Come," said a masculine voice from the other side.

She put her hand on the ornate crystal knob, squaring her shoulders and stiffening her spine as she pushed on the dark oak door.

One look at his grave face made her almost stumble.

"Who died?" she found herself asking before her brain had proper time to register she should likely hold her tongue.

He looked up, and that *thing* passed through her whole body again.

"I'm afraid I have some bad news."

It was a sign of how slow her brain had become that it took her a moment to realize his grave face might have something to do with *her,* and not the job she was doing with Gabriella. "What?"

He held up a piece of paper.

Mary swallowed. Hard. It was, indeed, her references. At least, she thought it was. Hard to tell from this angle.

"I have here a letter from someone who wishes to keep his identity a secret."

Bugger it. She *was* going to be arrested. Bloody, bloody, *bloody* hell. Who'd cackled to the bobbies?

"This person, whoever he is, has sent me a warning."

She could barely hear, the blood rushing through her ears so fast, she could feel it pound at the veins in her neck with a *thump-thump* that no doubt vibrated the frilled lace of her neckline.

"It appears as if my daughter might be in danger of a kidnapping."

So tense was she, so expecting different words, it took her a moment to actually absorb what he said. "*What?*"

"Kidnap her," he repeated, tossing the letter on his desk.

"Oh, gracious, m'lord," she said, placing her hands upon her chest in relief.

But he interpreted her remark as concern. "Indeed, I am quite upset myself. As you may or may not be aware, I command a revenue cutter for the Crown. Along with this letter came another post requesting my presence in Exeter. As such, I shall be forced to leave." He straightened. "Since it appears as if my daughter might be in jeopardy, I am forced to take her with me and by association *you.*"

She didn't glean his words at first. Fact is, it wasn't until he met her gaze again, the look upon his face that of a man who'd caught a whiff of bad milk, that she finally understood.

"I'm to go with you?" It was a statement for all that it came out a question.

He looked pained. Aye, like he'd swallowed a fat acorn, one that'd gotten lodged in his throat. "Believe me, Mrs. Callahan, I would not do so if I felt there was another option, but I cannot risk Gabby's care to anyone else save my own." He stared at her for a moment before saying, "And you."

Mary smelled a rat. A big, fat smuggling rat otherwise known as her father. She'd sent the blighter a letter the day she'd arrived. Told him she wouldn't be spying for him, and that he'd been a fool for asking her in the first place. The blighter must have decided to take matters into his own hands; flush his Lordship from his hole, so to speak.

"As her nurse, you will need to pack her things. And yours as well, of course."

She blinked five times before she suddenly blurted, "Have you gone daft?"

He looked at her as if she'd announced her intention to run for Parliament. "I beg your pardon?"

"You can't take me on a journey with you."

"Indeed, I can."

She crossed her arms over her chest. "Will we share a room?"

That got a reaction from him. He seemed to pale a bit, only to immediately turn red. "Of course not. You and Gabby will have your own room."

She lifted a brow.

"I assure you, Mrs. Callahan, I have no designs on your virtue."

"No? That's not what my eyes saw the other morn when they noticed the bulge beneath your breeches."

"The *what?*"

"Oh, aye. I know you got a rise out of seein' me in the buff. But I won't take it personal-like as I know a man is the weaker sex. Just as long as you keep your distance from me."

He was back to hanging his mouth open again, just as he had the first morning she'd met him. He shut it quick enough, though, flinging the paper he still held on his desk.

"Well, since we are clearing the air here, let me say that I know you are not as indifferent to me as you let on."

She lifted her head. So he'd caught that, too, eh? Hmm, she should have known he was no toad-faced fool. "Aye, and yet knowing that, you still want me to accompany you and your daughter to wherever it is you're going. I wonder at that."

"Ah, but you see, we are both adults and as such, perfectly capable of restraining ourselves, especially in light of the fact that you are a servant and I am your master. And while females of the lower order are often easy prey for men of my station, I assure you, I am not that type of man."

Why, of all the arrogant— As if being a nobleman and she being the daughter of a seaman had anything to do with it. She felt her eyes narrow. He was so busy playing the nobleman, he'd forgotten that he was a man. She almost told him so, too, but something made her hold her tongue, something that had to do with the sudden realization that if her father was behind this—and she had every reason to believe he was—then it might be best if she accompanied his lordship here just to keep an eye on his daughter. She should have seen that coming, she admitted with an inward sigh. Now she was honor bound to keep an eye on his lordship's daughter when what she wanted to do was let her father take the chit. It would suit the scaly cove right to be saddled with the hellion.

"When do we leave?" she asked because she admitted if his lordship's daughter was kidnapped, it was herself that would be to blame.

"As soon as possible."

"Very well. I'll pack Miss Gabriella and myself immediately."

He nodded, dismissing her with a hand.

Mary hated that. She truly did. And it was twice now he'd done it. She wasn't a dog to be shooed away from a dinner table.

Clenching her jaw, she gave him a curtsy, then straightened up as tall as she could. He didn't look up. Didn't even appear to notice her curtsy.

Ignore her, would he?

She would just see about that.

But to be quite honest, there was a side of Mary that positively looked forward to gallivanting about the countryside in his lordship's prime carriage even as another part of her dashed off a letter to her father warning him that she was on to his scheme of attempted blackmail through kidnapping (though she did wonder who'd tipped his lordship off).

So it was that when the time came to leave, her body

snapped with excitement even as a part of her wondered what the devil to do with Abu. She surveyed the little monkey now, wide, brown eyes staring up at her as if to say, "Don't you dare. Don't you dare stuff me in that satchel." But, she reasoned, what else could she do?

What else, indeed.

She should have known by Abu's look that it would be a battle to get him to cooperate. Mary was convinced that males of all species were difficult beasts when it came to listening to a woman.

So it was that when she descended the stairs, brown wool cloak thrown over her shoulders, leather satchel in hand (one that thumped and shifted about from the inside, though at least he'd stopped screeching), she tried to keep said satchel hidden beneath said cloak. But her concern over Abu was momentarily forgotten as she stepped out into London's dreary weather and caught her first glimpse of the marquis's coach and four.

Lord have mercy, would you feast your peepers on that?

She almost wished Abu were free so he could get a look at it. Four black geldings stood in gleaming black traces, the lead horse pawing the ground as if demanding to be let go. Beauties those horses were, their veins bulging in excitement at the task they were soon to perform, the coach rocking as they stamped their feet in frustration at being forced to stand. She noticed that his lordship didn't have their tails docked, a practice that turned Mary's stomach. Tall and long legged, Mary had no doubt the geldings would get them to where they were going as quick as could be.

"Coo, they're beauties, they are."

The coachman who sat high upon the driver's box

looked down at her, a smile spreading across his face from beneath his black top hat that collected rain and dropped it into his lap. "Indeed they are, miss."

Moving toward the lead horse slowly, she reached out to stroke one.

"Careful—"

But she'd already demonstrated her knowledge in the way she scratched beneath the headstall, the horse pressing against her hand as she itched beneath his bridle. So good did it feel, the black actually stretched its nose out in pleasure, his little whiskers fluctuating in happiness.

"Ach, know something of horses, you do."

If the man only knew, Mary thought, biting back a smile. For Mary made a living riding such animals, and not astride, but by standing atop or hanging off the side of them. As she inhaled that sweet scent unique to equines—a scent grown more potent by the rain—she realized she missed her team of horses. Missed hugging them and petting them and patting their necks. Missed the company. Prayed they were being well tended to in her absence, though even if they weren't there wasn't much she could do about it. They weren't hers.

She stepped away from the carriage, realizing if she didn't watch it, she might give herself away, so she covered her actions by saying, "'Tis a fine coach you keep, sir."

The man's smile grew. "Thank you, miss."

And it was. Even though the sky above flung annoying drops of rain upon all beneath it, the carriage still gleamed like black pianoforte keys newly polished by loving hands. Two postillions sat on a bench above the trunks, their green wool jackets collecting drops of rain that smeared their shoulders and the gray wigs upon their heads. The driver, too, was splendidly outfitted, though he had the advantage of that hat. And as she took it all in, Mary found herself wondering how many times she'd wished to ride in such an equipage. How many nights had she lain in bed dreaming of such a thing? And here was the real thing, a purple, ivory, and black crest painted on the rain-spattered door. Those drops beaded upon the paint, as if the wood dared water to seep into its depths.

"Abu, we're in for a treat, we are—"

"Mrs. Callahan, a word with you, please."

Mary jumped, turning toward his lordship. "Do you always have to sneak up on me?"

And had he heard her?

Apparently not.

He skidded to a halt before her like a barking dog, his multilayered greatcoat swirling around his legs, his hair mussed for all that it was drawn back in a queue again. He looked tall and powerful and arrogant and full of himself and utterly and undeniably angry . . . with her. *Blimey.* What had she done now?

She had her answer a moment later. "Did you lock Gabriella in her room?"

She almost clucked, stopped herself, then reluctantly nodded, Abu deciding then to make another bid for freedom by bounding around. Mary hid the satchel further beneath her cloak as she prayed the little animal wouldn't start to screech. "I did."

"Why?"

"Because she threatened to run away."

"So you *locked* her in her *room*?"

She let out a sigh, rolled her eyes heavenward. When she looked back at him again it was just in time to see a gust of wind catch his coat, open it, swirl it around his knees like a playful kitten, revealing a dark gray—nearly black—jacket beneath, his muscular and oh-so-masculine legs in buff breeches. She swallowed. Hard.

"M'lord, if she'd run away it would have taken until next Easter to find her. You know it and I know it. Don't be miffed. Truth be told, I thought about tying her to a chair, too. Lord knows how tempted I was to bleedin' do it. But I held back." And a good thing, too, judging by the look on his arrogant, irritated face.

"You—" It seemed the only word he could utter. "I can't—" he managed to get out next. "Of all the—"

"Nerve?" she supplied.

"How *could* you?"

"What do you mean, how could I? All I did was lock her in a room. Safe as a button, she was." And more importantly, safe from kidnappers.

"What if there had been a fire? What if she'd been unable to get out?"

"Was there a fire?"

"Of course not."

"And your point then would be?"

He lost his voice box again, but only for a second. "Mrs. Callahan, never, *ever* lock my child in a room again. Is that understood?"

"No."

"No?"

She shook her head. "Your daughter needs a stern hand right now, m'lord. If I can't have freedom to do as I wish, then I'm thinking this job isn't for me."

Abu let out a screech of anger.

Mary blanched.

"What the *devil* was that?"

"That was me. I make that sound when I'm vexed."

"You're vexed?"

"I am," she said with a lift of her chin, and she was.

"*I* am the one who is vexed. Why, I should release you without wages."

"Then do so. Doing me a favor, you would, like as not. And Miss Gabby would be beside herself with joy. She'll be able to go back to running wild again, making it easy for a kidnapper to nab her."

He drew up at the mention of a kidnapper. Well, good. That was her point.

"She needs reining in, m'lord," she added. "If not, she's apt to do something drastic, something that will put her in harm's way, if not in the path of a kidnapper, then something else. Aye, I've seen it before, with me youngest brother. Wild he was. And rebellious. I near tore my hair out trying to keep him in line. And then one day he fell in the river, a river that I'd warned him from approaching time and again. For hours we searched and all I could think was that I should have been more stern. Or kept a closer watch on him. Or a million other things that would have torn me apart if he'd drowned that day. He didn't, and from that point forward I refused to let him run roughshod over me. 'Twas the best thing that could have happened."

She leaned toward him a bit to make sure he was listening. "He's married now, has two bairns of his own, one of which is a fair way to giving him the same fits as he gave me. So if you don't like the stern way I handle your daughter, then I suggest you go ahead and dismiss me. I'll leave now. Make it easy on you and the kidnappers and save us both some trouble in the long run, I'll wager."

She waited for him to do it, to do what they both knew he *should* do. For even as she sat there, looking into eyes so stern and angry and wild, she felt the stirring in her belly. He looked so bleedin' handsome standing there. It fair made her want to cry. And having admitted that much, she also admitted to wishing she wasn't so common bred. That one day he might see her as more than a poor seafarer's daughter.

Ach, Mary girl. He doesn't even know *you're a seafarer's daughter.*

And he didn't. If luck went her way, he never would. Aye, two pounds richer she was already. A bleedin' fortune. And it was that, god rot her soul, that bloody greed that kept her from resigning herself . . . that and worry over what her father might do next.

"Well?" she asked when he kept silent.

"I appreciate your concern for my daughter's welfare, but I still say you went too far."

She lifted a hand, Abu strangely quiet, like as not because of her raised voice. "You're as blind as an earthworm, you are, but I'll not apologize. Nor will I leave, not unless *you* tell me to."

And still he didn't say the words. Still he didn't release her.

And in a flash she knew the reason why. "You don't want to deal with her any more than I do."

He looked like she'd stuck him with a hat pin.

"Do not be absurd. She is my daughter."

"'Tis true," she accused. "You're afraid of the whelp."

"How could I possibly be afraid of my own daughter?"

"That's why you leave her behind all the time," she reasoned. "She has you outmanned and outgunned and you're filled with fear at having to rein her in."

"You know not of what you speak."

"Don't use fancy talk on me, m'lord. I see right through you. What is more, I begin to realize why it is you hired me. Nothing puts the fear of God in a man faster than dealing with a berserk female. Aye. You've got the sloppy bowels because of her, and you want me to clean it all up."

He looked at her like she were one of those tonic peddlers who'd used their own product and turned their hair green. "You, madam, have lost your mind."

"And you, sir, are deluding yours."

He blinked at her for a few more seconds before he shook his head, saying almost to himself, "How do you do it? How do you get me so completely rattled that I forget 'tis I who is supposed to be vexed? How do you turn things about so completely that it's suddenly me who feels the need to apologize? I who wonders if I shouldn't have locked Gabby in her room to avoid a kidnapping?"

"I'm a woman, m'lord, we specialize in such things."

He stared at her for a few seconds more, then turned on his heel and went back to the house, the many capes of his coat brushing his shoulders.

He didn't dismiss her.

He didn't offer to give her a second chance.

He didn't do anything other than stamp back toward the house, only to turn suddenly when he reached the top step. "We will be leaving when the Bow Street Runners arrive."

Bow Street Runners?

"Since they aren't due here for another ten minutes you might wish to wait inside." His gaze moved to the coachman. "You, too, John. And the postillions. It will not hurt the horses to have them stand."

And with that, he turned and left, Mary trying to decide what shocked her more—the fact that he'd hired Bow Street Runners that might sniff around and discover she was no nurse, or that he cared about his staff enough to send them inside for comfort.

And from up above her on the driver's box the coachman said, "Well done, my lady."

Oddly enough, the words only depressed her all the more.

She wasn't *a lady.*

Chapter Five

Alex regretted his inability to release her every excruciating mile he was jammed next to her—thanks to his daughter's unswerving determination to sit as far away from her as possible. So Gabby was to his right, Mrs. Callahan on his left. Next to him. Touching him. Driving him mad.

Bloody hell, why hadn't he told her to leave?

Because you know she had a point.

And she had. He knew it, for it was one thing he prided himself upon, his ability to see both sides of an argument, if, indeed, one could call their discussion an argument.

She'd been right about Gabby's wild nature making it easier for a kidnapper to abduct her. The devil of it was, he hadn't even thought of it himself. Lord, he should be thanking Mrs. Callahan, not getting angry with her.

The coach lurched. Their bodies touched. Alex felt like he'd been jolted by the devil's pitchfork. Thoughts of the danger Gabby was in faded for a moment as his body reacted to Mrs. Callahan like fire reacted to dry grass. Frankly, he didn't know what was worse, his admitting she'd been right, or the way that sitting next to Mrs. Callahan made him feel.

He darted a glance at her.

The way Mrs. Callahan made him feel.

She, however, seemed impervious to it all. Her elegant profile was turned toward the window, her expression pensive as she watched the passing scenery. Gabby was asleep next to him, his arm her pillow. They'd passed out of London and by turn, out of the rain. Fluffy clouds tore apart like cotton and dotted the cerulean sky. They'd made their way through the park-like vistas of London's south country, having entered the wooded splendor of Surrey. Villages sprouted up in oddly square patterns, reminding him of a giant quilt whenever they chanced upon higher ground.

Oomph.

That was the undignified sound he made as the carriage passed in and then out of another nasty rut. Gabby stirred, but didn't awaken. That was a relief. He didn't think he could take another minute of his daughter and her nurse bickering. Frankly, he'd been on the verge of telling them to stop a half dozen times except he had the oddest feeling the two of them were bonding in some feminine way he didn't understand and didn't want to understand.

Oomph.

"Beg your pardon," he said, dismayed to realize the whole right side of his body was smushed against hers.

"At this rate, m'lord, you'll be in my lap afore long."

If only she *were in* his *lap*.

He blushed, a deuced ridiculous thing to do given his age, and yet the thought of her on his lap had him turning the color of a Dragoon's jacket.

"Frankly, m'lord, I'm surprised you didn't have me ride in a servant's carriage."

"Believe me, Mrs. Callahan, I am currently regretting

the Runners' decision to travel quickly and lightly in order to escape those who threaten my daughter."

She didn't respond so he glanced down at her. The look in her eyes took him aback.

"Rest easy, m'lord. She'll be right and tight."

"Indeed she will, for I shall kill anyone who attempts to harm her."

Her eyes widened, likely at the viciousness of his words. But just then the carriage tipped to the left and they rounded a bumpy corner, the motion bringing his shoulder into contact with her own. Again. Lovely shoulders, he suddenly realized. Elegant. Curved. Well, most shoulders were curved. But hers were *excellently* curved. The skin pale and soft looking—at least what he could see around the neckline of her gown. But what held his fascination most was the column of her neck where it sprouted up from those lovely shoulders. If he leaned just the tiniest fraction, he could brush his lips against . . .

He almost groaned. Instead he closed his eyes and clenched his fists.

"M'lord?"

Forcing himself to open his eyes, he looked down at her. Again. And he knew. He just *knew* she knew exactly what was going through his mind. The thought seemed confirmed when a saucy expression came over her face.

"It's hell being a man, isn't it?"

He didn't register her words, not at first, but then he looked into her eyes, saw the sparkle there, and the way she tilted her lips into an impish smile.

"Oh, aye. You may have a title, you may have blue blood, but beneath it all you're still a man."

"I don't know what you're talking about."

Liar, liar, liar, hurled a voice inside his head.

Indeed, but she *didn't know that.*

"Mmm-hmm," she said.

Or perhaps she did.

He forced himself to look straight ahead. Forced his hands upon his lap to remain still and not reach for her. Not pull her head toward him. Not—odd's teeth—kiss her senselessly as was his wont to do.

And yet, almost against his will, he found himself looking down at her again and, oh, how he wished he were the sort of man who didn't mind dallying with his staff. But he wasn't that sort of man. Point of fact: he prided himself on being the exact opposite. He was a lord. He'd schooled himself to have pride in King and country and all that rot and, by God, he should be able to control his base desires for one, pixie-faced woman.

"Do you have a mistress?"

Did he *what*? He jerked around to face her only to remember Gabby at the last moment and so he gentled his movements and hissed, "I *beg* your pardon?"

"A mistress. You know, a bunter, a bobtail, a blowen—"

"Yes, yes," he said as they bounced in and out of another rut, only to turn sharply left afterward. "I know what a mistress is."

She didn't seem to notice he was pressed against her as firmly as a saddle on a horse. "Well? Do you have one? You might need one if you don't. I've heard men who go unrequited for too long sometimes injure their privates, if you catch me meaning."

His mouth dropped open. "Injure their—"

She stared up at him, her expression utterly serious.

"You are—" He just couldn't go on.

"I am what?"

"You are, without a doubt, the most perverse female I have ever met."

She straightened, smiled. The carriage lurched back in the other direction, only she had a hand strap to hang on to so she kept her place. "Thank you."

"It was not a compliment."

"I didn't take it as such." She pressed her lips together, her nose wrinkling in that silly way she had. Then she leaned closer to him, dropping her voice. "But you really should take my advice. It's as plain as the holes in my half-boots that you're battling an overwhelming urge to kiss me. You need to do something about it afore things get out of hand."

She had holes in her half-boots?

"The only urge I am battling is to—" He broke off, trying to reel himself in before he said something ignoble.

"To what?"

"To do something detrimental to your health." Demme, that had slipped.

"My health? Why would you want to give me air and exercise? Not my fault you can't control yourself."

He could feel a pulse beating at his temples. "I assure you, Mrs. Callahan, I am in no danger of losing control."

"Do you deny wanting to kiss me mums?"

"I admit no such thing. What is more, this conversation is over."

"Don't try to bamboozle me, my lord. Horses make a low, throaty snort before they want to take a roll. You're making that noise now."

"Horses— Snort—"

"Or are you afraid?"

"Driver," he called.

"Aye, you're afraid to admit you desire me."

"Pull over," he ordered when the hatch opened.

"Aye, afraid to give in to the craving, not that I want you to. Don't get me wrong."

"Gabby should be allowed to stretch out as she sleeps," he said more to himself than as an excuse to her.

Mary Callahan's eyes narrowed. He could read the expression on her face. "Coward," she said.

Indeed, he was.

When they came to a stop, he couldn't escape fast enough, though he took his time making sure Gabby was settled first.

"If it starts raining again you can always come back inside."

He looked up, his hand on the door. The sight of her sitting there with such a gamine grin on her face made him realize that he would welcome a cold rain shower. Indeed, the colder, the better.

Coward.

Aye, that he was. But Mary couldn't be hard on him. No indeed. She should thank him, for she didn't want to ride with him any more than he wanted to ride with *her.* Except that she bleedin' missed sparring with him, she did. Aye, unbelievably, she'd started to like him. Ridiculous, for where the blazes could such liking lead?

Aye, but for a brief, silly second, she allowed herself to engage in a far-fetched fantasy. What if he fell in love with her like the fairy prince had fallen in love with the beautiful fairy princess in that bedtime story her mam used to tell her afore she went off and deserted her. What if such a thing were to happen? Not that it would, but what if? What would it be like to have a roof that didn't leak brackish water atop your head? To never again have a stomach scorch from the inside out when hunger got the best of one simply because her pet monkey damaged something on accident? To know that you were safe and secure and not at the mercy of Lady Luck. Aye. That would be a prime bit of fun.

She shook her head as she stared outside the carriage, scenery slowly slipping by. Fence posts, trees, sagging roofs on tiny cottages, and sheep . . . lots of sheep. Their two worlds were far apart, she admitted. Aye, she might give him trouble about his dealings with his daughter, but who was she to preach? She hardly spoke to her own father and brothers anymore. Fact is, she likely still wouldn't have spoken to her father if he hadn't summoned her back from London to help him in his fool scheme. She and her father didn't exactly see eye to eye, part of the reason she'd been so incensed that he'd dare to beg for her assistance.

She glanced down at the child lying next to her, a little girl that would never want for a thing. Who would always have her father's love. Such a pretty thing when she wasn't awake. Looked like his lordship, she did. There could be no doubt about that. She almost reached out and stroked her ink-black hair. Almost. Instead she dropped her hand back to her side, wrinkling her nose at the silly urge. The child didn't want kindness from Mary. And who could blame her? Mary wasn't the loving sort. She never had been. She'd begun to think she didn't have whatever it was women had that made them go goggle-eyed over a bantling.

You're goggle-eyed over his lordship.

Aye, she lusted after him, no doubt about it. And that were surprising. And unexpected.

She looked out the window again, her thoughts racing, and then without even realizing what she did, reached up and undid the clasp on her cloak. Cool air worked its way through the door, the air more chill as they passed beneath trees. As gently as she could—so as not to disturb the girl—she pulled the cloak off and laid it over her.

No reason for the lass to freeze now, was there?

Chapter Six

But four hours later, Mary felt less than smug. Rain had begun to fall again. Blimey. Would it never end? It was as if all the water in the ocean had been swooped into the sky to be dumped down upon them.

Now, Mary were used to rain. Fact is, growing up in a coastal town she'd seen more than her fair share of Nor'easters. But she had never, ever seen rain like this. It fell down the window in streams so thick, she couldn't see through the glass. It leaked through the roof, oft times pelting her smack in the face, making Mary wonder what the blazes the purpose of the roof *was,* if not to shield her from the elements?

But what chaffed her the worst, what made her want to tell the coachman to pull over so she could ride up top with his lordship (rain and all), was that Miss Gabriella had woken up and she was now engaged in the task of making Mary's life hell.

Mary: "Are you comfortable?"

Gabby: "Not with you in the same carriage."

Mary: "Do you need to empty your bladder?"

Gabby: "Only common people empty their bladders."

Mary: "Would you like my cloak again?"

Gabby: "It smells."

And so it went. On and on.

And on.

And on.

Mary wanted to clutch at her hair and jerk it out of her skull just so she'd have something less painful to do. It didn't help matters that she was worried about Abu, though truth be told, he was used to traveling in the confines of her satchel. Still, if he took it into his head to raise a fuss, the postillions above him, or worse, one of the Bow Street Runners behind them might hear him, though with the rain falling so hard they'd be lucky to catch any sound other than that of rain running down their ear canals.

Well, no sense worrying about it now.

And no sense in worrying about those Runners, either. If they checked her references and discovered the only thing she'd nursed was a headache after imbibing too much ale, she'd be gone afore they could say Tom'n Punch.

Gabby began to complain in earnest then, the rain falling harder. The hole in Mary's boot allowed a chill to spread that started at the arch of her foot and ended at her ears. She tried to warm herself by covering her lobes with her hands, accidentally smacking Gabby in the jaw with her elbow as she did so.

"Sorry, lass," she mumbled, rubbing at her freezing flesh.

"No you're not," Gabby said.

Mary rolled her eyes, too cold to argue. She looked out the window, and stiffened.

In the evening light it almost looked like a mirage, a figment of her imagination spun by a bored mind and soggy windows. "Lord above," she said, "would you look at that?"

Gabby reluctantly followed her gaze, the snide look on her face fading as she said, "Wainridge."

Wainridge?

"My grandfather."

Grandfather?

The *duke*?

But then Mary stiffened as another revelation dawned. One so startling, so unexpected, Mary could scarce believe it.

Wainridge, she'd said. Could it be . . . Wicked Wainridge?

Was the bleedin' duke of Debauchery his lordship's father?

She leaned forward, now all agog to see the place. "Lawks," she observed, could it be?

"It must have a hundred rooms," Mary said as they got closer.

"Two-hundred-fifty-five," Gabby corrected.

"And look at the park it sits in." Huge that park was, the trees having long ago been cleared by nature, or more likely, a man's hand. Green grass dotted with little white clover flowers surrounded the structure. Granted, they were wilting beneath the onslaught of rain, but Mary didn't care. Set behind a massive lake, the walls of the home—if one wanted to call it merely a "home"—rose *five* stories high. Square and long, Mary counted twenty chimneys before she gave up. Tall, oblong windows reflected a cloudy sky. And even though rain fell, even though a wind kicked up small waves on the lake, Mary knew she'd never seen anything so grand in all her life.

"Lord above," she found herself whispering. The

thought of going inside that home made her bowels loosen but good.

Then Gabby turned toward her and said, "My grandfather will put you in your place."

But the fact is, Mary already felt put in her place. What the blazes would it be like to live in such splendor? No worries about your toes being turned blue by the cold. No rats crawling over your blanket at night. No potato stew day in and day out. Just untold luxury that never went away and that you likely would never use up.

Gravel popped and crunched as they rolled closer. When they stopped, a liveried footman emerged from the double-wide front door, and even though it rained, the glass in that door still sparkled. The footman halted midway down the fifteen or so steps that had water pouring down it like a waterfall. Then he resumed his descent, bowing his head as Alex climbed down from the coachman's seat with a sway of the coach.

Mary couldn't hear what he said, but the footman darted back inside. Alex—no, his lordship; heir to a bleedin' dukedom, she reminded herself—turned toward the coach.

Mary felt her breath catch. Hell's fires, she couldn't stop herself. He were so handsome. So very, very handsome. Even with his hair slicked back from the rain, drops of it creeping down his face and moistening his skin, he looked so noble and so proud he reminded her of that hawk who'd liked to perch near the circus. His great cloak flirted with his legs, the fabric brushing away beads of rain from his sodden boots.

"Gabby, go inside," he said as he opened the door, allowing a gust of wind to sweep in rain.

Gabby wasted no time, shooting her The Look as she climbed all but over her to get out.

Mary made a move to follow. Alex—no, his lordship, she corrected yet again—stayed her with a hand.

"Henry will guide you and the Runners to the servants' entrance."

The servants'—

He shut the door.

Mary stiffened. She'd forgotten she was a servant for a moment.

It was warmer inside than outside, and for that Mary was grateful, even as she privately stewed for being summarily dismissed by his high and mightiness. But that warmth served to make Mary aware of just how cold she was. The wraith-thin housekeeper spared her hardly a glance as she bustled about, all in a dither because of the marquis's unexpected arrival, and the fact that he'd brought Bow Street Runners with him. Those Runners were getting the lay of the land presently, or so they'd told Mary before departing for parts unknown. Good. As long as they were busy they weren't looking after her.

So it was that Mary found herself waiting to be told what to do, alone, trying not to stare around her in awe. China the likes of which she'd never seen before filled a pantry near where she stood. A long corridor intersected the kitchen from other small rooms, maids in dark uniforms and footmen in maroon and white livery moving back and forth as they prepared for dinner.

"Who are you?"

Mary jumped. A woman who could be Mrs. Grimes's double stared down at her. Gray hair pulled back in a bun, lined face and watery blue eyes.

"Mary Callahan, mum," she said with a curtsy. "I'm Miss Gabriella's new nurse."

"You're in the way." She pointed. "Servants' stairs are that way. Someone will direct you to your room."

Why the devil Mary suddenly felt so small and meaningless, she had no idea. Always she'd prided herself on her self worth. And yet suddenly she felt like a grain of sand at the bottom of a pool.

She headed off in the direction pointed out to her, various people helping her along the way. It seemed to take forever to reach the long and narrow servants' stairwell, Mary blowing a hank of hair out of her face as she began to climb. Poor Abu, who'd suffered through the cold ride all alone in her satchel, moved about a bit.

"Almost there," she told the little monkey as she climbed what seemed to be the tenth landing.

"Actually, you've still a ways to go."

Mary yelped, so engrossed in Abu she hadn't seen the little man who stood four steps above her.

He moved toward her, though it was a slow descent and only done with the assistance of a silver-tipped walking stick. She couldn't make out his features in the muted light of the stairwell, but what she could see piqued her curiosity. He wore a wig, one of those old-fashioned kinds with curls and swirls that reminded Mary of an unshorn sheep's coat. A blue brocade jacket with a frilly white cravat beneath covered his frail form. Knee breeches with a pouchy front and white stockings tucked into fancy buckled shoes completed the outfit. His face looked painted, though on closer inspection she could see that his pasty complexion looked to be the result of years of bleaching. But the rouge could not be mistaken, nor the patch that sat on the tip of his chin.

Then he lifted a brow upon reaching the landing. And she knew.

Alex stared back. Well, Alex as he would look in a few decades.

"You're the duke," she whispered in awe. And in that same instant she realized he was, indeed, Wicked Wainridge.

He bowed slightly. "At your service, madam." When he straightened he said, "And you are?"

For some reason Mary found herself standing taller, and when she did, his gaze dipped down, just like his son's did. "Mary Callahan," she said, narrowing her eyes.

He stepped closer, Mary stiffening as he pulled out a quizzing glass, then began to circle her. It was a very large landing—as big as her room in London—with a small window so she had a perfect view of him as he circled like a buzzard. "Mary, Mary, quite contrary—" he began.

She held up a hand. "Don't say another word. Not if you value your life, your grace."

She could see his rheumy old eyes light up with an odd sort of sparkle as he contemplated her. For half a second she wondered if Alex's father were batty, but, no, he didn't look crazed. She'd seen crazed before.

"You're a saucy one," he pronounced. "Are you new to my son's staff?"

"I am."

Mary felt his gaze rove over her again and if she hadn't been so certain she could tip him over with a breath, she'd have been a wee bit nervous. As it was she said, "You're looking at me like I'm a *petit four,* your grace, and I don't like it."

He smiled. "Why of course I'm staring at you. You're

a bonny one, you are. Rather makes me wish for the old days when I would have pounced on you with alacrity."

"If you did, you'd find yourself pounc*ing* down the stairs with alacrity."

He chuckled. Mary stared in fascination. *This is what the marquis would look like if he laughed.* She found herself amazed by the sight.

"Remind me of my first mistress, you do. Rose was her name, as fair and saucy a wench as ever crossed a London street." And then, to her absolute shock, he moved behind her and settled himself on a step, his breath wheezing out a bit as he did. "What has my son told you about me?"

If someone had told Mary she'd have a duke sitting at her feet, she'd have laughed herself silly over the idea. Yet here one was. "What do you mean?"

"Has he mentioned me at all?"

"I didn't even know we were coming here."

"Ach. Likely you wouldn't be here, either, if it hadn't been for the rain."

She stared.

"So he's mentioned nothing of me?"

"No."

"Hmm. Pity. Must be losing my touch. I was certain he'd have warned you against me. He must think me too old and infirm to be of much danger now, and I'm afraid he'd be right."

"I assure you, your grace, I've no idea what it is your son thinks."

"Hmm. I suppose not."

"Though if it makes you feel better, I *have* heard of you."

"Have you?"

She nodded. "Aye. Saw a drawing of you in the paper. 'The Current Duke of Wainridge' was the heading. And below that was a caption saying, 'Wicked Wainridge lives up to his family name,' and below that was the drawing of a maid and your face in her, um, bubbys."

"Is that so?" the duke guffawed.

"Aye, though I never thought in a million months of Sundays that I'd actually meet you one day."

He wheezed in a way that could only be a laugh, but didn't truly sound like one. "I bet not," he said. "Though those days are long gone. But tell me, my dear, what do you do for my son?"

"I'm his daughter's nurse."

The duke winced. "Poor lass. I wouldn't wish the little hellion on anyone. 'Course I hardly get to see her." He turned to stare at her with light blue eyes which had gone rheumy with age or excess. "Alex doesn't approve. He's afraid I'll corrupt her." He looked down at his hands, his expression turning sad.

Mary found herself staring, a part of her still disbelieving that she was having a conversation with an honest-to-goodness duke, another part of her finding it odd that even noble families had skeletons in their closets.

"Well," he said, pushing himself to his feet with more creaks than a ship's deck. "It was nice chatting with you, Mary Callahan." He stared down at her. "By the by, this is not a servants' stairwell. The maids here are a bunch of old hens. They ofttimes play pranks on visiting staff. You'd best go 'round back and use the stairwell to the north. I'll show you, if you like."

Northern stairwell? Bloody hell.

"Come, come," he said, motioning her to follow him down the stairs she'd just climbed.

And so Mary found herself following a duke, even clutching his elbow when he teetered a bit on one of the steps, Abu strangely quiet inside her traveling bag. But the toff didn't lead her down the servants' hallway, instead he led her toward the main living quarters, into a hall that made Mary's breath catch when they stepped through a double doorway and into a massive area that reminded her of a cathedral she'd once peeked inside of back in London.

"I *knew* it."

Both she and the duke gave out a yelp that echoed off the high ceiling above, though it was the duke that recovered first. He turned toward one of the windows, toward a body that'd been obscured by a tall, red velvet drape.

"Alex," the duke said. "What the blazes are you doing there?"

"Waiting for you." His eyes moved to Mary. "Are you well?"

Her brow knitted in puzzlement.

Alex's gaze moved back to his sire. "Father, I am appalled."

"Here now, don't you go spoiling my amusement."

Amusement? Mary turned to the duke and it was then that she noticed the old duke didn't look quite so old anymore. His stooped shoulders were now straight. His watery eyes took on a crafty brightness. Even his hands had stopped shaking.

"Why, you old rudesby," Mary said.

She'd been had. By a man who looked to be a hundred years old. Who looked old enough to be put out to pasture, but who apparently still ate wild oats. "You were going to accost me, weren't you?"

"I was," he said with a gleeful smile.

Mary almost laughed. Almost. "You old buzzard."

"Hah," he barked. "Did you hear that, Alex? An old buzzard she called me." The words turned into a laugh. "Has a mouth on her," he said to his son. "I like that."

"Leave her alone, father."

"She fancies you, you know."

Mary gasped. "Why I— Whatever gives you that idea?"

"You do," he said. "What's more, dear boy, I'd take her up on the unspoken offer."

"That's enough," Alex said, crossing to his side and turning him toward the door. "I wish to speak to Mrs. Callahan alone."

"What if *I* want to see her alone?"

"You shan't be given that chance."

The duke frowned. "Spoil my fun, what, what. Very well, if you insist." He turned to her. "It was a pleasure meeting you, Mary Callahan. I'm only sorry I won't get to further the acquaintance."

"I'd have acquainted you with my fists," Mary said.

The beard splitter gave her a slow smile before turning away, but not before he gave her a swat on the rear that made Mary yelp. She turned, prepared to go after him.

A hand on her shoulder stilled her. "Don't," he said. "You will only provoke him."

She turned, her eyes narrowing as she said, "Is it a family thing, this habit of accosting me?"

"When did I accost you?"

"In my room. With your eyes."

"That was not accosting."

Mary decided not to argue the point. Abu was getting restless as evidenced by the way he shifted about. She covered the motion by shifting the bag to another hand. "You knew the old bloke was going to do this, didn't you?"

"I was a bit concerned, which is why I hid here. I knew he would move in quickly, before the other servants had time to warn you of his tendency to pounce on visiting staff."

"You should have bleedin' warned me."

"And I beg your pardon for that, Mrs. Callahan. You are correct. I should have warned you."

It always amazed her the way he could take the wind out of her sails. But her pique was forgotten as a new realization dawned. It made Mary stiffen, made her study him more intently. But it all made sense: The stodgy behavior. The holier-than-thou attitude. The princely airs.

"Why, you poor sod."

He stiffened like he'd been poked in the behind. "I beg your pardon?"

"*Now* I understand why you're such an indignant bag of wind. You grew up with The Scarlet Pimpernel as a father."

"Scarlet Pimpernel?"

But sure as sin it were true, Mary thought. Why, look at him right now. All moral affront. She placed a hand on her hips. "You're the most arrogant man I've ever seen," she said. "Controlled, you are. And yet a part of you fights that control. You hate the fact that you find me attractive. No, no," she said, holding up a hand. "Do not deny it, for I know it's true."

"You go too far."

"Do I?"

"Yes, damn it, you do."

"And yet you don't leave."

"No."

"Why not?"

"Because I need to apologize, curse you."

"Apologize? For what?"

"My father's behavior. It was unconscionable and out of line. I should have taken steps to protect your virtue. I did not. And for that I am sorry."

She drummed her fingers, a bit insulted that he would think her so silly as to be bothered by his father. "My lord. If you think that's the first cakey old man to accost me, you've got another think coming."

He stiffened, his shoulders tensing in a way that meant her words had surprised him.

"I see," he said. "I had not thought of that. You are, indeed, uncommonly pretty. I should have realized that that might have presented a problem in the past. But I assure you, you have no need to fear for your virtue here . . . or anywhere as long as you're in my employ."

She didn't move. Aye, she likely couldn't have said a word if she'd wanted to, for she was suddenly struck by the notion that he made her feel like a lady when he looked and spoke to her thus. A genuine, blue-blooded, bona fide mort.

"Thank you," she managed to squeeze past her stupefied lips.

He inclined his head just like she was, indeed, a proper lady. "Would you like me to escort you to your room?"

"No."

He seemed to color. "Then I bid you goodnight." But he stared down at her still and Mary found herself wishing . . .

For what? That you'd been born noble?

She almost winced. Aye. Almost.

Got bats in your belfry, Mary girl.

Likely she did, for there was no sense in denying it. She couldn't shake a feeling, one that told her beneath the stuffy shirt, beneath the arrogant airs, was a genuinely caring man.

Chapter Seven

The next morning Alex woke to the sound of rain, and a pain in his groin from the dream he'd had of Mary Callahan naked in his bed.

Odd's teeth. He needed to stop.

He took breakfast in his room (he didn't want to run into Mrs. Callahan in the halls, though that was hardly likely in an estate of Wainridge's size). He made sure the stairs were clear before checking with the Runners that all was well, and then with his father's head groom about the condition of the roads. (Poor. They would be stuck at Wainridge at least another day unless he wanted to risk Gabby taking a chill. Bloody hell.) Next he took himself off to a room he knew for certain Mary Callahan would never enter: the fencing gallery (located in a rectangular room one could only reach by passing through three salons, a ballroom and the *pièce de résistance*—a room with a multitude of game staring sightlessly at anyone who happened to venture inside, certain to turn any lady's stomach). There he took vengeance on a straw dummy that he pretended had his father's face, his blade jabbing into it with regular force. This jab for the embarrassment he felt at having to rescue the newest member of his staff. That jab for daring to tell Alex to take Mrs. Callahan for himself. Another jab for the realization that he wanted to.

And so it went, which was why when he heard a feminine voice call out, he missed the hay-filled dummy he'd been thrusting his rapier into and hit the wall instead. His whole arm vibrated from the impact, his blade arcing and then *whaw-whaw-whaw-whawing* as the thing flapped about like a dying fish.

"Bravo, m'lord. A pox on that nasty wall."

"What the blazes are you doing here?" he asked as he turned.

She wore a different dress today, was his first thought.

How the blazes did she manage to look so lovely? was his second.

Unlike some women, Mary Callahan appeared to look good in any light. In fact, the rain-drenched light only darkened the shade of her lashes, making her eyes appear huge, her red hair a splash of color against the room's marble walls.

"Looking for you."

And what could he say to that? Except he suddenly had the urge to loosen his cravat, only he wasn't wearing a cravat. No. He wore a white shirt tucked into fawn breeches that would alert the ubiquitous Mary Callahan to the fact that he found her presence this morning something less than disagreeable.

Hell and damnation.

He turned away, more to hide unwanted evidence of his attraction than to grab the towel that rested on the floor near the dummy. But that towel served two purposes. One, to wipe his face—which he did—for he was suddenly sweating. Two, to make himself look busy, which it did, for he pretended an urgent and industrious need to clean his blade with said towel.

"What is it you need to see me about?" he asked over his shoulder.

"*I* didn't want to see you," she said with a lift of her brows. "'Tis your daughter who wants to see you."

"Does she?"

"Yes."

"You should have sent a servant," he said rather rudely before realizing such a demand was hardly gentleman-like.

"My lord," she said. "In case you hadn't been noticing, I *am* a servant."

He stiffened, though he still didn't face her. But he was sure if he did, she'd be staring up at him with her bloody twinkling eyes. "Indeed you are, Mrs. Callahan. Indeed you are. I beg your pardon."

She didn't say anything and for a moment he was almost tempted to turn and find out why, but he couldn't risk her seeing the overwhelming evidence that he didn't think of her as a servant, but as a woman. And damned if he knew what to do about it.

"And since, as you point out, you are a servant, you may return to my daughter and tell her I shall be with her forthwith."

No response. He refused to turn.

"As you wish," she finally said. "If I can find my way back to her afore the day ends," he heard her mutter.

He waited for her to leave, but she didn't.

Leave, please, he said to himself. *Leave, leave, leave.*

"May I be frank with you, my lord?"

He almost cursed. Hell's fires, just the sound of her voice—

"Of course, Mrs. Callahan."

He risked a glance over his shoulder.

She was looking up at him, her head tilted in such a way as to make her look even more lovely.

"I know what it is you're hiding."

That made him jerk a bit.

"And I know it's hard."

Hell and damnation. It was *what?*

"But you shouldn't be ashamed."

She couldn't be referring to his erect manhood. Could she?

"It's not your fault."

She *was* referring to that. Bloody hell. Very well, if she wanted frankness, he'd give her frankness. "I know it's not my fault, Mrs. Callahan. My reaction to you is completely involuntary."

Only when he spun around, her gaze dropped, and something about the way she popped off the ground . . . about the way she jolted right up off the floor, alerted him to the fact that he'd made a serious tactical error.

"Good lord," she said, her gaze fixing on his privates. Then her expression changed, her hands going to her hips as she met his gaze. "I mean, *good lord.* No wonder you've been keeping your back to me."

He promptly turned his back again, a blush such as he'd never felt turning his cheeks scarlet. "You weren't talking about my, ah, my—"

"Whore pipe? No. I was not."

He closed his eyes. And on the heels of that action came the realization that Mary Callahan always seemed to catch him at his worst.

"Then what, might I ask, were you talking about?"

"Your father," she said. "I was going to say that I know what it's like to have a relative you're less than proud of."

He almost let out a groan. Could he have blundered it so bad?

He could.

"I see," he said.

"And I was going to say that you don't need to be ashamed. I've been doing some talking to the other servants here and they all agree that you're a stand-up cull. A man as unlike his father as a boar is from a hound."

He stilled, her words penetrating the edge of embarrassment. She'd been trying to set him at ease about his father.

"So while I understand how you might think that I was . . . ah . . ." she paused and her eyes lit up in that shooting star way of hers, "talking about something else, I can promise you right and tight that it wasn't me with my mind in the gutter."

She turned, and Alex couldn't stop the curse that escaped as she headed out the door, and he wasn't sure, but he thought he heard . . .

Laughter.

Part Two

This little pig went to market,
This little pig stayed at home . . .
And this little pig cried, Wee-wee-wee-wee-wee,
I can't find my way home.

Tommy Thumb's Little Story Book,
c. 1760

Chapter Eight

Mary couldn't sleep the whole night, something that'd gotten to be a common occurrence since being employed by his lordship.

His lordship.

George Alexander Essex Drummond, marquis of Warrick. Heir to a bloody dukedom. And he desired her.

She rolled over, socking her pillow at the same time she smiled. A marquis. And he desired her. *Her.* She almost giggled like a young miss when she recalled the look on his face as he'd turned around, only to have her grin fade. She desired him, too. And therein lay the crux of the problem.

Abu sighed, stretching out beneath the covers. So far she'd been able to keep him hidden, though she didn't know for how much longer. And if that happened, they'd want to know where she'd gotten the little monkey, and she sure as certain couldn't tell them that she was really a performer with the Royal Circus. A female trick rider, to be specific, one who led such a lonely life only Abu could be claimed as a friend.

And then her thoughts returned to the marquis again, only to be interrupted by concern for Abu, only to circle back round to his lordship until she finally said, "Blimey. I give up."

Her toes sank into plush, wool carpet as she climbed out of bed and padded across the floor to stare out the window. It was one of those nights when the night looked blacker than a pot of coffee, mist streaming in tendrils outside her window. Tiny pinpoints of moisture clung to the glass. She raised a finger and drew a smiling face. Next she drew a horse (well, as close as she could). And when that failed, she drew the marquis, complete with long thick lashes, just like he had. She wished she had pots of paint, for she'd like to try to catch the blue of his eyes . . .

Bloody hell.

She needed to stop this nonsense. There could be no future between her and a marquis, at least not the respectable kind, and she refused to get involved with the other, so that—

A flash of light caught her eye.

It was so out of place, so unexpected, Mary forgot all about the marquis and her attraction to him (well, for a moment, at least). She squinted, rubbing at the window with the sleeve of her white dressing robe to get a better look. A mist could be seen hanging at the base of a grove of trees, and she wasn't sure.

Flash.

She jerked upright.

Flash, flash.

And Mary Callahan, smuggler's daughter, recognized the pattern of that flashing.

"Holy mother of God."

Mary raced down the stairs. She hit the bottom floor with a slap of her bare feet, all but running down the hallway that separated the kitchen from the pantry, washroom, and servants' parlor. A hearth that burned brightly enveloped her in heat and light as she paused in the middle of the hallway. Where to go? Would they take Gabriella out the servants' door? Or some other side door? Perhaps one of the doors leading out to the gardens?

Where the blazes were the Runners?

"Hurry up, you daft fool, we're going to drop him."

Mary dived into the kitchen, pressed herself up against a wall. A braid of garlic hung above her head, nearly falling from the wall before she caught and steadied it.

"Hurry," the voice urged again.

Moving from her spot against the wall, she darted behind the massive oak table that dominated the center of the room. Leftover flour on the floor caused her to lose traction. She fell onto her rump with an *oomph* that caused her to grunt, then freeze, every hair in her ear canal tuned to sound.

"Where's the bloody door?" a second voice asked.

"Straight ahead."

Lord, they didn't have her already, did they?

She lifted herself up, peeking over the edge of the table just as two men came into sight. They carried something. Mary almost came to her feet when she realized what it was.

The marquis.

Alex knew something was devilishly wrong when he woke with a splitting headache and the taste of old shoe in his mouth.

Granted, he had done something he rarely, if ever, did; have a drink before bed, but that wouldn't account for his head feeling the way it did, nor the fact that the bed he lay upon seemed uncomfortably hard. And that he couldn't move. Nor yell for help because, good lord, his mouth was gagged. And his hands were bound.

What the devil?

Dank and musty air filled his nostrils as he inhaled in shock. He tried to move, but he was wedged as tightly as a billiard ball in a pocket.

He hated small spaces. Absolutely loathed them. 'Twas one of the reasons why he sailed the high seas. Alex needed air and freedom. He needed light. He needed to be able to move.

He jerked sideways, but he couldn't move. Not even an inch. And—devil take it—his feet were bound too. He tried to draw his knees up. That he could do, but it did little good, for his kneecaps came in contact with the lid of what he'd begun to suspect was a coffin sealed tightly shut above him.

Bloody hell. All right, he was close to panic now. He could admit that. He jerked around in a futile attempt to free himself.

And suddenly the lid opened, a dawn sky the color of pewter above him, with Mary Callahan momentarily blocking the view.

"Shh," she said, making a shushing motion with her finger. As if he could speak. As if he wasn't lying in a bloody coffin and staring up at the one person in this world he least expected to see.

She reached in, her hand grabbing his arm in a way that meant he should try to sit up. He was only too happy to oblige, but the moment the blood drained from his head, it left behind a mind-numbing ache that almost made him lie back again. Almost.

"Hurry," she hissed at him, her eyes darting around. "They'll be back any moment."

Who?

She shook her head, pursing her lips in a way that clearly answered back, *not now.*

It was then that he realized his casket was in between other caskets. Mary atop the one to his left, her red hair hanging loose around her, the gown she wore—no, not a gown, a *night shift*?

Egads.

The fabric hung open, her breasts nearly spilling out. He blinked twice at those breasts before realizing this was clearly not the time to be having lascivious thoughts about Mrs. Mary Callahan.

He'd been kidnapped.

Silly how the thought struck him then. It should have been obvious such was the case long before now. And on the heels of that realization came the realization that he'd interpreted the letter wrong. It was *he* the letter had referred to, not Gabby.

Gabby.

His daughter would be frantic.

"Hurry," she ordered.

Devil take it. No time to worry about his daughter now. He lifted himself to his feet, though it was damn hard with his hands tied behind him. Next he tried to move, but he couldn't because his bloody feet were tied. He almost fell atop her.

"Careful," she hissed up at him, her gaze darting around. "And squat down, will you?"

"Mii feetth rrr tddd," he tried to tell her.

"Shhh," she immediately ordered.

He looked around for what had her so concerned. They

were parked in a thin sort of wood. And yet just beyond the trees, visible through the mossy trunks and branches, was a tiny village. It was early morning, Alex noted. Roosters crowed a welcome to the chilly morning air, the reason for the village's desertion apparent. Everyone was still abed, only the dogs were awake, judging by the way they barked nearby.

"Miii feetth rrrr tddd," he repeated when he spied no kidnappers, nor even a farmer.

She shook her head, her manner one of lost patience as she stared down at him. "Here," reaching behind him to jerk the gag off his face.

"Ouch," he cried, for she near ripped his nose off, too.

"Hop out," she ordered again.

"I can't," he hissed back, and he could feel where the gag had left a mark on his face. His patience ended. "In case it's escaped your notice, Mrs. Callahan, my feet are bound. I cannot lift my legs over the edge."

She glanced toward the appendages in question. "Bloody hell," he thought he heard her curse. "Sit down and swing them out."

Good thinking. Alex felt miffed he hadn't thought of it himself. Demme. They must have struck him harder on the head than he'd thought.

He did exactly as instructed, Mary staying behind to close the casket lid, then replaced the tarp that had obviously been pulled over them.

"Lean on me," she said, after he'd hopped down.

Lean on her? "Devil take it, untie my legs and hands first."

"We can't. There isn't time."

He leaned on her, her small arm wrapping around his waist, Alex surprised at how easily she took his weight.

It seemed to take forever for them to reach the woods, Alex feeling like he played a childhood game of hop in a sack. Only this was worse. She forced him on until they both nearly fell, Alex cursing, Mrs. Callahan doing the same.

"This is silly," she said, dropping down to her knees after darting a glance at the village. Not a night shift, he realized, but a chemise with a white cotton robe thrown over it, one that allowed him a view of her voluptuous breasts. He swallowed. Bloody hell. He refused to have more lascivious thoughts about her. They were running for their lives—well, he was running for his. She was an innocent bystander who'd happened to get involved.

Come to think of it, how *had* she gotten involved?

He was about to ask her, but she stood suddenly, untying his hands next, and the feel of those nimble fingers on his flesh made him groan inwardly.

Bloody hell. He *was* having salacious thoughts.

When she finished, she wadded up the rope and tossed it into the branches above where it caught on a bough.

"What the devil are you doing?"

"Evidence," she said. "Don't want them to know we came this way."

He almost pointed out their traipse through the grass was hardly invisible what with the grass having folded down where they trod. Snails couldn't have left a better trail, but she was off and moving again before he could say a word. And, besides, it *was* a clever thing to do.

"Do you have any notion where we are?"

"How the bleedin' hell should I know?" she asked, her robe catching on the bottom of the thick grass, wetting the fabric, and brushing the ends of the blades flat some more.

"Then you have no idea where you are going?"

She stopped. He bumped into her, automatically reaching out to steady her. She didn't appear to notice for she turned, hands on hips. "I was under the bleedin' tarp the whole way here—same as yourself—freezing me cooler off in the pouring rain, on a road that shouldn't be travelled, if you don't mind me saying. And I'm not pleased about that, m'lord. Not pleased about any of it. I rode in the back of that bleedin' cart stuffed between two eternity boxes half afraid the carriage would shift and I'd be crushed flat like a run-over possum. So, no, I don't know where we are."

And without another word, she turned again, running toward a stand of oak, their trail no longer obvious now that they trod atop last fall's leaves. Gradually, the wood thickened, the village faded from view, and still Mary pushed on, darting glances behind them. And she likely would have kept going, too, if she hadn't pulled up suddenly, her gasp of "Ouch," bringing him to an abrupt halt.

She wore no shoes.

He felt his body buzz with the shock of it. She'd been running—No, they'd been charging over twigs and prickly oak leaves and the whole time she'd been—

"Bloody hell, I'm bleedin'."

Bleeding?

"Lord love a duck, this day just couldn't get worse. Stuck in the country with some fancy bred swell with no shoes, no blunt, and no bleedin' clothes. Someone should just shoot me and put me out of me misery now."

And her words made him feel an odd combination of pity and amusement mixed with . . . tenderness?

"Here," he said, "I'll carry you."

"Not on your bleedin' life," she said, putting her foot

down, turning and moving off again. But he noticed she didn't put her heel all the way down, though she tried to make it look as if she walked normally.

"Did you catch a glimpse of my kidnappers?" he found himself asking.

"Only briefly."

"Is that how you became involved?"

"Aye," she said. "I saw a signal lantern from my window, and since I figured whoever was up to nonsense would likely not use the front door, I went to the servants' entrance only to discover the nonsense was *you*, which reminds me, my lord. You need to hire better Runners next time."

"They were stationed at Gabby's door."

"Aye, but someone should have been patrolling the boundary."

And suddenly the enormity of what she'd done—all of it—struck him. She'd charged in to help him, unclothed, in the dead of night, not knowing what fate she might face, but committed to her course. She'd rescued him, handily, he might add, then run for her life with him in tow.

Amazing.

"Here," he said again, unable to stand her limp a minute longer. He crossed to her quickly, bending so he could scoop her up.

"What the devil are you doing?"

"Carrying you," he wheezed because, good lord, she was no milk and water miss.

"Are you daft? Put me down, you nodcock. You cannot carry me. We need to hurry. Asides, you're not strong enough."

He drew himself up. "I beg your pardon."

"You are not"—her green eyes narrowed—"strong enough."

"I am, too," he said, even though his arms already began to feel the strain. But Demme if he wasn't committed to carrying her. At least for a bit. He owed her that much.

And so he did, carry her, that is, though it wasn't until the weight of her near bowed his back that he began to think he might, perhaps, do as she asked.

She must have sensed his growing weakness. Or perhaps it was the way he kept stumbling over roots, his feet feeling oddly heavier as he carried her. Whatever it was, she said, "That's enough, my lord."

His arms began to shake, either from the strain of carrying her or the lovely way having her up against him made him feel—

"Put me down."

He didn't want to. He truly didn't want to, though he'd begun to suspect it was because he rather liked the way carrying her made him feel. Still, he did as asked, gently, though reluctantly, setting her down.

She immediately sat on the ground, lifting her foot up for inspection. "I think I might need a bandage," she said with a frown.

He followed her gaze, and his abdomen clenched, his heart almost seeming to stop and then ache as he spied her foot. Good lord. "Mary, why did you not say something?"

He sank to his knees beside her, picking up the foot and cradling it gently. It was torn to shreds.

"We needed to escape," she said simply.

He felt the biggest of cads. "You should have told me."

"Why, when we couldn't stop?"

And George Alexander Essex Drummond, marquis of Warrick, heir to the duke of Wainridge, simply marveled. Her courage took his breath away. She may be a nurse. She may be of common blood, but, odd's teeth, she comported herself as nobly as any blue-blooded miss.

"Bloody hell, they hurt."

Well, some of the time.

Chapter Nine

Mary noticed Alex staring at her oddly, but she told herself to ignore the gleam she thought she saw in his eyes. Weren't no sense in the either of them getting all mushy, not when she were shivering from cold now that she was away from the heat of his body and the cool morning air felt as freezing as the pads of a dog's foot.

"You're cold," he pronounced.

"And hungry," she added. "And tired. And wondering what the blazes we're going to do out here in the middle of nowhere with no blunt, no horses and nothing to recommend us to a person other than my good looks."

He looked past her and beyond, his lips compressing into a frown. "Indeed, Mrs. Callahan. You have a point. We are in a fix, although I find myself grateful that it's *me* in this predicament and not my daughter."

And oddly enough, Mary was, too. Not even Gabriella deserved to be kidnapped. Nor did his lordship here. She studied his profile, the worry he felt for his daughter evident by the white parentheses which cupped his mouth.

"She'll be all right," she found herself saying. "I doubt she'll even notice you're gone what with her constant tantrums and the like."

It was an attempt at humor, but it fell woefully flat.

"Indeed, Mrs. Callahan. Indeed."

And then Mary jerked. "Abu," she gasped. Lord above, she'd forgotten about her pet. She hadn't closed her bedroom door, which meant her pet was running loose—

"God bless you," he said, frowning down at her. "You're sneezing. The cold must have gotten to you."

Sneezing? She almost corrected him before realizing she couldn't tell him about her pet presently loose at his father's estate. Hell's bells.

"Here," he said, sinking down to his knees and then grabbing the hem of her night shift. "Let's see if we can't at least get your feet warm."

"What the blazes are you doing?"

"Makeshift shoes," he said, tugging at the fabric which gave—in Mary's opinion—all too easily, which likely wasn't surprising considering it was the cheapest fabric on God's green earth.

"Here," he said again, tugging a long strip off the edge. "Wrap it around your feet."

Funny. He didn't even take a peek as he worked. She'd never seen a man pass up an opportunity to stare at a woman's walking sticks.

He tore off another strip which she then took from him, trying to ignore the way her bum sopped up mois ture.

"The tighter the better."

"I know. I know," she mumbled, trying not to wince as she did as instructed. Hurt like the very devil, they did.

"Here. Let me help you stand." He held out his hand. Mary stared at it for a moment, then reluctantly placed her palm into his. Hot, his hand was, making her realize she felt near to freezing.

"Do you want me to carry you again?"

No, she did not. His kindness had begun to make her weak in the mind. Why else would she feel the urge to say, "Yes," when all she wanted to do was keep her distance from him.

"I can walk," she grumbled.

He didn't look like he believed her. Well, bully for him. She took a step, biting back an oath at the stinging pain which shot up her heel and into her leg. Bloody, bleedin' hell. Why the devil did it hurt so badly all of a sudden?

"Are you certain you do not wish for my help?" he asked.

She waved a hand at him in dismissal. She would walk, confound it all, even if it meant she'd have bloody stumps when she got to where they were going, wherever that was.

The shadow of a bird floated on the ground near them. Terrific. Like as not a carrion bird come to feast on her stumps when she keeled over and died. She gritted her teeth and pushed off.

And walk she did, for what seemed like forever and likely was. Through it all, Alex was right there to catch her when she stumbled, which was often, his expression all that was kind as he helped her along. It fair drove Mary mad. She didn't want him to be kind to her. Frankly, she didn't want to react to him at all. The men in her life had never been what one would call soft on her. Yet here one was, a bleedin' lord, for goodness sake, who treated her like fine china.

And you love it.

Aye, she did. Wished for just a moment—

Ach, you're having those fairy-tale notions again.

And she was, even though she knew it would end. It always did.

* * *

The house came into view suddenly, Mary coming to a halt when she spied it through a break in the trees.

"Let's go around," she said, turning in the opposite direction.

"Around? Are you daft, woman? You need clothes, shoes, and ideally, a warm fire. Not to mention, the sooner we secure help, the sooner we can return to Wainridge and Gabby."

She looked up at him, unsure if she'd heard him correctly. "And you think they'll help us there?" she asked, pointing to the house—well, more of a manor, really. Square it was, and three stories high, but large enough to tell those who came upon it that the owner was landed gentry. Ivy covered the front of it, white-trimmed windows that sparkled in such a way as to denote an army of servants with washrags in their hands.

"Of course, once I tell them who I am."

Lord, would you listen to him?

"You think they'll believe you?"

"Why wouldn't they?"

She almost laughed. They were both covered in dirt, the hem of her robe torn, and now tattered and frayed. Her hair hung down her back like a gypsy with dandelion hair and he wanted to go calling on the neighborhood lord.

Dicked in the nob for sure.

But she shrugged, convinced that when his silliness here knocked on that door, it'd be slammed in his face almost as quickly as it'd opened, but there'd be no convincing *him* of that. So her expression said, "Suit yourself."

He half-bowed.

She rolled her eyes, thinking the man would try the patience of a glacier. When he turned away, she hobbled behind him as he led the way.

The house seemed to grow as fast as a two-year-old as they approached. Oh, it were nothing compared to the duke's home. But it was a country gentleman's home, no doubt about that, and in Mary's experience, there was no bigger snob in all of Christendom than the landed gentry. They didn't have titles, aye, they didn't even own a fancy crest, but they acted like it.

"We should knock on the back door," she said simply because she knew they stood a better chance of gaining sympathy from one of the under staff than a butler, or any other member of the upper staff. That much she'd learned in her brief stay at the marquis's home.

"Don't be silly," he said, "we shall ring the front."

Mary rolled her eyes. *Ring the front,* she silently mimicked. The man had bangers for brains.

"Stay behind me," he ordered, trotting off across the lawn and strolling toward the door like they were in bleedin' London. Mary half expected him to pull out a card. She almost snorted.

There were no steps, just a plain gravel path—didn't it just figure?—that led to the front door and had Mary wincing the whole way, though she tried to keep to the carriage ruts where the stones had faded to dirt. For the first time she found herself wishing she'd be wrong. Aye, how nice a warm fire and a tub of water to soak her feet would be. And then later to return to Abu. And, aye, even Miss Gabriella. Cold must be getting to her because she actually missed the little termagant.

They reached the front door. Alex knocked on it. Actually, what he did was lift a brass ring attached to the nose of a lion and let it fly. Fancy door that, she noted, elegant scroll work carved into S-shaped patterns, a brass kick plate that shone so brightly, she could see her bandaged feet in them.

The door opened.

Mary took one look at the man who answered the door and said, "Lord, we're in for it now," under her breath, even as she almost closed her eyes in delight at the warm air that filtered out to them and stirred loose strands of her hair.

"May I help you?" he asked Alex in as pompous a tone as she'd ever heard from his lordship. Tall he was. And thin, with gray hair. When his hazel eyes slid past Alex to land upon her, they widened a bit, then just as quickly narrowed.

"I wish to speak to the master of the home."

The eyes moved back to Alex, a condescending brow lifting. "Do you now?" he asked.

"Yes." And Alex only made it worse by saying, "Immediately."

"I'm afraid he's not receiving guests today."

"But—"

The door slammed in their faces.

Alex jerked so violently, Mary thought he might launch himself to the moon.

"Impudent man," he said, turning to her. "Did you *hear* his tone of voice?"

Mary had heard that tone all her life, especially where swells were concerned, and so she only shrugged.

Alex turned back to the door, reaching for the door knocker again.

"I wouldn't."

"Why ever not?"

"Because if you annoy him, he might set the sheriff, or magistrate, or justice of the peace, or whatever passes for law in these parts, and then we'll be in a fine kettle of fish."

"But I should welcome a sheriff's intervention."

"If a fancy butler doesn't recognize you for what you are, what makes you think a sheriff will? And I should remind you, m'lord, that vagrants are incarcerated for wandering the countryside. Transported for being guilty of nothing more than having no place to call home."

"I am the Marquis of Warrick. I am not without a home."

And with that, he turned, lifted the brass handle, and let it fly.

Mary looked heavenward again.

The door swung open and a blunderbuss emerged.

"What'd I tell you?"

"What the blazes do you *think* you're doing, man?"

"Go on. Get out of here," the butler said. "The both of you afore I report you to the squire."

"What'd I tell you?" Mary repeated, clucking her tongue.

"Then report me, you fool. I am the Marquis of Warrick," Alex said, drawing himself up to his full height. "I am a member of the House of Lords. Heir to the Duke of Wainridge and I demand to see your master."

Mary had to give him credit; if she'd been that butler, she might have found herself wondering if Alex spoke the truth. Alas, she forgot the one cardinal truth; people only ever saw what they wanted to see and it was far easier to see the worse.

"Off with you," the butler repeated, waving the firearm.

Mary took a step back. To give him credit, Alex did, too.

"Now," the butler added with another wave.

"I shall come back," Alex said. "Someday I will come back in my coach and six and speak to your master about your abominable treatment—"

The butler lowered his weapon and slammed the door. Again.

"Why that—" She watched as his fists clenched. "Of all the—" The tips of his fingers reddened, he squeezed them so hard. "I ought to—"

"Finish a sentence?" Mary asked, crossing her arms in front of her. With the door closed, it'd turned as cold as an icebox again. It made her skin start to sting, made her body jerk with a great spasm of a chill, made her wish, for just a moment, that his lordship had succeeded with his silly plan. Ach. She hated always being right.

"I simply cannot believe—"

"That without your fancy horses and carriage you weren't recognized as a lord?" He gave her a non-blinking stare. "Let me tell you something, m'lord, people are cruel to those they consider beneath them. It doesn't matter if you have fancy talk or expensive clothes. We look like dredges, you and I, so that's what we are. No amount of caterwauling will change that."

And yet he looked like he might give it another try. Well, she wished him well. She, for one, wasn't going to spend the night in a college, no matter that it might be warm.

She would give anything to be warm.

Anything.

But the cold had settled deep into her bones and she was bleedin' tired of it. And worried about Abu, and the fact that some fool duke might kill her pet after mistaking it for an exotic animal that he could add to his collection of trophy heads.

"Where are you going?" he called out after her.

"To find me some clothes."

"And where do you plan on doing that?"

"If I knew that, mayhap I'd be there already."

But she'd only taken two wincing steps when a voice cried out, "There they are, Sir Thorton."

Alex and Mary turned, Mary groaning at the sight of the bewigged man that trailed behind an outraged butler, two fart catches following behind the fancy toff. Mary had been around long enough to know there were wigs and there were *wigs.* This wig was a magistrate's wig. She'd stake her favorite costume on it.

"Damn," she heard his lordship mutter.

"I'll wager we won't be seeing your daughter any time soon," Mary added.

Chapter Ten

"I don't bloody believe this." Alex paced from one end of the small room they were being held in, to the other. "It is beyond belief. Ridiculous. Absurd."

Mary Callahan silently moved her mouth along with his, which incensed Alex all the more, even as he felt a pang of guilt as he watched her cradle her foot in her lap. Someone had given her a tattered brown cloak, not out of kindness, but to shield her indecency. Her legs peeked out from that cloak, the edge of her nightclothes creeping up. She glanced up, her long red hair catching the early afternoon light even though the room they were in had one small window set high in the wall.

Alex looked away, feeling utterly embarrassed and, yes, ashamed. *He* was the reason they were in such a muddle. He was the reason why Gabby and his father would go a full day without knowing where they were. He and only he.

"I am the Marquis of Warrick," he said. "One would think my breeding and lineage would show upon my face."

"You forget who your ancestors are."

He looked at her, about to give her a serious set-down for slandering his lineage so, until he thought about it for a moment. His mouth closed.

The room they were in was actually an antechamber of a rectory, the church, they'd been told, doubling as a court when the occasion warranted it. As such their window was made of stained glass, the image of two white doves in a field of blue filtered by sunlight. It turned the wood floor topaz.

"What you need to do is concentrate on how to get us out of this ramshackle cell," she said, gingerly trying to clean out her wounds, "instead of dwelling on no one believing who you are."

"There is no way out," he said. "It would appear as if we've been tried and convicted simply because we happened to be passing through a town that had had the sad misfortune of just being robbed."

"Welcome to the world of the poor, m'lord. Sometimes all you have to do is simply exist to be punished."

He didn't want to admit it, but he thought she might have a point.

But what had Alex feeling even more buggered, what made him wish for the thousandth time that he'd never knocked on that damn squire's door, was not the fact that his daughter and father would be worried about them. No, what worried him was that he'd have to spend the night in a room. A tiny room. Small. Really, really, minuscule.

His heart began to beat in his chest like he was a man with a string wrapped around his tooth, and a horse on the other end. His hands began to shake. And—devil take it—his skin began to itch like a nest of ants had crawled on it.

Bloody hell.

He tried to distract himself by concentrating on Mary, and for a moment it worked. She looked better than she had earlier, he noted. At least he had that to be grateful for. The squire's cook had given them some stew, Mary having all but devoured it in a gulp. So had he. And though it seemed an inconsequential matter, he suddenly realized she had the prettiest of noses. Small and tipped at the edge.

And then his gaze caught on the door, and all thoughts of Mary fled.

He itched the skin at his neckline. It was exactly five paces from one end of the room to the other; he should know. He'd counted. Numerous times. But it did no good to keep on the move, for his heart only seemed to beat faster, his gaze fixing on that damnable locked door. Locked. Locked. Locked.

"You got fleas, m'lord? Never seen a man itch as much as you."

He had no idea he'd stopped before that door, that he stared at it, breathing hard, hands clenching and unclenching in between itches. He turned to her, her feet apparently forgotten as she stared up at him.

"Here now," she said, "don't tell me you've taken on a chill?"

He opened his mouth, about to tell her that was, indeed, the problem, but he couldn't do it. And so he said, "I'm afraid I'm a bit claustrophobic."

"Claustorfic?"

"Claustro*phobic*," he repeated. "Afraid of small, enclosed places."

She blinked, her brows lifting. "Well now, waking up to find yourself in a coffin must'a been a wee bit hard on you then."

She almost startled a laugh out of him. Almost. "Indeed."

Her brows lowered, eyes following the motion of his hands as he itched again.

"And I get hives when I'm nervous."

"But there's nothing to be nervous about. We're safe as jewels in a box in here."

Box was not the correct word to say. Not now. Not ever.

He felt his breath hitch, felt his heart rate ramp up. Felt new hives break out on his legs.

"M'lord?"

He didn't answer, just bent down and scratched his legs. Why should he say something when there was nothing to say? He was a coward. A lily-livered, itching coward when it came to confinement. He could admit that. To himself.

"Here now. Don't go all blubber-kneed on me now. You're a man. You're supposed to have a stiff upper lip."

He nodded, scratching at his arm.

"Careful. You might give yourself welts if you keep goin' on like that."

And she actually looked amused. *Amused.*

"Come, m'lord. Sit down beside me."

"No."

"Do it."

And like a five-year-old child, he did as ordered. Scratching the whole way. He sat down beside her, though his knees shook and his breath jigged like a spirited horse.

"There now. That's better. Now, tell me what it's like to be a great lord."

Her words almost didn't penetrate the pressure that had begun to build in his brain. Indeed, to make it impossible to think. But he forced himself to listen.

"Did you have your own pony as a child?"

Pony? Who cared about a pony? He almost snapped the words at her, but of course, he knew 'twas only his anxiety that made him on edge.

So he said, "Of course," hearing himself as if from a great distance.

"And did you order that pony about like you order everyone else about now?"

Bloody hell. He needed air. He needed freedom. He needed to get up again, if only so he could itch his back.

She stopped him with a hand, quickly, reaching out as if they were the best of friends, her smile oddly endearing as she said, "Did you act like bloody Wellington? Bring me my pony," she imitated a male voice. "Now, now, what, what."

The words sounded farther away. He had trouble focusing, had trouble breathing. He clutched at her hand.

"Alex," she said sternly. "Look at me."

He didn't, tried, instead, to calm himself, to tell himself that what he felt was simply a reaction to being enclosed in a room. He would be all right. He had no choice. He *had* to be all right. For Gabby's sake.

"Alex," she ordered.

And then he felt warm hands on either side of his face, was startled into gazing into her concerned green eyes. "I'm here, Alex. You're not alone. I'm here with you." She patted his cheek.

He looked at her, and god help him, he almost didn't recognize her. But then she put her nose right up next to his, the tip of it touching his own. He caught the scent of her, a smell that was earthy and warm and that made him close his eyes and simply breathe. A calm began to settle over him again, the itching faded a bit. He closed his eyes, inhaled even more deeply. Lovely, she smelled lovely.

"Don't think you're going to work that energy o' yours off, m'lord, for I tell you here and now, there'll be no lechery in this room to pass the time."

His eyes sprang open.

She smiled.

He could only stare, looking from one eye to the other as he waited, waited for . . . something.

Her smile slowly faded. Time seemed to freeze for the both of them. Alex leaned toward her.

And then she released him, faced forward, messing with her cloak as she said, "Now, go on. Tell me about your childhood." But in her gaze, right before she'd turned away, he'd seen something in her eyes. Something rich and warm and remarkably like longing.

And god help him, he'd felt the same thing.

But he was not his father. He would never take advantage of her. Not now. Not ever.

"It was," he forced a breath in, "a childhood like any other young lord's."

"Well, then, I suppose you can stop right there for I've heard it all before, me knowing so many lords and all."

It took him a moment to realize she was being sarcastic.

"What do you want to know?"

She was staring straight ahead still, her eyes having gone unfocused. "What was it like?" she asked again. "What did it feel like to have a roof over your head always? To know that you had a place in this world. To know that you are and always will be Alexander Drummond, Marquis of Warrick, heir to a dukedom?"

He found himself staring at her. Found himself suddenly swallowing. "It felt like nothing for it simply *was.*"

Her profile in the waning light looked strikingly pretty, and wonderfully perfect. Alex suddenly found himself forgetting about his anxiety, though he scratched at a lingering itch on his neck.

"Aye," she said. "I suppose that's true. You were born to greatness while I," he watched her swallow, look down for a moment, "I grew up wanting greatness."

"You did?"

She nodded, her eyes once again growing distant as she tipped her head up and back, her voice low as she said, "Sometimes I would face the stars—just gaze into the heavens and know that someday I would be *someone*."

He hardly dared move, feeling almost afraid to breathe, for fear she'd remember his presence.

"Some days, it was all I could do to hang on to the dream. My mother died when I was five. Then it was up to me to raise me brothers, and raise them I did, and I took care of me father, too." She swallowed. He could see the way her throat worked as she did so. "It wasn't easy feeding six mouths. Sometimes it was all I could do to make the food stretch a week, only to realize too late that I should have figured for a week more. Da was never happy when that happened." She shivered as if the memory chilled her, and he had a feeling it did. "But somehow I lived through it, all the while vowing that one day I'd leave, make my way to London where I could be a *somebody*."

"And did you?"

She started at his words, and he knew then that he'd been right. She'd forgotten his presence. "I went to

London, all right. I learned the hard way that it's a man's world out there, and that a young, naïve female has no business trying to work in it."

"How old were you?"

"Sixteen."

Sixteen? He'd been at Oxford at that age. Still learning Latin and Greek. Still trying to understand the world and his position in it, while she . . . she'd been out living it.

"But enough about me, m'lord. Tell me about your fairy-tale childhood. Tell me about your pony." She rested her cheek against the wall, and Alex almost thought he saw a tear track on her cheek. But, no. He must be imagining it. Mrs. Mary Callahan didn't cry.

So he told her about his pony, Rosie, and the time he'd fallen off the little horse and broken his leg. And the talking helped, for it kept his anxiety at bay, his hives fading away.

Time passed. Eventually she leaned into him, though he doubted she even realized what she did. And still he talked. And then the weight of her body made him realize that she might have fallen asleep. He shifted and looked down at her, and she had, indeed, drifted off. Her lids closed against her cheeks, the thick lashes a smudge of shadow. And as he stared at that face, he wondered how she'd survived it all. How she'd kept her wits, and her sense of humor, and her undeniable charm. But what struck him most about her was what she didn't say, what she didn't complain about. He had a feeling it might have been a lot, that her childhood had been one notch above miserable.

How long he stared at her, he had no idea, but from nowhere came the urge to touch her. He had cause, then, to be grateful that she slept, for she remained blissfully unaware of his reaction to her. Unaware that he stroked the side of her cheek softly, her only response to his touch a small moue of irritation, almost as if she thought a fly crawled upon her skin. That almost made him smile. And then, because he couldn't seem to help himself, he lowered his head, a craving he knew he should never allow prompting him to taste the forbidden. One kiss. Just one.

He pressed his lips against her own, his heart beating as it had earlier—hard, frantic pumps—only for an entirely different reason.

She stirred as he kept his lips against her own. And there was a part of him that wished she would open her eyes. That she would meet his gaze, and that in that gaze he would see the desire he himself felt.

Alas, all she did was turn her head into the crook of his arm, sigh, then nestle closer to him; Alex inhaled deeply.

Lord help him, he wanted her. Badly.

Chapter Eleven

"Alex Drummond, you're being charged with theft and fraud."

It was the next morning after what had been a very, *very* long night. Alex stood in the center of a small room, a rail behind him separating him from the masses of people who'd shown up at the small church/court.

"Fraud?" he said. "Are you mad? What the blazes for?"

"Impersonating a lord."

"I am not impersonating one, you oaf. I *am* one, which you would know if you were near my own shire."

Very well, it had been a child-like slur, but it was the best he could come up with given his lack of sleep and his general state of anxiety.

The magistrate didn't seem to notice. He sat behind the pulpit, the squire apparently wearing many hats in this part of the country, or wigs as the case may be. Landowner, vicar and Justice of the Peace. He had assumed absolute power in the region, much to Alex's dismay. Spectators filled the oak pews behind him, Alex standing at the foot of the pulpit. No one recognized him, but of course they wouldn't for they were far from Alex's lands. A big hulking farm hand with shoulders as wide as a draft horse's stood behind him. Alex had a feeling that if he made a break for it, he wouldn't be chased; the giant would simply stamp on him.

"How do you plead?"

"Why, not guilty, of course."

The magistrate looked pained. "Very well, what is your defense?"

"I demand an attorney."

"This is not London, sir. We have no fancy attorneys to defend you. Beside, have you the coin to pay for one?"

He bit back an oath of frustration.

"I will grant you, sir, that you do a remarkable impression of your betters. Most play actors do. However, the fact remains that we have had a series of thefts in the area, thefts that coincide with your arrival. As such, I am quite convinced of your guilt."

"But that's ridiculous—"

"Silence." The man banged his fist. "Alexander Drummond, if that is indeed your real name, you are hereby convicted of theft and fraud, sentenced to be taken away from my shire and sent to London where you will be remaindered to one of the hulks."

"A hulk? Are you mad?"

"Take him away."

This couldn't be happening, Alex thought. It just couldn't. He was a revenue commander. An officer of the Crown. *He* was the one that did the arresting. Not the other way around.

"Come with me, sir," the giant said.

But, alas, it was all too real, Alex wondering for a brief, panic-stricken moment if he'd ever see Gabriella again.

They led him outside, the sun hidden behind clouds that were firmly clasped closed, yet the gray light felt bright enough to make his eyes ache and his lids lower. It was an old Tudor town with narrow streets and M-shaped buildings, dark wood beams intersecting their white fronts. A few people milled about, but most, he decided, were inside the church with the tall, white spire.

"I am telling you, sir, you are making a mistake," he said to his guard, but the farmhand ignored him, leading him toward what looked to be an ice cart converted into a makeshift prison transport. It was completely enclosed, with not even a window cut into the side.

Alex felt his mouth go dry.

"Here you go," the man said, opening a door. For a brief moment Alex thought about struggling, but what was the point? Thus, when the man opened the narrow door at the back of the transport vehicle, Alex climbed inside. But by the time he took his seat upon the flat wooden floor, he'd begun to feel a deep-seated rage. Less than five minutes later Mary joined him.

"Well, now, this is much better than roaming the countryside. Thank the good lord above you thought to knock on that squire's door. I fancy the hulks will be much warmer than your home in London."

"Sod off, Mary."

She jerked as if he'd hit her, blinked a few times, clucked her tongue.

"And why the blazes do you always sound like a chicken when you're irritated?"

"Habit," she said simply.

"Well, I'm in no mood for your smart mouth *or* your clucking."

She stared a bit longer, her expression lightening as she said, "Very good, m'lord. I see you're growing a spine."

He didn't answer.

It was, Alex realized, the lowest point of his life.

And far away, at an estate called Wainridge, Gabriella felt low, too.

Her father still hadn't returned. Worse, she'd woken up this morning convinced he'd run off with that horrible nurse.

She stared outside through a pane of glass dotted with rain, hardly noticing the cold that seeped through the small crack where the wooden frame met the casing. The window seat had a comfy blue and white down blanket covering it, but Gabby ignored that, too, as she recalled the way her father had looked at the nurse . . . and what the nurse had said in the carriage when they'd thought her asleep.

You want to kiss me.

Had he? Had he truly? How could he want to kiss a woman with such horrible red hair? And who talked so much?

Gabby felt another tear teeter down her cheek, zigging and zagging so that she had to wipe at half her face to catch it. And if he did want to kiss her, did that mean he'd run off with her? One of the downstairs servants seemed to think so. She'd overheard her say exactly that. Her father had run off. He'd become a Wicked Wainridge, though she didn't know what the last part meant.

And as she sat there, the fear within her grew and grew and grew.

And then something jumped in her lap.

Gabby shrieked. Which made the creature screech. Which made Gabby shove the thing off her. Which made the creature leap down . . .

It was a monkey.

Her shriek died mid-scream.

A monkey.

She sat up, hearing footsteps outside her door. The monkey must have, too, for it turned and darted under her frilly bed.

"Miss Gabriella," a housemaid cried as she burst into the room, her white mob cap knocked askew, the black dress she wore a stark contrast against her white face. "What 'appened?"

"I saw a spider," Gabby said, with a look at her bed.

"Lord above. Gave me a fright you did. What with the Runners off searching for your father, and you screamin' like you did. I thought you was being taken—" The maid stopped abruptly, seeming to realize that she shouldn't mention a possible kidnapping. "Well, glad it is you're well," she said, stepping back, curtsying and then closing the door.

Gabby waited a breathless ten seconds before slowly leaving the window seat and approaching the bed, her cold feet appreciating the warmth of the plush ivory rug.

"Here, monkey, monkey." Silence. "Come here. I won't hurt you."

It was as if the little thing understood her, for she saw it lift the edge of her coverlet as if they were engaged in a game of hide and seek. A white face peered up at her, pink skin around his nose and mouth and eyes looking almost human-like. And then the creature smiled.

Gabby couldn't help but smile, too.

"Come here," she said.

The monkey listened, leaping into her arms and snuggling under her chin like they were the best of friends.

And as the two lonely creatures comforted each other, a friendship was forged, one that would last a lifetime.

Alex felt like yelling. The driver of the cart they rode in took pernicious delight at finding every rut and hole and bottomless pit he could find on a road that, by all accounts, should be impassable. Alex's cranium smacked the roof every time. Worse, he could barely see his hand in front of his face, the only light that which shone in through the paper-thin cracks between the boards. He couldn't breathe, though he told himself that was likely a good thing given the poor quality of the air. Mold filled the interior of the vehicle with a sour smell, not even a small breeze brushing it away.

"Devil take it," he said after one particularly hard knock. "Can he not endeavor to go around?"

Mary Callahan reclined against the very back of the box, her eyes closed as she wound one strand of her hair around and around her index finger so that the thing looked like a Christmas ribbon when she was done. "The roads are rough, m'lord, or have you forgotten we were stranded at your father's place prior to your kidnapping?"

Since the moment she'd entered the cart, she'd been quiet playing with that strand. She hadn't even spared him a glance. Not this morning when she'd woken. Not before they'd been taken away for their trial—if one wanted to call it that. Not even when he'd been served a deplorable breakfast of some kind of lumpy floury thing that might have been gruel.

Alex could stand it no longer. "Do you not care that we are on our way to the hulks?"

She shrugged, her red hair shifting over one shoulder. In the dim light he could see that she'd pulled her cloak around her dressing gown. Why no one had offered to supply her with a dress, Alex couldn't fathom. He was certain it wouldn't have been hard for the local magistrate to arrange such a thing.

"Ain't no sense in worrying over that. Isn't a bleedin' bloody thing we can do about it."

"Mrs. Callahan, your sublime unconcern over our fate worries me ill."

Finally, her eyes snapped open. She flicked the ribbon of red hair over her shoulder. "At least I haven't turned cross."

"Cross? I am not cross."

But he knew he was. More than that, he knew the reason why, and it had nothing to do with the farce of a trial he'd been forced to endure and everything to do with the way his skin began to itch.

"You've got the hives again," she said.

He did, damn it. Worse, his pulse raced. Could hear the blood buzz in his ears, signaling the onset of yet another one of his blasted attacks, as if his itching skin wasn't warning enough.

"Lord love you," he thought he heard her murmur. "Shall I try and turn your mind with a tale?"

And though he hated to admit weakness, though he reminded himself that he was the Crown's best revenue commander and as such, above such a silly thing as a fear of confined spaces and—of all things—hives, his voice was barely audible as he said, "Yes, please."

"Very well. What?"

"What what?"

"What would you like me to talk about?"

It was a challenge to concentrate, to force the words into his brain and then assimilate them.

"Tell me about your childhood," he finally said.

"Isn't much to tell and what little there is, I told you last night."

Sadness poked through his fear for half a heartbeat, but it quickly retreated as he itched his belly. "Very well. Then tell me . . ." He had to all but mush his mind into working. "Tell me your happiest memory."

If Alex could have seen Mary's face when he asked the question, he might have changed his mind. But he was too busy trying not to let his panic get the best of him again, and so he didn't notice the way Mary grew as still as a startled bird, the way her hands clenched in her lap. Then again, chances were he wouldn't have been able to see her anyway in the stuffy darkness and gloom.

"I'd rather you tell me more about your own childhood."

He shook his head. "Already done that. Need you to distract me." And it was a testament to his state of mind that he didn't even care that the words made him sound weak. He closed his eyes, trying to regulate his breathing as he'd done last night, trying not to scratch at the bloody, silly welts.

When she didn't immediately answer, Alex opened his eyes, trying to find her in the darkness.

"I was ten years old," she said at last.

He almost released a sigh. Her face was in profile, a knothole allowing a thin beam of light to shine upon the floor. That light illuminated her toes, reminding him that she didn't have any shoes.

His fault. They might have been home by now. He might have been reunited with Gabby. Instead they rolled toward an uncertain destiny.

"What happened?" he said over a lump of guilt.

“I found a horse.”

It wasn’t the answer he expected, though he’d be hard pressed to say what, exactly, he’d expected.

“He just appeared one day.” And the smile he saw was one he’d never seen cavort playfully across her face. Beautiful. Unexpected. Like a gift from the heavens.

“There he was grazing on the side of the road, free as a bird, and the ugliest beast you’ve ever seen. Skin and bones, he was. A big bay with feet the size of dinner plates and huge ears to match.” She laughed softly. “Looking back on it, I think the reason why his owners turned him loose was because he was too ugly to sell and too skinny to use for meat. Poor thing.”

The smile dimmed a moment, but then returned full bore. “So I kept him. Oh, I asked if anyone knew who he belonged to, but no one ’fessed up. Truth be told, he looked so rackety he might have traveled a long way before coming to stop by that roadside. I didn’t care. He was a horse. I claimed him as mine.”

Her eyes found his in the darkness. “Have you ever wanted anything so bad that you’d have done anything to get it, and then once you had it, to keep it?”

Had he? He honestly couldn’t recall. But then again, their worlds were so far apart as to be the sun and the moon, he admitted as he absently scratched his thigh.

“My father hated that horse, but I told him I’d take care of it. Feed it. Clean up after it. Whatever I had to do to keep him. And I did, too, working odd jobs for anyone I could find, in between taking care of my brothers. ’Course, once I started making some blunt, my dad demanded I give it to him. But I learned to hold back just enough to buy food and oats for my horse. And when Admiral—that’s what I named him because he had so many battle scars—when Admiral got strong enough, I began to ride him." Her smile grew wistful. "The first time, m'lord, is a day I shall never forget."

And all he did was stare, marveling that she would consider riding a sway-backed old nag one of her life's greatest pleasures. That she should have gone to work at the tender age of ten, when the young ladies of his social set were still sitting at their governess's knee. That she thought nothing of the obvious squalor and strife that she'd endured as a child. But most of all, that she'd managed to mature into a woman with a sense of humor and a zest for life that was evident in her every word.

"Do you still have him?"

What a silly question. Of course she didn't still have him; he knew it the moment her smile snuffed out.

"He died."

"Died? How?"

She shrugged, her happy smile falling away like old timbers. "He was a horse. They die."

There was more to the story than that, for he'd glimpsed something in her eyes, something painful and unmistakable: a look of loss nothing could hide.

"What happened?" he asked softly, his anxiety forgotten as he reached forward and clasped her hand.

She met his gaze, and like last night, something passed between them. Unlike last night, she wasn't asleep, and so the connection felt deeper, his need to comfort her so great, he felt helpless with a longing for it.

"I was sixteen," she said. "For six years I'd managed to keep and feed Admiral, no easy feat, let me tell you, for my father resented that horse with every breath he took. It was a battle day in and day out, my father unable to understand that I needed Admiral as much as he needed me. He was my only friend. A confidant who knew my deepest fears, and dreams. I would have done anything to keep him, and just about did, and then one day my father decided to use him as a plow horse."

Alex realized then that he'd probed a wound best left undisturbed. A horrible premonition overtook him, made his breath catch. Made him squeeze her hand even more, his own discomfort forgotten in the face of her pain.

She didn't seem to notice. "I don't know what Admiral used to do before he came to me, but I'd bet he wasn't used as a plow horse. Or maybe he was, and that's why he ran away, but whatever the case, he didn't want to be one the day my father tried to hitch him up."

Her face had gone oddly lax, as if the telling of the story was so old, that she was beyond emotion now.

"He kicked my father in the leg that day, nearly snapping it in two. It didn't matter that I told my dad not to do it, that Admiral was mine to do with as I pleased. In his eyes, the horse was his." She shook her head. "I think that kick sent my father over the edge. He said he was tired of feeding him, tired of the time it took me to clean up after him. The horse had to go. God help me I thought he meant I'd have to sell him. I never, ever thought he meant to shoot him."

Oh, God.

"When he grabbed his hunting rifle, I thought he meant to bring it with him into town. It wasn't until he stopped outside the small paddock I kept Admiral in that I realized what he intended to do."

"Good God, Mary," he said. "I'm so sorry."

She shrugged, the absence of a single tear in her eyes somehow more painful to him than if she'd sobbed buckets.

"I tried to stop him, but there was nothing I could do. In the end I consoled myself with the fact that Admiral died a quick death."

Lord, he'd never heard such a sad tale in his life.

"I wanted to kill my father right then. I truly did. Even told him so. But he said if I didn't like what he'd done, I could leave." She met his gaze. "So I did."

And it all connected together then . . . how she'd left when she was sixteen. He'd thought it a young age to strike out on one's own. Now he knew why.

"I left. Never looked back, either. Well, mayhap once or twice. Being on my own was a frightening thing, at first. But I survived, as you can see." She splayed her hands. "Though I never got meself arrested like you managed to do the first time you were on your own."

"I did not get us arrested."

And he argued with her not because he felt slighted, but because the change of subject was needed. He knew that. Pounced on it.

"Indeed you did," she volleyed back. "If not for you we'd be long past Shopshire and on our way to your father's house unfettered."

"Shopshire?" he asked, for a moment disbelieving the words that entered his ears.

"Aye. That pitiful town we were in was called Shopshire. And who, might I ask, names a town Shop? That would be like naming a dog Bark, or a horse Neigh."

"Good lord," Alex shouted, ignoring her logic, though she did have a point. "Do you mean to say all day yesterday and this morn we were in *Shopshire*?"

"We were."

"But that is not above ten miles from Sherborne."

Mary just stared at him blankly.

"My cousin Reinleigh Montgomery is the Earl of Sherborne."

That got a reaction from her. She shot away from the wall as if an ant had bit her back. "Why didn't you say that afore?" She moved toward the back of the cart. The air stirred as she passed, some of her hair tickling the side of his face.

"What are you doing?"

He watched as she pried a rather large splinter from one of the timbers, inserting it between the crack of the door. From there it was a simple matter for her to flip up the swinging latch so that it spun out of the U-shaped holder outside.

"Good lord," he said as the door opened with a blast of sweet-smelling air, tiny drops of rain pushing in until the warmth of the carriage pulled them back out.

She gave him a cocky smile that was almost endearing in the way it conveyed her absolute pride in herself. "I was going to wait until we got nearer to London, but since you've a cousin nearby, and what with you being afraid of small spaces and the way you get hives and all . . ."

Alex wanted to kiss her. He truly did. And he would have, too, but in the next moment she was giving him a wink just before she slipped out the door.

Chapter Twelve

He looked like he wanted to kiss her. And as Mary recalled the way it'd felt to have his lips cover her own last eve, she realized she wanted him to. Instead she held out her hand, saying, "And if you get us arrested again, m'lord, you're on your own."

His lordship just stared up at her. Rain fell in miserable drips from the sky, made his shirt even muddier than before. But Mary thought him still the handsomest cull she'd ever seen.

"Thank you," he said simply.

And the look in his eyes . . . it made her feel like Mary Callahan—smuggler's daughter, former turnip-cart operator, lately of the Royal Circus—was Somebody, which, if she were honest with herself, was something she'd longed for all her life.

He pulled himself up, his body standing tall and firm. And she thought—*oh*, how she held her breath because he seemed so handsome then.

But in the next instant he was turning away, saying, "Let us be off, before that driver realizes we've escaped."

A half-hour later, Mary's feet felt like they'd been scrubbed with a rock, a sharp-edged, porous volcanic rock. Lord above, every step she took made her wince, his lordship's stockings doing little to shield the pads of her feet.

They were wending their way through the countryside, Alex utterly convinced he knew exactly where they were.

Ach, Mary had heard that before.

But he'd been insistent he could find his way to Sherborne blindfolded. Mary certainly hoped so. She were wet, in pain, and so cold her nose dripped like melted wax. It had just stopped raining, water pooling on leaves that little fairies dumped on her head just as she crossed beneath. Her hair hung like dog fur around her ears, and she'd begun to suspect the cloak she wore was infested with fleas. Her skin itched like a hound's.

So immersed was she in wallowing in her own misery, she almost smashed into Alex's back when he stopped suddenly.

"There it is."

Mary followed his gaze, her frozen spine popping into place as she straightened suddenly.

Another bleedin' castle. Coo, would you look at that.

Alex chose to look at her with an expression of near boyish enthusiasm. And Mary decided then and there that when he weren't looking like someone hung off his testicles, he seemed almost human. Oh, he were still a handsome gent—he always would be—but that handsomeness suddenly took on the shine of a coin that'd been spat on, rubbed and polished clean. Hidden dimples came out to play. Wrinkles by the sides of his eyes loosened and shaved years of seriousnessness off his face. It all made Mary long to swipe his wet hair off his forehead.

Argh, lost your mind, you have. He's a lord, Mary girl, best you remember that.

And if ever she needed evidence of the world he lived

in, she need only look off yonder. Sherborne was a shire of rolling green hills and thick woods with acres of green pastures between them. The castle itself was a true castle with parapets and turrets and the like. They'd been slowly climbing a hill, one that crested above the castle, Mary forgetting her disgruntlement as she stared at the place. It looked just like a drawing she'd once seen of a castle in a fairy story. Granite walls, large arched door in the front, and a gold and red standard that tried to fly in a half-hearted breeze.

"We need to walk down this hill to the road visible just there through the trees." He pointed down below. "That will take us to the main entrance."

He bounded off with all the enthusiasm of a squirrel carrying a nut. But they'd hardly taken a step when someone said, "I'm afraid you won't be welcome at the main entrance."

They both turned. A horse and rider had broken through the trees. Mary felt her breath escape in a rush, for the man looked like the very devil himself as he sat atop his black stallion, twin streams of steam shooting from the horse's nostrils.

"Don't tell me to leave, you silly cawker."

Mary felt her gaze whip to Alex's. Silly cawker? Where had he learned *that* from?

You.

Mary straightened in pride. The man's eyes narrowed. He clucked his horse forward—not that the beast needed much incentive. And then it was almost comical the way the expression on the man's face turned instantly to one of puzzlement.

"Alex?"

"Aye, you wretch. 'Tis I."

He pulled his horse to a stop. "What the devil are *you* doing here?"

"Walking to Sherborne castle, as you can see."

"But where is your coach?"

"'Tis a long story, one that I almost hate to regale you with, so I shan't. Not till later."

The man Mary now suspected was the earl looked at her. Or, rather, he studied her, his gaze lingering on her breasts (thus proving to Mary that the two men were, indeed, related) before meeting Alex's eyes again.

"I see the company you keep has improved, though her feet are bleeding all over my land."

Mary looked down. Blimey, her feet *had* started to ooze.

"Mary, why didn't you tell me?"

She looked up, shrugged. "What was there to tell?" she said. "We needed to keep moving. Weren't no sense in stopping over a little blood."

"Take her up before you," Alex said to his cousin.

The earl looked like he'd just been asked to push her off a cliff. "On this stallion? Are you daft? She'd be dumped before her backside hit the saddle."

Mary decided then and there that she rather liked Alex's cousin. Weren't no fussiness to his manner of speech.

"Fine, then I'll carry her."

"No," Mary ordered, stopping him with a hand. "You'll fall on your backside trying to traverse this terrain with me in your arms, and beggin' your pardon, m'lord, but I don't ken to more injuries."

"Very well. Rein, dismount. She shall ride. You shall walk."

"Ride Onyx? I think not. I can easily ride back and fetch another—"

"She's bleeding, Rein."

Mary was about to point out that she'd been bleeding for hours, but just then another chill racked her body. Aye, she'd be frozen into a block of ice if she were made to wait for these two sapskulls to figure out what to do.

"Get off your horse, m'lord."

The earl blinked down at her.

"Quickly now."

Two pairs of eyes turned toward her.

"My lady," the earl said. "You do not understand—"

"Get off the horse," she insisted, the way he called her *my lady* making her draw up.

Reluctantly, the earl dismounted, the stallion dancing around the moment his feet touched the ground.

"Careful," Alex warned.

"I told you, this is a silly idea."

"Stand back, m'lord earl."

The man looked over at her, his eyes narrowed. "I don't think—"

Mary ran at him. The horse saw her, splayed all four legs in opposite directions in shock. That gave Mary time to come alongside of him.

"Mary, don't—"

The horse whirled. Mary grabbed at the mane just as the beast dug in hooves and took off at a run.

The technique came to her instantly. Using a combination of strength, the horse's momentum, and the ground itself to propel her forward, Mary vaulted onto the horse's back, landing in the saddle with a softness that took even her by surprise, given the fact that she hadn't performed the trick in months. She'd worried that her chemise might get in the way, but she needn't have. The thing ripped, exposing her legs to her stunned audience of two. But a man staring at her legs wasn't anything she wasn't used to, so she didn't care.

The hardest part was fighting the horse's forward motion to grasp the reins that his lordship had thankfully left over the horse's neck, but she managed to do the deed. A big brute the horse might be, but he had a mouth like butter and the manners of a gentleman once he realized it was no gentle*woman* who rode his back.

"Easy now," she coaxed, the animal's gallop turning into a canter, then a trot, until, finally, a prancing walk.

"Easy," she repeated, turning him toward the two men. Though she told herself she didn't care what his lordship thought of her "talent," and though she warned herself that such an upright cull would likely be aghast at her unladylike skill, Mary still sought out Alex's gaze.

She had the rum-eyed pleasure of watching his mouth slap closed, the look on his face not one of disgust nor even dismay, but shock followed close on its heels by admiration as she pulled the horse to a stop, the animal's front hooves leaving skid marks in the grass.

"Where to, m'lord?"

"Where did you find her?"

They were walking back to his cousin's home, Alex unable to take his eyes off the sight of Mary Callahan as she cantered the horse off ahead of them, turned around, then cantered back. Expertly. Perfectly. And with a perfect seat rare amongst men, much less women.

"She's my daughter's nurse."

"She's *no* nurse."

Alex had begun to suspect the same thing. The first

time he had wondered had been when she locked Gabriella in her room. No nurse he'd ever met would have done such an outrageous thing. But he'd truly begun to suspect something wasn't quite right when she'd used such skill when evading their pursuers. There'd been an air about her as they'd fled, the air of someone who'd been in such a situation before.

"How did she come to be with you?"

"She rescued me from a kidnapping."

"Did she now?"

"And then she flipped open the lock of the ice cart we were imprisoned in."

"The tale grows more interesting. Perhaps you should start from the beginning?"

And so Alex did, knowing his cousin would be amused and entertained. And, indeed, he was, laughing when Alex described his outrage over not being recognized by a mere butler.

"Of all the things to happen to you," his cousin said. "You're such a stick in the mud, I can only imagine what you must have looked like when you were charged with theft."

"It was not at all amusing. The first thing I shall do when we reach Sherborne is dash a note off to my father and daughter reassuring them we are well. Once we have both eaten and rested, we shall return to Wainridge post haste."

"You'll not get far with the roads in their present shape."

"I am determined to try, if only to head for Shopshire and that silly squire so that I may rebuke him for daring to incarcerate me."

"Indeed, I'm not surprised."

"And what is that supposed to mean?"

Rein shrugged. "I meant no offense. 'Tis a matter of truth. *I* would have laughed to find myself in such a situation. You, however, will act the indignant lord, making certain that all involved are brought to task. You are, as always, determined to bring order back to the land."

"And what is wrong with that?"

Rein looked ahead to where Mary turned around his mount. "Nothing, nothing, but it makes me wonder what you will do with her. I have a house party in attendance."

"Devil take it."

"Aye, I invited Lord Falkner over to discuss our East Indian investments and before I knew it, five females and two matchmaking mamas were coming along with him. I tell you, Alex, it makes no sense. I am a blackguard. A rake. A certified lecher, and yet these two women think I would make a lovely husband for one of their innocent young daughters. Demme, they are like flesh peddlers, only worse."

"Mary's arrival will cause a stir."

"Likely, it will, not that I care. Perhaps it might scare them away. Then again, they will think her your tart, especially if she shows up on my doorstep dressed as she is. Then again, she might have to show up naked in order to truly startle them. I don't suppose you can convince her to shed her clothes?"

"Rein," Alex chided.

"No? Oh, well, I suppose we could sneak her into the servants' entrance. My staff will take excellent care of her."

"And gossip about her, too, no doubt."

Rein inclined his head. "Indeed, however, they have

proven themselves quite discreet in the past, thank the good lord above."

"Have they?" Alex asked, knowing his cousin referred to the other type of guest that frequented Sherborne, his cousin the earl's mistresses.

"You could likely trust them."

"But not your guests's staff should they catch word of Mary's presence."

"That, I'm afraid, I can do nothing about."

Alex thought for a moment, straightened, then looked Rein in the eye. "How do you feel about discovering a new cousin?"

"Are you bloody daft?"

Alex glanced up and down the barn aisle, making sure they hadn't been overheard, which would be unlikely since Rein had told his grooms to make themselves scarce. He stood outside a stall in a U-shaped courtyard, Mary inside one of the spacious foaling pens. She'd been brought here to hide until proper attire could be found. Alex had just broken the news to her that she was to become the newest member of the Drummond clan, but just for a night, as they would set off to Wainridge in the morning.

"You can't be thinkin' bleedin' straight."

It had begun to rain again, word having reached his cousin that a storm was headed their way. Alex wondered if that might impede their departure on the morrow, but at least they'd been able to send word to his father.

"You're not answering me, m'lord, which makes me think you know your idea is a bleedin' daft one."

She stood inside the stall, the fog having dropped down from the sky to coat everything it touched with dew. She was still cold, for he could see her shiver beneath her cloak, no matter that she'd settled herself upon a mound of straw in the corner, then scooped some of it over her legs for warmth. Alex was no warmer, though staring down at her with her hair loose about her shoulders made his body beat in places he didn't want to think about.

"Mrs. Callahan, please, hear me out."

"Hear you out? I'm done hearing you out. I'm tired, cold, and fair on me way to starving to death. All I want to do is go back to the duke's so I can fetch my things and leave."

"Leave?"

She nodded. "I'm through being a nurse. Through with kidnappers and smugglers and upright lords what think they rule the world."

She had, indeed, been through a lot. And it was his fault.

He turned away, resting his weight against the stall door, but the image of her stayed in his mind. Even Rein had commented upon her extraordinary good looks, Alex feeling an unexpected surge of protectiveness at the interest he saw in his cousin's eyes. It didn't matter that she wore a tattered brown cloak. That her hair hung wild and wet around her head. That she looked tired and worn and cold. Her spirit illuminated the stall as brightly as a new moon, and he knew she was exactly the sort of woman Rein would be attracted to if his cousin put it into his head that he wanted her. And he would.

He jerked around to face her again. She rested her head against the back of the stall, her eyes closed now. And for a few moments he allowed himself to admire the way her nose blended into her face. He truly loved her nose. And the way her forehead seemed just the right height. And the way her hairline swept up, then back down, then back up again. There was a perfection to her features one rarely saw and Alex found himself wondering if she'd return Rein's interest.

"You have no choice in this matter," he said, suddenly feeling out of sorts. "I do it to protect both your reputation and mine."

Her eyes opened at the same time she snorted. "What reputation?" And her lips quirked up into a smile, and for the first time he noticed an edge of cynicism to that smile. Indeed, and a hint of sadness. "I have no reputation to save."

"Be that as it may, I am not giving you a choice. You will do this, Mary Callahan, or—"

"Or what?" she asked, red brows lifted. "You'll release me without wages? I wish you would."

He swallowed, refusing to say the words, though he realized after everything they'd gone through he'd be hard pressed indeed to think of her as a nurse. If, indeed, she was one. But he couldn't escape the fact that she'd rescued him. Twice.

"I hope that you understand I truly do have your best interest at heart." And he did, damn it, he did. "You will be treated like a queen, waited upon hand and foot, given the best of care. Please say you'll do it."

Chapter Thirteen

Mary wanted to call him daft again. Had he been conked in the head too hard? Was his brain box damaged? Had his noodle stopped working due to lack of sleep?

"It won't work."

"It will," he said. "With my help."

She almost laughed. That were rich. His lordship teaching her to act like a proper lady.

And suddenly there were two faces outside the stall, the earl's and Alex's. "I had a devil of a time securing this gown," said the earl. "Had to fabricate a tale of a lost trunk and an overturned carriage. The bad news is that Lady Dalton is all agog to meet my long-lost 'cousin.'" The earl peered into the stall. "What did she say when you told her of your plan?"

"I told him to sod off." And then she caught sight of the gown Alex's cousin held. She pushed herself to her feet, no matter that it hurt like the very devil to do so. "Coo, is that for me?"

Rein nodded. "It is, though I've no idea if it will fit. Like as not it will be too big for you. Lady Dalton is not the most svelte of women. But it was the best I could do, her ladyship the only person I felt comfortable involving, though she does not know the truth, of course."

Mary wouldn't have cared if it were as big as a circus

tent. Coo, would you look at that material? Silk it was, she would stake the piece of precious chocolate she had stashed in the side pouch of her satchel back at the duke's. And, oh, how she longed to take it. Lord, she hadn't received something so nice since the time that groom at the circus had given her that piece of tin with the horse engraved on it. She still had the thing stashed in with her chocolate.

"May I touch it?"

She saw the two men exchange a glance that clearly said, "We've got her." But Mary was far from convinced the idea would work. Granted, she did a fair imitation of her betters. Better than fair, but the rest of it? Eating, dancing, conversing with the swells? She'd make a muddle of it for certain sure.

But the dress . . .

Too big it might be, but beautiful without question. The color of her eyes it was, Mary wondering if the earl hadn't chosen it for that very reason. But what caught her attention were the sleeves, for they were made of the sheerest green lace with little flowers and dots stitched onto the fabric. Around the waist was a piece of thick, forest green ribbon, and beneath that, covering the long skirt, more of the fancy fabric. It was the prettiest gown Mary had ever seen, and it shocked her how much she longed to put it on.

"I can't," she said, more to herself than to the men.

"Certainly you can," Alex said, taking the dress from his cousin. "Go ahead, at least try it, for we need you to get dressed no matter what your decision."

Mary almost told him no again. Instead, she found herself reaching for the garment. Her hand shook, almost afraid to touch the bleedin' thing, it were so fine.

"Go on," he prompted, waving the dress out in front of him.

She grabbed it from him, quickly, before she changed her mind, the fabric all but slipping through her hand it was so soft and slippery to the touch.

"Coo," she said, holding it up before her. "Will you look at that? I could dance in Covent Garden in this."

The two men exchanged The Glance again.

Mary tugged the dress up against her. "Oh, you wicked, wicked men. Come to tempt me like the devil, you have."

"Tempt you?" said the earl. "My dear woman, we are merely trying to protect your reputation."

"As I said to his lordship here earlier, I don't have no reputation to protect. And if you're going to call a kettle black, you may as well do so. You're worried about what will be said about the marquis here. Worried that people will assume I'm his ladybird should I show up at your home with him. And don't tell me otherwise, for I know no one cares about Mary Callahan."

They had the grace to look abashed. But as Mary held the fabric against her, aye, smelled a floral scent that lingered upon it, a longing she'd never felt before rose up within her.

Just for a night, Mary Callahan. Just for a day, wouldn't you like to know what it's like? What'd it feel like to sleep in one of those fancy rooms? To wear beautiful clothes? To be waited upon and served like the finest of ladies?

"Oh," she shot, clucking her tongue in irritation before she said, "I'll do it, devil take you. But if I blunder it badly, you won't be blaming me."

"What the devil is that noise she just made?" the earl asked.

"She clucks when she's irritated," Alex explained.

"Does she? How unique."

"You have no idea," the marquis said drolly.

Which made Mary wonder if she'd just been insulted or not. But then her hands slid across the silk of the dress and she decided she didn't care. Not one little bit.

It was exactly like a fairy tale, only better, Mary thought as she stared out the window of her second-floor room. Second floor. With a view. She almost spun around and did a dance. In hindsight she felt silly for raising a breeze over everything. Fool. What was so wrong with spending a night amongst such splendor?

Rose-colored walls with white wainscoting surrounded her. A flower arrangement the size of a shrub sat on an ornate wardrobe, empty, of course, but still the most beautiful piece of furniture she'd ever clapped eyes on. A screen with Oriental figures upon it sat in one corner, a tall mirror with real French glass sitting next to it. A plush rug with large, red roses stretched from one side of the room to the other. Windows with maroon draperies sat one after another along one whole wall. Five of them there were. Five! Mary was hard pressed to decide which one to stare out of.

But what had her all agog, what made her want to twirl around in glee, was the dress. She crossed to the mirror, swishing her hips from side to side like a grand lady. Never mind that the gown hung off her sides like an animal gone too long without food. Or that the hem dragged on the ground. It were the finest, most beautiful gown Mary had ever seen and as she stared at her reflection,

Mary was overcome by the silly urge to—oh, she'd gone crackers for certain sure—to cry.

Ach. What a fool you are.

She inhaled before a silly tear had time to form. There were better things to cry about in this world than the way a body looked in a dress.

Oh, but what a dress, a voice said.

The only thing that she'd worn as fine was the too-short tunic Samuel forced her to perform in, the one with all those fancy paste gems sewn into the bodice. But Mary hated that bloody costume and the catcalls and whistles that went along with being the Royal Circus's star female performer. Well, actually, the only female performer. In England. Mary was still a bit astounded that she'd carved a niche for herself simply because she'd spent years playing around on old Admiral's back.

But she wasn't performing tonight. Well, not on a horse, at least. And if the rain continued on, they'd be forced to stay another night, Wainridge a good day's ride away. And though she worried a bit about his lordship's daughter being let alone with that bosky-minded duke—not to mention Abu—she consoled herself with the thought that the two were likely safe as seashells in that giant ocean of a house. In the interim, by heaven, she'd enjoy herself.

She threw back her head, clutched the skirts of her dress and spun around, feeling her upswept hair tug at her scalp. A fancy maid had styled it and so the locks now sat atop her head in loops and coils and fine little wisps, making Mary feel like the grandest of ladies.

"Are you ready to go below stairs?"

Mary stopped and turned toward the door. Oh, how she loved the way Alex's eyes instantly widened, the way his gaze swept her up and down, the way he suddenly looked speechless.

"Well?" she asked, holding her skirts out. She tipped from side to side again, saying as she swayed, "Look like a grand lady, do I?"

If he agreed, Mary didn't know, for he still stared at her. Those river-blue eyes of his swept a current through her. They dropped down again, lingering for a bit on her breasts (or so she thought), then up again. And suddenly, the usually redoubtable Mary felt a bit self-conscious. Blimey, her face even heated a bit, her body reacting in rackety fits and starts as she waited for him to say *something.*

"You look—" he finally said, only his bleedin' words dribbled off.

Mary waited, feeling an odd combination of anxiety and pique.

"You look—" he tried again.

Pique won out. "Get on with it, me lord. Is it good or bad."

Finally his gaze met her own, and when it did, she realized she needn't have worried, for she could see how she looked in his eyes: Marvelous. Spectacular. Absolutely top of the trees.

She straightened with pride. "I look well, don't I?"

"You'll do."

She smiled, aye, the biggest smile she'd ever smiled before, she realized, for it tugged at her cheeks and made her nose wrinkle. Walking toward him, she ignored the small stab of pain in her feet—what was a wee bit of pain when one felt as fine as Harriet Wilson—and swung her hips, noticing that he looked rather fine himself. He must have borrowed a jacket from his cousin, for he wore a dark gray coat and buff trousers that fit a bit too snug around his thighs, making them bulge in a very stallion-ish way. Mary realized he had fine thighs for a swell.

"Do you think the nabobs downstairs will be fooled?" She stopped, placed her hands on her hips.

His eyes narrowed, his face taking on that odd look he got when he tried hard not to gawk. Lord love her, she almost felt sorry for him. But Mary had never, ever felt as fine as she did now. Like a proper lady, she looked. Aye, as fancy and pretty as any of those women what came to watch her ride. And she'd have a fancy gentleman on her arm, too. And a fancy dinner to eat. Aye, all the things she'd often dreamed about.

"I believe, Mrs. Callahan, that the people downstairs will see what they want to see. That being an uncommonly pretty young woman who talks and acts like a commoner."

She stopped like she hit a wall. "A commoner?"

He nodded, and though he still looked at her like she were the sweet cream on his pie, he no longer had that dazzled look in his eyes. He recovered himself most quickly, though how he'd done it Mary had no idea. Usually, a man could no more control his base urges than a male dog could stop from lifting his leg.

"Indeed, Mrs. Callahan, for you need to learn how to walk and comport yourself as a lady."

She almost glared at him. Almost released a huff of frustration. Instead she said, "I don't need no lesson."

"Any. You don't need *any* lesson."

"That's what I said."

"No, you used the word *no,* not the word *any.*"

"And now you're giving me lessons."

"Yes, I am."

She waved a hand in front of her, some of the wispy tendrils she'd been so proud of a moment before fluttering like spider-web strings. Wanted a lady, did he? She'd give him one right and tight.

"I assure you, sir, you have nothing to fear from me." And she took great care to enun-ci-ate. "I am quite adept at mimicking my betters." She had the rum-eyed pleasure of seeing his mouth flop open again before she said, "Now, if you would be so kind as to escort me below stairs?"

"Why you little—"

She lifted a brow.

"How did you *do* that?"

She walked toward him with all the grace and finesse of a true aristocrat. "Simple as rum, m'lord. When you've watched as many lords and ladies as I have, you pick up their ways."

He looked at her like she was a spider that had emerged from a crack in the wall. "And you watched these lords and ladies where, exactly?"

Too late she realized she'd revealed too much. He knew her as Mrs. Mary Callahan, nurse, and not as a famous equestrian.

"Why, how do you think?" she improvised. "When working for them." Which was true if one twisted it about a bit, which she did.

He didn't look like he believed her, not surprising since she'd demonstrated more than one non-nurse-type talent in the past few hours. But she told herself not to worry. In a couple of days she'd return to the duke's, collect Abu, and leave.

Aye, though why the blazes that made her feel strangely low, she had no idea.

"And I suppose jumping onto a horse's back is another talent you 'observed'?"

"I learned that trick back at home," which was true.

"And jumping from moving carriages?"

Once again, she didn't need to lie. "My brother James taught me that handy trick. We used to practice on the wagons that used to take the fish to market."

He stared down at her, Mary realizing she needed to do something before he asked her a question she would be forced to lie about. "Are you through, m'lord, or would you like me to take the bar again?"

Her words had the desired effect, for he gave himself a bit of a start. "I beg your pardon, Mrs. Callahan. I did not mean to pry."

"Lady Callahan," she corrected with a lift of her nose.

He half bowed, and she could have sworn she saw his lips twitch. "Lady Callahan," he corrected. And then he did the strangest thing, something that made Mary wonder if she hadn't been a bit hasty in her desire to rattle him a wee bit. He offered her his arm, just like a gentleman would do to a proper lady. "Would you care to go downstairs?"

She stared at that arm, wondering if she should take it.

Take it, Mary, it's not a bleedin' tiger's tail.

"Indeed you may," she said at last. Bugger it, she was Mary Callahan. Afraid of nothing.

Only the moment she touched him, it all came back. All too vividly she remembered the way it'd felt to be snuggled next to him. Remembered how she'd had to fight the urge to simply revel in the way he held her so safely and securely in his arms. Aye, the way his fingers had felt gliding across her face. Tenderness. He showed her that, and lord help her, she'd never had it before . . .

"That is a fine jacket," she said to cover her sudden anxiety.

"It is my cousin's," was his expected answer.

And Mary suddenly found it hard to swallow. What had happened to the sultry vixen? To the saucy wench? To the self-confident Mary Callahan?

Gone by the wayside, she had. And it angered her because all her life she'd fought to stand on her own two feet. Aye, she'd done some things she weren't proud of to get to where she was. And now here she stood in a nobleman's house, touching a nobleman's arm and she'd gone as soft as freshly oiled reins.

What a pea goose.

Lifting her chin, she reminded herself that this was all a farce. That she would enjoy the next few hours, whatever they might bring. Memories were what she'd take away. Aye, and that was all, for she wasn't fool enough to believe there would ever be anything else.

Such as a happily ever after.

Chapter Fourteen

Her bravado lasted until the moment she entered the main hall.

What was it with the bleedin' nobility that they all owned spectacular homes? Grand did not begin to describe either the duke's or the earl's, though each was as different as a cat was from a dog. While the duke's hall had been wide and spacious, the earl's hall was dark and dull, only . . . not. To their left and right were open doors that allowed light to filter in from windows in the exterior walls. She gawked until she caught sight of the trees. Aye, trees. Four of them there were, two on the left and two on the right, and taller than herself. Only as she got closer did she realize they were giant ivy topiaries, the pots they stood in bigger than Mary's bed back in London. Lord.

She glanced up at Alex who, of course, looked completely impervious to it all as they headed through the center of it, though how someone got used to such surroundings, Mary sure as certain didn't know. Just then she spotted a moth fluttering above their heads, the creature's presence amongst such a pristine environment somehow out of place.

Mary felt a lot like that moth.

"Are you ready?" the marquis asked, pausing before a closed door, the servant who stood next to that door standing so upright, Mary was certain a stick was strapped to his back. Inside she could hear muffled laughter mixed with the murmur of voices. And for just a second Mary felt a great fear come over her. Aye, almost like the time she'd come face to face with a large, snorting bull that'd escaped from a nearby pasture back in Hollowbrook.

But years of quelling a nervous stomach enabled her to look up at him and say, "I am."

Alex nodded. The servant opened the door, and conversation in the room stopped. As Mary glanced inside the room, she realized she might, just might have bitten off more than she could chew.

Ladies dressed fancier than parade horses stared back at her. Five of them there were, two of them wearing, of all things, fortune-teller turbans with ornate feathers tucked into the front of them. Jewelry as grand as the Queen of England's sparkled on their bodices and on their heads. Real emeralds with diamonds encrusted around the sides. One young lady even wore a coronet with a diamond as big as her pinky nail for a center stone. And though she'd felt rather fine in her green dress, only now did she realize that the gown she'd been given could only be called second rate. The women before her wore satin and lamé in various colors: burgundy, yellow, even pristine white. And with various stripes and prints that made her own dress appear dowdy.

And the way they stared. It always amazed her. A noblewoman could look a person up and down in a way that made a person think they'd been born and raised in a dust bin.

"There you are, cousin," the earl said, crossing an Oriental rug so plush, Mary's feet hardly hurt at all as Alex led her across it. The room had a fireplace made of green stone, and despite the pristine environment, she noticed that not even nobles could keep the smell of smoke from invading their room. But it was a grand fireplace, indeed. Gray and black marble. And a matching clock that rested upon a marble mantel so large, Mary imagined she could play shuttlecock upon its surface. Everything looked clean and neat and so new, Mary ached to touch the precious objects on the shiny inlaid side tables. Only the earl stood before her now, Mary admitting he was nearly as handsome as the marquis. Nearly.

He took her hand—and it only went to show how bosky-headed she'd gone for that her hand shook with fear—raised it to his lips as he murmured softly, "Curtsy," with a smile.

Curtsy?

Oh.

She started, then sank down. The earl looked down at her in approval. So she sank even lower.

He frowned, leaning toward her under the pretext of kissing her cheek only to say, "Not so low, for I am only an earl, and your cousin."

She jerked. Too abruptly it turned out, for her head cracked him in the face.

"Oh, good lord," she said, realizing what she'd done.

"Rein, are you all right?" Alex asked.

"My nose," the earl mumbled from behind his hands.

Everyone stared; Mary wanted to dive beneath the bleedin' fancy rug. It didn't help that when the earl removed his hands, blood smeared his face.

"Oh, my goodness," Mary gasped.

Someone else gasped, though it was more of a moan. Mary turned just in time to see a portly lady hit the ground like a giant pine. That started a trend—and Mary would swear later it was like watching one tree knock down another. One by one the females of the room listed to the floor. Mary's mouth dropped open. She turned to Alex, saying, "Either someone passed foul wind, or they're overreactin'."

To which Alex choked, or laughed, Mary couldn't be sure.

Rein followed her gaze and said, "Oh, for God's sake. Ladies, 'tis just a little blood."

"Here," Alex said, holding out a white handkerchief. "Cover yourself before we have to fetch a physician for the whole lot."

Rein dabbed at his nose, Mary noting that it did, indeed, look awful.

"You're going to have a nasty bump on the bridge," Alex observed.

"Lord," Mary said. "I'm so sorry, m'lord. I'd never curtsied to a bleedin' earl before. His lordship here, yes, but he's a nabob what doesn't count."

And after she said the words, it was one of those moments, one of those awful moments when you realize you've shot yourself in the arse by opening your big, fat flapper. Mary glanced around. From the floor their ladyships' eyes popped open, one by one. The men who kneeled over them looked up, too, froze, one portly chap going so far as to say, "Never *curtsied* before? What the devil does she mean, never curtsied before?"

"My thanks, Mary," Rein said an hour later. "You managed to empty my house faster than I thought possible."

Indeed, she had, Mary thought miserably. She looked

at the earl, lifting her chin a notch as he lifted a glass of brandy in her honor. And though she made sure to place a look of sublime unconcern on her face, there was a large knot in her throat, one made up of humiliation and, of all things, disappointment.

"I tried to cover my slip."

And she had, only she'd made it worse, forgetting her fancy accent and muddling the whole thing. She glanced over at Alex. He sat near the fire, staring into its depths as if contemplating the troubles of all mankind, or simply himself. And he had cause to be contemplative, Mary admitted. She'd gone and caused him trouble, for Alex had tried to explain to the earl's guests that her appearance at Sherborne was an accident.

They hadn't believed him. And, really, Mary was surprised Alex had thought they might. Hadn't he learned by now that people actually *wanted* to believe the worst? That mankind lived for the latest scandal? Odd's teeth, it was such a basic lesson, Mary had a hard time understanding how it'd escaped him.

"And Alex," the earl said next. "Why such a long face? Welcome to the ranks of rakes. You should be honored, for not even I would ever dare to pass my mistress off to the *ton.* You've outdone me, old boy. Handily, I might add."

"Oh, stuff a fist in your mouth, m'lord," Mary finally said, unable to take his sarcasm a moment longer. "Can't you see he's ready to shoot himself? He's a man what spent his whole life trying to escape his father's reputation. And in one night—one bleedin' night—I have to go and open my mouth and now all of London will believe he's as bad as his sire."

"Worse, actually," Rein added with a smile. "For as I said, he tried to pass you off."

"Worse," Mary agreed.

"Oh, stop it, the both of you." Alex stood up abruptly. "What's done is done." He looked over at Mary with an expression of self-flagellation. "You cannot be blamed for what happened, for it was I who came up with the idea of dressing you as a lady. 'Tis not your fault that you lack the skills. Not your fault at all."

His words stung, Mary feeling the ridiculous urge to tip her chin up. She did have the skills. She'd just forgotten them in the resulting melee. If only . . .

But it was ridiculous to wish for "if only." As his lordship said, what was done, was done.

"Let us go eat instead of hanging our heads," Alex added. "I dare say it will do me some good not to have such a sterling reputation. At least the more discriminating of matchmaking mamas will turn their noses up at me now."

And that was when it dawned on Mary why she truly felt wretched. It wasn't that she'd failed at being a lady. It wasn't even that she'd failed herself. It was that she'd failed the marquis, though why it should matter was beyond her ken.

"Indeed, cousin," the earl agreed. "Mary, if you do not mind dining with two disgraceful wretches, I should like to eat as well."

Mary didn't think she could eat a bite. "As you wish, my lords," she said softly, coming to her feet.

The earl looked at her in surprise, then smiled widely. Mary tried to smile back, but she couldn't shake the funk she'd sunk into.

Not even the beauty of the room the earl and marquis

took her to could shake it. Nor the fact that the table she dined at was as big as the sweet shop she frequented back in London. Nor that, for the first time in her life, she was waited on hand and foot. Mary noticed none of it. Well, she did notice a particularly large spoon made of silver so shiny, she could use it as a mirror if she had a mind to. And that the sausages were particularly tasty. But that was it, because there was one thing that didn't escape her notice, and that was the feeling that she was a fraud.

Silly chit, she scolded herself. *You should be used to feeling like a fraud.*

Aye, and it were true. For the person who performed so brazenly in front of hundreds of people had always hated it. She despised the exhibitionism of being a trick rider for the Royal Circus: the catcalls, the lewd whistles. She hated the men thinking she exhibited herself to catch their attention. She hated that women thought the same thing when all she wanted to do was show the world how special a horse could be.

"Are you finished, Mrs. Callahan?" asked the earl.

Mary looked up. His lordship had been nothing but kind, while Alex . . . well, Alex had ignored her. And though a part of Mary felt like she should enjoy the earl's solicitous attention, another part of her admitted she wasn't in the mood. Her black spells happened rarely, but when they did, she knew enough about herself to know it wasn't worth the effort to try and lift her spirits.

"I am, m'lord," she said softly, deciding that what she needed was fresh air. Aye, the smell of candle wax was giving her a headache. And the flower arrangement. And all that rich food. She needed to breathe. To be herself. Not Mary Callahan, nurse. Not Artemis, famous female rider. Just plain old Mary.

"If you will excuse me, m'lord," she said, rising suddenly. "I believe I shall retire early."

The earl nodded, looking not surprised. "Indeed, you've had an eventful day."

She looked at Alex, but all he did was give her a brief nod, his eyes not even meeting her own.

So that was the lay of the land, eh? Very well.

Throwing her napkin down on the table, she turned away, uncaring where she went, just wanting to get away.

"Which way to the gardens?" she asked the first servant she could find, a footman by the looks of his fancy white and gold livery.

"Why, I'm sure I don't know, madam," he said with a look of affront, and the way he did it, aye, the very way he looked her up and down was exactly like those fancy lords and ladies.

It was funny how a body could keep forging ahead, and then, *blam,* one person could come along. One, inconsequential person could say something rude and cause a body to crumple.

That's how Mary felt. Like crumpling.

Why? she yelled at herself. Why did she suddenly feel like crying? Was she worried again about Gabby and Abu? Or were her menses coming on? Was that the trouble? For as sure as she wore borrowed clothes, those were tears she felt at the back of her eyes.

"I see," she said, lifting her chin as she'd done so many times before. "Well, then, if you would be so kind as to point me to the privy, I'd appreciate it very much. Of course, if you'd rather I toss my accounts all over this fancy marble floor, you could tell me you don't know where that is, too."

He pointed to a door beneath the stairwell. Mary turned.

"Thank you," she said as ladylike as she could. But each step she took, she felt closer and closer to collapsing like a sandcastle doused by a wave.

It was a small room with a slanted roof, thanks to the stairwell above it, but it was clean, and surprisingly spacious, with a wooden privy this time. And it occurred to Mary as she stood inside the tiny, little room: a person's worth could also be measured by the type of commode he sat upon. The marquis's had been marble. The earl's was wood. Hers was a bucket. And so, too, was her life. In a bucket of, well, never mind.

Of course, she didn't really have to use the privy, she just wanted some privacy and a water closet seemed as good a place as any. There was even a bench next to a dark oak washstand, and so she sat down, placing her chin in her hands and fighting the urge to cry. Silly thing, tears. A monumental waste of energy, she'd always claimed. They made your eyes burn, your skin redden, and in most cases, branded you a fool.

Yet a tear still fell.

She wiped it away angrily, wondering what the blazes was wrong with her. She hadn't cried since she fell off that big stallion of Mr. Hughes; it'd hurt like the very devil. Demme, she hadn't even cried when she'd been laughed out of London for wanting to ride horses for a living. Nor when she'd been unable to find a place to sleep and food to eat and been near starved to death before some fancy swell had taken pity on her and handed her a shilling. And yet here she was, in an earl's bleedin' privy and turning into a water pot. She'd gone crackers for sure.

"Mrs. Callahan?"

Mary stiffened.

"Mrs. Callahan, are you in there?"

Mary wanted to bury her face in her hands. Instead she wiped her ridiculous, silly, unwanted tears away and said, "What do you want, m'lord?"

Silence. Mary thought Alex might have gotten the hint and left her alone. But one thing Mary had learned after working with the masculine persuasion. They were a bunch of slow-topped fools.

She should have known better.

"The footman told me you were ill," he said.

Indeed. Likely he'd been worried she'd mess up the bloody water closet. "I'm not ill," she said. "I just needed to empty my bladder."

Silence again. Good. Perhaps she'd embarrassed him into leaving.

"You're lying."

Mary lifted her head. Lying— Why that—

"Go away, m'lord."

"No."

She couldn't believe her ears. And what really fair bogged her mind, what made her feel like screaming, was the silly, daft-witted urge to cry all over again.

"You're not overwrought by what happened, are you? My cousin says that you are, but I find that hard to believe."

She was. Damn it all to hell. She really, *really* was.

"Go away," she said again, feeling the soddin', ridiculous urge to cry. And it prickled at her heart that he didn't know it.

The door opened.

Mary gasped, wiping away tears before he could see them.

Too late.

"You're crying," he accused, all but pointing an imaginary finger at her.

"I am not."

He stared at her as if she'd jerked off her arms and handed them to him. "Why are you upset?"

"I'm not upset. And if you're finished disturbing my peace, you can leave."

But he didn't leave. Instead he stepped into the small room, his height making the walls seem shorter. "Why are you crying, Mary?"

Sod it all, why did he use her given name? She didn't like it when he did that. She truly didn't.

"Please, m'lord. Go away." And then—oh, blast it all—a tear darted out of her left eye and made its way down her cheek like an errant bug.

He knelt in front of her, clasped one of her hands, stroking it in a way that made it suddenly hard to breathe.

"Don't," she said, trying to draw a breath.

But he wouldn't let her. "Tell me why you cry."

"I started me menses."

He drew himself up, then just as quickly narrowed his eyes, still holding her hand, still rubbing it tenderly.

Funny thing about that hand, for as Mary turned her gaze to it, it didn't look like a nobleman's hand, it looked like any other man's hand. Long fingers. Soft skin. And that disturbed her to the point that she pulled her hand away, under the pretext of wiping her eyes, of course.

"You're lying to me, Mary Callahan, and I want to know why."

She remained mutinously, determinedly silent.

"I want to know why a woman who walks across English fields, shivering with cold, feet bleeding, stomach raw from hunger—but who never once shed a tear—is suddenly crying."

"I told you, I started my menses."

He frowned, even shook his head a bit. "Are you upset over injuring the earl? For if you are, you shouldn't be. The bump is near gone, in reputation, that is."

"Well, there you have it," she said, beginning to lose patience. "'Tis exactly what I'm upset about. I caused a nobleman a great injury, one I'm sure he'll never recover from. Indeed, I shall never be able to live with myself again."

He stared.

Mary returned it.

"Well, if that's not what's bothering you, then what? Is it my daughter you're worried about? If so, have no fear, I'm sure all is well with her at Wainridge. The Runners I hired will see to that."

No, she wanted to scream. Couldn't he see? Couldn't he? She stood up on her aching feet, brushing by him, went to the door, swinging it open, hoping, nay, praying, he would leave.

"I told you what was bothering me, but if you don't want to believe it, I suppose there's not much I can say that'll convince you otherwise. So I'm asking you to leave. Again. Leave me in peace, m'lord. And while you're at it, tell Lady So-and-so that I'll have her dress back to her just as soon as I get up to me room. Beg her pardon for my thinking I might be good enough to wear it. For thinking maybe someone in the room might like me for all that I'm common bred. For daring to want to experience what it's like to sit down at a fancy table and eat a fancy meal."

"But you did get to sit down at the dining table."

"Oh, you silly, daft, fool man. You don't understand."

She thought she heard him hiss in frustration before he said, "Then *tell* me."

"I wanted to see how the ladies ate. Wanted to hear what they conversed about. To experience, for once in my life, what it's like to be gently bred, and not be treated like a boil on a pig's bum by some fool footman what thinks I'm your tart."

He appeared suddenly thunderstruck. Mary wanted to shake him. Wanted to say, "Do you finally understand? Finally?"

Instead she turned on her heel and, unfortunately, she forgot about her lacerated foot. Pain shot up her legs and made her gasp, "Bloody hell." Lord, she thought, why didn't someone just chop off her feet and put her out of her misery? And the bloody tears were back. Damn. Bloody. Tears.

"Mary, stop."

But Mary had had enough.

"Mary," he repeated, tugging on her arm. She tried to resist, but resisting put too much weight on her feet and so she gave in and turned around.

And when she met his gaze—oh, horrors—to her utter and absolute embarrassment, she started to sob. Good lord. Big, gasping sobs. What the *devil* was *wrong* with her?

And then he pulled her into his arms.

"You're far and away the most courageous, headstrong, outspoken woman I've ever met, and sometimes you drive me daft, but those ladies who left should have been fortunate to make your acquaintance, Mary Callahan. At least, in my opinion."

Funny how one could stop breathing, how one's whole world could still and time could stop. For that was exactly what happened to Mary. She froze. Didn't breathe. Didn't move. And as she was held in his arms, as she was tenderly held, for the first time, no, for the *only* time in her life, she realized that *this* . . . this one moment, was one she would never forget. Never. Held by a marquis.

No, held tenderly by a man.

Her tears abruptly ended, Mary's mind completely taken over by wonder. And then he pulled away, as if suddenly recalling where they were, or perhaps who he was, or more importantly, who *she* was: A servant. Trash. Nobody.

And Mary felt the absence of his arms like the loss of a friend. He stepped back from her, straightening his waistcoat and cravat as if afraid it might've gotten mussed.

"Now," he said, "if you would be so kind as to join my cousin and myself in the drawing room, we would like your opinion on some verses Edward favors."

Verses? Didn't the man know what holding her had done to her? How just the feel of his arms had made her feel things she'd never felt in another man's arms? How for a fleeting moment their two worlds hadn't seemed so far apart?

Ach, Mary, no. He hadn't.

He's a man, *yelled another voice.*

"I—" and the words just bottled up in her throat. How to play it? As if she hadn't been melted by his kindness.

As if she hadn't just been sobbing in his arms? As if she hadn't a care in the world.

Aye, answered the voice again, *for isn't that what you always do?*

And it was.

He offered his arm, bowing slightly, just as he had upstairs, only this time, she didn't think he was mocking her. So she took it.

Chapter Fifteen

Love is a fart
That permeates a heart;
Oft times it don't smell;
Other times it repels
Like a rotted cabbage fallen off a cart.

Alex stared at Mary, aghast at the utter crassness of the verse, while his cousin Rein, that wretched man, doubled over in laughter.

Good lord.

He blinked, looked at Mary in wonder. What had happened to the crying woman? What had happened to the tender sparrow he'd held so closely and wanted to comfort? She'd disappeared behind the face of a naughty harridan.

"Oh, my good lord, Alex," Rein gasped, hand across his stomach. "Wherever did you find her? She's a treasure."

That treasure was smiling brightly, the ridiculously big dress that she wore looking all the more silly now that she sat upon a large couch. Rather like a child playing dress-up, Alex thought, only the face above that gown was far from childlike.

"Do you know any more?" Edward asked.

"I think that is quite enough," Alex said.

"Indeed, I do, m'lord," Mary said. "Quite a few of them, actually."

"Tell me another one."

"I'm sure Mrs. Callahan is tired—"

To which Mary began again:

There once was a maid named Gert,
Whose master was oft up her skirts,
He'd call for the duck,
Then say, 'Let have a quick—"

"Enough," Alex shot. "Mrs. Callahan, *really.* Surely you must own that to use such a word is highly un-ladylike."

"What word?"

"*That* word."

"What word?"

"Mrs. Callahan, I can hardly say the word aloud. To do so in the presence of a lady would be highly unseemly."

"Well, m'lord, as the earl's guests have determined, I'm far from a lady."

And whereas an hour ago she'd been in tears over that, now she smiled.

Lord, he would never understand a woman's mind.

"And I was about to say 'nip n' tuck' for the last line deals with what he had to drink for dinner."

Alex narrowed his eyes, not liking the way Rein laughed at her comment while somehow managing to eye her up and down. Never before had he been bothered by his cousin's reputation as a rogue. Certainly, he didn't approve, preferring to lead a more restrained life. Only now he found himself wondering what it would be like to be more like his cousin. A ridiculous thought, but there you had it. And, indeed, that was the problem. He'd been having those thoughts about Mary Callahan since the moment he'd first met her.

Why? Never before had he been so tempted to seduce a woman, and yet there could be no denying it. After yesterday's brief kiss, and then being with her this evening, there was little doubt that he desired her. No, even that was too tame a word. He wanted. Oh, how he wanted . . .

To bed her.

"Well," Rein said, leaning forward to place a hand over hers. Alex's eyes narrowed further. "You are lady enough for me."

"Why, thank you, m'lord."

Lord, the way the two were going at it, she'd be Rein's mistress by night's end.

Over his dead body.

And, indeed, there was no sense in fighting it any longer. Though he'd fought all his life against the stigma associated with his family name, against being held as much a rogue as his father, suddenly Alex wondered if asking her to be his mistress wasn't exactly the right thing to do. He could return to Wainridge, ensure Gabby was well, then head to London where he could secure lodgings for Mary.

And once the idea took hold, he couldn't seem to dispose of it. He sat there, watching her trade sallies with his cousin. Sat there quietly as Rein made every appearance of being as besotted with her as she was with him. Sat there silently and stewed, mulled and then ultimately, made the decision. And in the end, he had to ask himself, had there ever been any doubt?

"Well, I think I shall go off to bed," he said, standing, his heart thudding in his chest in the same way it did when chasing a smuggler. "Mrs. Callahan, I should be happy to escort you upstairs."

And now that he'd made his decision, he allowed himself the fantasy of bringing her to his room, of removing that ridiculous dress she seemed to all but cherish. Of seeing her with her hair down again, in her chemise—

"If it's all the same with you, m'lord, I think I'll sit with the earl a bit more."

He stiffened. *I should say not.*

"Mrs. Callahan, leaving you here with my cousin would be highly improper."

He thought he heard Rein choke back a laugh. Or perhaps a snort, Alex couldn't be sure, only knew it was time his cousin got the message.

She's mine.

"I don't think we'll need to be worrying about that," she said with a smirk.

No, of course not. Ridiculous thing to say. He knew that. But *demme* if he could have something to say other than being blatantly honest.

Leave us, Rein. I want her for my own.

But he couldn't say it aloud, so he said it with his eyes, Rein seeming to instantly get the message, judging by the way he sat up.

"Actually," Rein said, "I think I shall retire for the night, too."

Alex relaxed a bit. Apparently his cousin wasn't such a nodcock after all.

"Care to join me, Mrs. Callahan?"

"I *beg* your pardon?" Alex said.

Rein looked up at him. "I don't believe I was asking you, old man."

"No, but your suggestion that Mrs. Callahan might be

willing to engage in a liaison with you is an insult to her character."

"I didn't invite her to my room. I invited her to join me in retiring for the night."

"In your *room.*"

And if Alex had been looking closer, he would have seen the devilish gleam in his cousin's eye. Would have seen the way he leaned back against his settee, his arms splaying out on either side before joining at the back of his head. Would have seen the gleam of unquestionable amusement. But he didn't see it, and so when Rein replied, "I never said any such thing, but now that you say it, 'tis a smashing good idea. Mrs. Callahan, would you care to join me in my room tonight?"

"Devil take it, Rein. You go too far."

"Enough," cried the object of their discussion.

They both turned to look at Mary, Rein lifting a brow.

"I don't know what gave either of you the idea that I wanted to go upstairs with you, to your room or otherwise. So while I thank you for your offer, m'lord earl, I assure you, I have no interest in joining *either* of you for fun and frolic." She stood. "Thank you, m'lords, for a pleasant evening. I bid you goodnight."

"Mary, wait."

"Mary, is it?" he heard his cousin say.

Alex shot him a look, one that clearly said, *Bugger off,* not that he took the hint.

"I wish to speak to you privately," Alex said when she'd turned back to him.

"I'll wager you do," Rein added.

"What about, m'lord?" she asked with narrowed eyes.

"I truly do like the woman," his cousin muttered.

"Will you please leave?" Alex all but shouted in Rein's face. Good lord, would the man not take a hint?

"Why certainly, my good man," Rein said in a tolerable imitation of him. It made Alex want to plant him a facer.

"Don't leave, m'lord. Stay. I've a feeling whatever it is the marquis has to say, can be said in front of you."

"That, my dear, I doubt." He smiled. "If I read my cousin correctly." He turned back to Alex. "I wish you luck, cousin. Rest assured, if she tells you no, I am next in line."

"The devil you say," Alex shot.

"Ask me what?" Mary asked, and much to Alex's surprise, she appeared genuinely curious. Could she be that naïve? Could she truly not understand the undercurrents swirling around her? It seemed extremely unlikely given her knowing airs. And yet . . .

He shook the notion away, glad when Rein gave him a nod, then a bow, then took his leave.

"Ask me what?" Mary repeated, hands on her hips.

But now that the moment had arrived, Alex was surprised that he wasn't at all sure he knew how to proceed. He'd never asked a woman to be his mistress before. Oh, certainly, he'd had women, but he'd never felt strongly enough to settle upon one or the other. But as he stared at Mary Callahan, he knew that this was one he wanted.

"Are you going to answer, or are you going to stare at me all night?"

He took a step toward her. And perhaps it was the look in his eyes that tipped her off. Perhaps it was the carnal need that not even she could be so innocent as not to see. Whatever it was, suddenly her eyes widened. She took a step back.

"You're going to ask me to be your mistress, aren't you?"

And damned if she didn't look surprised. He'd expected her to be shocked. Flattered even, but never surprised.

"You are, aren't you?"

"I am," he admitted aloud. No matter that it went against his moral fiber, the very essence of who he thought he was. No matter that he'd sworn to never have a mistress such as his father kept. He wanted Mary Callahan, and in the end, that was all he could think of.

"Well, now, that's rich."

"I beg your pardon?"

"A home in London," she went on to say. "Fancy clothes? An allowance, and more than likely a bairn or two? That's what you're offering, isn't it?"

"You needn't worry about children," he added in case that was an issue. "I am well versed in ways to keep a woman free of child."

And then she looked amused. It threw him for a moment.

"Well, in case you hadn't noticed, m'lord, your technique needs some finessing. Or have you forgotten about Miss Gabriella?"

"No, I have not forgotten. An unfortunate lapse on my part. It will not happen again."

"Are you sure?"

"Quite."

"Absolutely sure?"

"Devil take it," he said, frustrated. "You are teasing me."

"I am. 'Tis either that or I slap your face."

"Slap my face?"

"Aye. Isn't that what most women do when propositioned by their lord and master?"

"I am not propositioning you."

"Are you not, m'lord? Oh, I'll grant you, what you offer is marginally better than a quick tumble and a few quid for my services. But asking me to earn blunt on me back is a slap to *my* face, so tell me why I shouldn't slap yours?"

"Is it money you want?"

"No," she answered quickly, too quickly for there to be any doubt as to her honesty.

"Then what *do* you want?"

And lord help him, he'd begun to feel desperate. Only now did he realize that to have her in his presence and not actually have her would be the worst torment of all.

She tossed her chin up, her eyes suddenly and completely serious. "I don't want nothing from you, m'lord."

And then she turned on her heel and left.

As the door closed all Alex could do was mutter, "Damn."

It seemed amusing that Mary finally found the garden when she wasn't looking for it, but that was exactly what happened.

His mistress.

She wanted to howl at the moon. She even tipped her head back as if about to do that very thing, rain dotting her face and pelting her dress so that it spotted like an ermine stole. No, it was Lady Dalton's dress. For such a fine garment was never to belong to the likes of Mary Callahan. No, indeed. Mary Callahan were only good enough to be a man's mistress. Never anything more.

Aye, and what were you expectin'? The offer of a ring and a fancy title?

She closed her eyes, wrapping her arms around herself for warmth. Light from the windows spilled out to illuminate a wet walkway, the rain starting to come down in earnest whilst she'd been flirting with the earl.

And she had been flirting. Some reckless need to act like a tart had made her say and do things she would never have had the courage to say under normal circumstances. But things were far from normal. They hadn't been since the moment the marquis had lifted her chin and gazed into her eyes.

And for the second time that day, nay, likely the second time in her life, Mary felt tears rise.

What the devil was wrong with her? First those nasty nabobs had turned her into a watering pot, and now the marquis—

No, Mary, said a voice. *Do not think about how his offer stung.*

Blindly she headed for the glass house she'd spied from her room earlier. It jutted out from the side of the house like a finger, light from the second-story windows shining down upon it.

Mary headed straight for it, pushing on a door that dragged on her hands due to the difference in room temperature. The warm, sticky air was a shock to her system after the cold of outside. Her hair hung on her head, drenched already. The door closed behind her with a *boom,* Mary pausing just inside the door as she hugged her arms close to herself again. Rain fell onto the glass above, sounding like a dull roar in the silence. Three rows of plants stretched before her, the smell of roses and citrus mixing with chives and basil. Lightning flared.

Mary jumped, looking up at the sky just as thunder boomed above.

"Tell me you feel nothing when we touch and I will leave you be, Mary Callahan."

Mary whirled. Another flash of lightning revealed Alex's face, his jacket, the shoulders dark and drenched with rain.

"Tell me, Mary Callahan. That is all you need do."

But she couldn't. Lord help her, she couldn't. He'd held her gently in his arms, cradling her when her feet hurt so bleedin' bad she'd wanted to cry. He'd kissed her tenderly when he'd thought she was asleep. He'd lifted her chin, calling her more worthy than any other woman of his acquaintance. Until a few moments ago he'd treated her with more respect than any man before him.

Until a few moments ago.

And it was that which made her step back, that made her shake her head. Made her realize what a fool she'd been. For because of that very kindness, she'd thought—she blinked away another ridiculous tear—lord help her, she'd thought he might have actually come to respect her.

She should have known men like him didn't respect lowborn females like herself.

"Go away, m'lord. Go away and never come near me again, for I've had time to review your 'offer' and I've decided that I must regretfully decline."

He stiffened, she could see that though his face was shrouded in darkness. Could see the way his body tensed though only the dullest of light shone through the roof. Could tell that her answer wasn't what he'd expected, no matter that she'd laughed in his face a few moments ago. It had been the hardest thing she'd ever had to do to force that laughter past her lips.

"I see," he said.

"Do you?" she mocked, because, God help her, mockery was all she had. "That I doubt."

"No, Mary, I do."

"How could you possibly understand what it's like to be me? To actually be tempted by your offer, but not because of the pleasure it'd bring me—oh, aye, I'm woman enough to admit that—but because of the luxuries it'd bring me. M'lord, do you have any idea what it's like to be so hungry you're half tempted to boil your boots, just so you'd have something in your stomach? To look down at the ground, spy a rotted vegetable and think that don't look half bad. To be so hungry your mind seems to buzz, and your body to shake to the point that it's all you can do to stay afoot, but that you can do nothin' about because your last week's wages were withheld?"

He didn't say anything. But, really, what *could* he say?

"When I first came to London," she said, "I'd been trying to find work, but times were tough what with the war going on and trade interrupted. It seemed everyone were looking for work."

She shivered, the clarity of the memory startling her. As if she stood back in London again, she remembered the dirty streets. The angle of the shadows as the sun sank behind buildings. The multitude of carriages going what seemed like twenty different directions at once. The cries of the street vendors. The mud and gunk that caught on the bottom of her half-boots and made them heavy and hard to walk. And the smell. Lord, the smell. "My stomach rolled with that hunger, and with every step I took, I was more afraid of not finding food than anything else. Starving I was. Literally, I think."

He peered down at her and Mary found herself saying, "I would have done anything then for coin. Anything."

He seemed to know where she was going, seemed about to ask her to stop, but she wasn't about to stop. She'd begun the journey, now she'd finish it.

"The man came out of an alleyway. At first I didn't see him. Truth be told, I was half-blinded by fear and exhaustion. But he made his presence known. Offered a shilling if I'd go with him and lift my skirts." She shook her head. "And I actually considered it for a moment, I truly did, but in the end I couldn't go through with it. I may have been raised a poor man's daughter. I may not have the manners you gents call 'grace,' but I knew better than to go off with him."

And here's where the memory got vague. Here's where, in her dreams, her nightmares began. "Only he didn't want to take no for an answer. He dragged me into an alley, kissed me," she swallowed, "touched me. But I hadn't raised four brothers for nothing and watching them taught me a thing or two. I knew where to kick him, aye, and I didn't hesitate to do it.

"He dropped fast enough, but by then others had gotten into the sport. They came from nowhere, pawing at me, grabbing me. One of them threw me onto the ground. Another held my hands above my head."

She turned away, staring out the glass at the darkness beyond. "I think—I don't know, the memory is foggy—but I think they began to argue over who would be first. By now they'd gotten most of my clothes off. I remember looking up, remember seeing a flake of ash fall down from the sky. It headed right toward me. I followed it with my eyes, wondering if it was snow, thinking how odd if it was for there wasn't cold enough. I remember wanting to be that piece of ash, remember thinking how grand it would be to fly so free. And, I don't ken, they must have decided who was to go first, because one of them lay atop me, and I remember feeling something on the inside of my thigh and I knew then, I just knew that I'd rather die than, than—" She couldn't finish, just shook her head, amazed at how she could so perfectly recall the rage that had filled her. How that rage filled her once more.

"They must have thought me subdued. When I jerked away, my limbs slid through their grasp. I fought like a madwoman, screaming and yelling. I'd no idea what damage my fists could do. One of them fell. Another ran away. And then more arms were around me. I thought at first it was the first man, the one I'd kicked, but then I realized it wasn't that at all." She turned, met his gaze. "It were a man, a stranger. My screams had brought help at last. The man helped me to my feet, brought me to a watchman, even gave me a coin before he left, but do you want to know the irony of it all?"

He stared at her mutely.

"The watchman didn't try to find my assailants. He wanted to charge me with solicitation." She shook her head. "He thought I'd been trying to sell my wares, that things had gotten out of hand."

It'd been a bitter lesson, and the rage she'd felt brought tears of anger to her eyes even now. "I was sixteen years old. Alone. Frightened. And this man thought I was a whore." She swallowed tears.

"I got away that day, but I learned a valuable lesson, m'lord. I learned a woman only has two things of value in this world. Her mind and her morality. That day taught me that I didn't have what it takes to sell myself to a man, and if you think the fact that you're a lord changes that, you're wrong. If anything, it makes me more determined to steer clear. So while I thank you for your offer, I must again, regretfully decline."

She turned away then, though her limbs shook and her heart raced. Turned because it was time he realized something.

She was a fraud. Brave little Mary Callahan didn't really exist. It was all an act, her sauciness meant to foist the image of a woman of the world. She'd learned while working side by side with men that the surest way to keep them at bay was to make them think she'd seen and done it all. Aye, and it had worked. Only now came a man that she couldn't ignore, that made her wonder for the first time what it'd be like to be with a man. Made her wonder, lord help her, if she'd ever know.

Chapter Sixteen

Mary skipped breakfast that next morning. She couldn't stomach facing either of their lordships. Besides, it wasn't as if they were going anywhere. The roads were washed out. Again. At least judging by the amount of rain falling outside her window. Little rivers ran down the gravel drive, thick streamers of water falling from the cornices of the roof to land with a *splat.* She could see nothing of the hills they'd crossed, the clouds so thick and heavy they hung over the tops of the pines and elms like floating blankets.

Someone, one of the maids, likely, had furnished her with a serviceable brown gown, though how much longer it would be serviceable was anyone's guess. The hem frayed so badly, she could sweep the floor with the streamers of threads that hung down. Brown slippers, too, had been given to her, the kind with drawstring around the ankle. They were old and worn, but—thank the Lord above—comfortable on her still sore feet, and at least she was able to walk a wee bit better this morn.

"There you are."

Oh, no. No, no, no.

She turned, hands on her hips, clucking her tongue for a moment before she said, "Bloody hell. Have you no care for my privacy?"

The earl of Sherborne merely lifted a brow, saying, "That noise you make is truly extraordinary. And actually, no, I do not care. I need to ask you a question."

"You didn't even knock."

"Why, when you would not have answered?" He smiled, Mary realizing that he looked a lot like Alex. Well, close. The earl's hair had no gray, however, making him appear raffish rather than distinguished. The eyes were different, too. Green, they were. But both were tall, too, and broad in the shoulder. Yet, if Mary were to choose who was the more handsome, she'd choose Alex.

Alex, who wanted her to be his mistress.

She lifted her chin. "What do you want, m'lord?"

He strode into the room . . . well, glided, really, like a weasel slinking into a hen house. "I hear you refused Alex last eve."

She crossed her arms in front of her. "Aye, and if you've come here to offer yourself next, you're in for a disappointment."

"Not at all," he surprised her by saying, stopping before her, his eyes seeming to twinkle mischievously, though why she couldn't fathom.

"Actually, I've come here to invite you to a ball."

She stiffened.

He nodded. "The locals in these parts hold an assembly Saturday nights. I thought you should like to attend since my own guests have abandoned me. Shocking lack of manners, that."

She stared for the longest time, a million thoughts going through her mind.

"You want me to attend a ball?"

He nodded.

She felt her mouth snap like a lobster claw. "Lord above, you're as daft as your cousin."

"Am I? And here I thought I was the more intelligent one."

"If you were the more intelligent one, you'd know I have no desire to be seen with either of your lordships."

"Why ever not? I assure you, my dear, despite my reputation, I am very good *ton.*" He strolled deeper into her room. The flower arrangement on her dresser still gave off a fragrant odor of roses and lilies, his lordship reaching out to stroke one of the rose petals with a hand. His touch seemed almost gentle. Like a caress.

He turned back to her suddenly. "Well, what say you? Will you join me?"

"Have you not been listening? No."

"Then I shall have to work harder to convince you."

So great was her irritation that she could think of absolutely nothing to say. Oh, but their lordships would frustrate a rock.

"Come now. It will be great fun."

To that she said, "Oh, indeed, going out in this downpour would be quite amusing."

"We shall use my carriage."

"Fat lot that will do us when the roads are impassable."

"Only the main roads. Our local roads will be tolerable enough."

"And what shall I wear to this ball? My chemise?"

His smile turned wicked. "Oh, I dare say something could be found." That smile lasted a few seconds longer, his teeth as hale and hearty as the marquis's. Then his face went suddenly lax. "Of course, if you'd rather stay cooped up in the house all day, trying to avoid my cousin, you may certainly do so. I should advise you, however, that you would no doubt give Alex a fit of apoplexy by agreeing to be seen with me. And does that not render such an endeavor worthwhile?"

His words almost poked a laugh out of her. Almost. "No, m'lord, it does not."

"No? Too bad. Well then, what is it? If you're afraid my intentions are less than honorable, you would be right, but I will gladly give you a small pistol to carry with you, loaded, of course, should my passions get the better of me."

She did laugh then, though two minutes ago she wouldn't have believed such a thing possible. "Why, m'lord? Why would you offer to do such a thing?"

He smiled again. "Because I should like to see Alex rattled about. Such a stodgy old man, and only one year younger than myself. And because, quite frankly, I enjoy bringing my paramours to these events, though not," he quickly added, "that I think of you as such. It is merely that I rather like passing women off to the local gentry as members of the *ton.* It amuses me no end to see them curtsy to a commoner. Sometimes, I even put it about that they are uncommonly wealthy heiresses, and then you never saw such a bid for a woman's attention. Quite amusing, actually."

So he would bring her because she was common? Lord, that hurt. She told herself she was silly for letting it. After all, she'd be the first person to tell a body that she was no lady. But that didn't mean she liked it thrown in her face.

She lifted her chin again, saying, "No, thank you, my lord," in as cultured a tone as she could muster. "If it's all the same to you, I'd rather spend the evening peeling my nails off my fingers."

He jerked, blinked, then looked almost disappointed. "Are you certain?"

"Quite."

The light in his green eyes almost seemed to fade. "As you wish, my dear," he said with a bow. "Though I do believe you shall miss a most amusing time."

"No doubt," she said sarcastically. At her expense. Oh, the pompous, pompous ass. Their lordships insulted a body without even realizing it.

"If you should change your mind, you have only to say the word."

She smiled tightly, nodding. And it was odd, for she had a feeling he stared at her most curiously then. Not at all like he had earlier. Then there'd been a sort of warmth to his gaze. But now he looked at her rather watchfully. Aye, like a man what didn't know if cream or sour milk sat in a bowl before him.

Then he bowed again, turned on a booted heel, and left the room.

"You will not go."

Lord, Mary thought, turning away from the window again. Would they never leave her alone?

"I forbid it," Alex said, striding into her room not five minutes later. And Mary felt the hurt return with a bloody vengeance. "You are a member of my staff, not someone to be . . ." he jerked to a halt, "to be trifled with."

Member of his staff now, was she? My, how things changed.

"I insist you go to my cousin immediately and tell him that you've changed your mind."

Mary's temper soared. "I will do no such thing," she said, realizing too late that by saying such a thing, she was committing herself to the earl. Her eyes narrowed. Why that crafty-faced fiend. He'd manipulated her into going. And she'd fallen for it, too. Marvelously fallen for it. But she'd be damned if she backed down now. "I am determined to go, m'lord, and go I shall."

"You cannot."

"Indeed, I can."

"But you have no notion how to behave."

That made her temper flare anew. "I assure you, my lord, I can behave as well as I ought."

"You didn't last night."

That stung. Oh, how it stung.

He must have realized he might have insulted her, for he tried to change the subject by saying, "What will you wear?"

"I am told something will be provided."

"I will not allow it."

"You cannot stop me."

And Alex could only stew. All morning long he'd wanted to come to her, wanted to see how she fared, wanted to beg her forgiveness, for he'd realized by the light of the morning that he'd behaved as a complete cad. And yet the first word he had of her came from his cousin, Rein seeming to be overjoyed that Mary Callahan was to join him at a ball. And then he'd come up here and insulted her further. Damn, but she rattled him.

"You do not know my cousin as I do, Mrs. Callahan. You would be wise to keep your distance."

"I would be wise to keep my distance from all your relatives, I should think."

And what to say to that? Likely she was correct, for

even now he felt that damnable stirring for her that he always did. No matter that she'd refused his offer last eve, and refused it flatly. No matter that he knew, given her adamant stance, that an alliance with her was far from likely. Still, he could not seem to stop himself from admiring her. From wondering what it would have been like should she have said yes.

Lord, how I wish she'd said yes.

"Very well. If you insist upon this."

"I do," she said with a tilt to her chin, and she could look no more proud, no more full of herself than the haughtiest of society ladies. Indeed, if the gown she wore was not made of such poor fabric, if her hair had been dressed more elaborately, he would have been hard pressed but to think her anything but *haut ton*.

She crossed to the door, standing by it in an obvious manner. "Goodbye, my lord. I wish you a pleasant evening."

"And you, Mrs. Callahan," Alex all but growled. And, *Demme*, he wished for a hat that he could cram upon his head—except he didn't have one—or perhaps a walking stick to jab into the ground as he made his exit, something that would afford him some dignity as he made his retreat. Alas, he had neither.

So he left, brushing by her and trying not to remember what it felt like to stare into her eyes. To kiss her lips. To lift her chin with the tip of his finger.

She slammed the door behind him.

He jumped, more piqued than he could ever remember feeling. And the devil of it was, he felt jealous, too. He didn't want her to step out with Rein. Nor with any man.

Damn it, what I want is for her to step out with me.

* * *

By the time lunch rolled around, Alex had worked himself into a fine fit of temper.

By teatime, he was ready to go to her again and demand she stay behind.

By the time dinner was announced, he'd convinced himself that he didn't care. Mary Callahan could do whatever she wanted. She was his servant, by God, and as such beneath his notice. He should be concentrating on who had tried to kidnap him, and getting back to Gabby at the first possible moment, though he'd received a missive from his father that all was well and that he was taking great care to keep Gabby safe.

But that didn't make him feel better.

And then Rein popped in his head right as Alex scooped himself to another stomach-bulging helping of beef. "We'll be leaving in a few minutes, old man."

Alex turned toward him.

Rein smiled sublimely. "Don't wait up for us."

Alex almost lunged at him. Bloody hell, his whole body tensed in anticipation of the move. For a moment he indulged himself in the fantasy of wrapping his hands around Rein's throat, finger by finger. Of bashing his head against the floor again and again and again, before he reminded himself that Mrs. Mary Callahan was not his concern.

"Have a care for her feet."

He looked up in time to see Rein straighten, his expression turning almost pleased for some devilish reason known only to himself. "Yes. Of course, though I'm hoping she'll spend most of the night *off* her feet."

The napkin in Alex's lap became an instant substitute for Rein's neck. So did the fork he held in his right hand, the soft silver bending.

"Enjoy your beef. Cook does an excellent job of making it look not at all like cow tongue."

And then he was gone, only Alex could hear him out in the hall, whistling. Whistling, for God's sake, as if his success with Mary was a foregone conclusion.

Ah, but he didn't know what he was up against.

And neither did Mary.

And therein lay the crux of the problem, for it hadn't been mere jealousy that had prompted Alex's anger. Rein truly was an uncouth rogue. And while Alex was certain his cousin would never go so far as to force himself upon Mary, he was in no way certain that he would couch his interest in her in such a way that it would not be upsetting to her. Not certain at all.

"Devil take it," he hissed.

"Is something the matter, sir?"

Alex glanced up. A footman in off-white and gold livery had entered the room, his expression one of concern.

"No, no. Everything is as it should be."

Except it wasn't. Devil take it, nothing was as it should be at all. He'd crossed a line with Mary, one that could never be taken back. And that line dictated that he look out for her. Watch over her, if you will, even if she had turned him down.

He stood abruptly.

"Will there be anything else, sir?"

"No," he said, leaving the room, leaving because it was the very conscience that made him realize he could not leave Mary Callahan to her fate.

He'd come to care for her too much to do that.

Chapter Seventeen

To say Alex was in a foul mood when he arrived at the assembly would be a severe understatement. It was beyond foul. One could say it was quite repugnant. Disgusting, even, for he certainly had a disgust for himself.

It didn't help matters that the minute he entered the room he could hear murmurings that included the word *Marquis*, though how the local gentry knew who he was when he'd arrived in his cousin's carriage wearing his cousin's borrowed black jacket and breeches, he had no idea. But it seemed ironic that when he didn't want to be recognized, he was, and when he wanted to be recognized, he wasn't.

The good news was that the room was rather small, the threadbare and scarred furnishings so sparse as to be nonexistent. A number of people stood about, but the size of the room made it easy to see the whole of it, or more specifically the dance floor, at a glance.

And there she was, sitting upon one of the many chairs that lined the wall, his cousin standing over her like a male dog protecting his bitch. And she looked quite splendid. Alex hadn't been able to bring himself to see her before she left, only now he wished he had. Seeing her earlier might have given him time to prepare. As it was, it caused everything inside of him to collide in a mish-mash of emotions that excited and irritated and flummoxed him all at the same time.

She wore a green gown shot through with gold, her red hair once again dressed in a fashionable style with a green feather sticking out at the back. For half a moment he wondered where Rein had gotten the ball gown, only to catch a glimpse of the front of it, the answer thereby immediately presenting itself: She wore one of his mistress's castoffs.

Bloody rake. How could he give that to her?

There was a simple answer for that, for Rein was . . . well, Rein. Nothing was too outrageous for him to do.

And the irony of it all, the thing that made Alex realize how truly naïve she was, was that she likely didn't realize that the neckline was far too low to be considered proper. That the skirt was cut a tad too close to the hips to be thought acceptable. That the neckline alone would proclaim her a member of the very profession she'd fought so hard to avoid . . . if she'd been at a proper ball.

But this wasn't a proper ball. Conversations were too loud. Dancers moved through the steps too exuberantly. The clothes both the gentlemen and ladies wore were of a fashion that proclaimed them to be not quite *à la mode*.

Alex shook his head as he took it all in, though his gaze fell quickly back upon Mary. She looked vexed with Rein, he noted, though what his cousin had done to pique her, Alex had no idea, but it was a pleasure to watch them trade sallies, to observe the way her face mirrored everything she felt. To see how her nose wrinkled whenever she was particularly peeved, the way she rolled her eyes at something ridiculous Rein must have said. She didn't flirt with his cousin, didn't invite with her eyes. In fact, she seemed content to insult and trade barbs with him all evening. Alex felt monumentally better.

Someone came up to him, even attempted to converse with him, and Alex sent the man away with a freezing glance. When he looked back into the room, Rein was gone. What the devil?

"Good evening, Alex."

Alex jerked, abashed that Rein had managed to skulk up to him.

The two engaged in battle waged with their eyes until Rein said, "Are you claiming her, Alex? Is that what you're doing here?"

"No. I'm protecting her."

"Hmm. That is a very odd thing for you to want to do."

"Not at all, cousin. Not when you consider how well I know you."

Rein smiled. "I see," he said. "I should have known you would never actually state that you want her for yourself. Such a common emotion as desire would be beneath you, wouldn't it?"

"Leave it, Rein. I've no wish to engage in a verbal battle with you."

"Lust, Alex. That is what you feel. And the sooner you admit it, the better off you'll be. Frankly, I'm quite relieved to see you succumb to the thing. I'd begun to fear you incapable of the emotion."

"Do not cast me in the same light as yourself."

"Oh I'm not, I'm not. For while I would continue to pursue her even after she'd turned me down, you will not." He turned back to stare into the ballroom. "Such a pity, for she really is exquisite. Alas, I will stay away from her since that seems to be what you wish." Their gazes met again. "I bid you good eve, dear cousin. Happy hunting."

And without another word, he bowed, turned and left. Alex stared at the spot he'd been, wondering why he should feel somewhat concerned over Rein's easy acquiescence. Rein made a hobby out of chasing women; it wasn't like him to simply bow out of the competition now.

Could it be that his cousin truly thought Alex meant to try and claim her again?

Are you, Alex?

His gaze fell upon Mary. She sat exactly where Rein had left her. Of course, with her feet the way they were, she would likely not want to move. Something caught her eye, though what it was, he didn't know, but it made her smile slightly. Lord, but there could be no doubt that she was the prettiest woman in the room. In the whole shire, likely. And in addition to that, she had more integrity than half the people in this room.

And he'd asked her to be his mistress.

Odd how he'd never considered doing such a thing an insult before now, but indeed it must have been.

She began to turn, her gaze skimming over the tops of people's heads, stopping for a moment here, darting around there, until finally, inexorably, it came to rest on him near the door.

She might have gasped, for he saw her mouth open a bit. Then she stiffened, much the way he did, too. The slight smile disappeared, and Alex was sorry for it. She looked away, her cheeks coloring, her hands clenching in her lap. Obviously, she was every bit as piqued to see him as she had been to be with Rein. And he didn't blame her.

Lord, he'd fumbled it with her. Badly. He could admit that now.

He moved toward her, ignoring the people around him. Stepped around a couple so engrossed in each other they didn't see him approach. Ignored an old matron whose simpering daughter smiled up at him. Neatly avoided a man who tried to stop him with a hand.

He walked up to her, conversation around her dribbling to a stop—more than one person overheard saying the words *heir* and *dukedom.* He stared down at her for long seconds. Then slowly, with great care, he bowed.

"My lady," he said softly, "would you be so kind as to favor me with a dance?"

She looked up at him and snapped the word, "No."

He straightened, feeling—good lord, of all the unexpected things—the urge to laugh. To smile even. Perhaps it was the saucy way she'd looked at him just before she turned away. Perhaps it was the way she'd shot out her answer like the word was a rock in a slingshot aimed directly at his arse. Perhaps it was because he knew he deserved her pique. Whatever the reason, he suddenly found himself admiring her even more.

"Mary," he tried again, speaking softly, and for her ears alone. "I am sorry for coming to your room as I did. For demanding you not come with Rein tonight. Sorry for insulting your virtue by asking you to become my—" he lowered his voice, "—mistress." And she looked up at him in surprise then. "I promise to treat you with the utmost courtesy from now on, if you will but let me."

She didn't say anything, which Alex supposed was a good sign, though with Mary one never knew. But then he knew she was still irritated with him because she started to cluck that damnable tongue of hers.

"Come," he said, holding out his hand.

"My feet hurt."

"Then let me carry you around the dance floor."

Her gaze darted to his. "Don't be a fool."

He laughed. He couldn't help it. Lord, he loved her frankness.

"Please, Mary. Just one turn. If it hurts too badly, we'll stop."

"I'm angry with you, my lord, thus I refuse to dance with you."

"And I told you I'm sorry. Can you not forgive me?"

"No."

"Come, just one turn."

"I'd sooner dance with Old Scratch."

"He's already left the ball."

She gave him a look that was an odd mix of confused disdain.

"My cousin. He's already left."

To which he saw her lips tighten and then twitch. Ah. Progress.

"Come, Mary. Just one turn. Confess. I know you well enough to know you're dying for the opportunity."

The look she gave him was visual snake venom.

"You are," he reiterated.

"I am not."

"You've never wanted to dance? To move in time to the music? To feel, just for one night, like a princess at her first ball?"

How the blazes the marquis knew that, Mary didn't know, and, oh, how it irked her that he knew . . . and yet she'd wanted to dance since the moment she'd arrived, the fancy swells bowing and smiling at each other. The music stirred her soul. The soft candlelight warmed her skin. The cool breeze coming from outside energized her spirit. But dancing with him would be like dancing with the enemy.

"You're a vile beast, do you know that?"

He smiled a bit, obviously sensing victory. And that irked her all the more.

"Dance," he repeated.

"I don't know how."

"I'll ask them to play a waltz. That way I can lead."

She almost said no, even parted her lips a bit to do so. It still stung that he would ask her to be his mistress. And yet, he'd asked for her forgiveness most sincerely. And one thing she knew of Alex, he was always honest.

"One turn," she found herself saying instead, because devil take it, this would be a once-in-a-lifetime opportunity, just as he said.

"Just one."

"And then we leave."

"If that is your wish."

"It is."

"Very well." He bowed before her again. Mary felt herself straighten. She'd lost her mind for sure. She shouldn't dance with him, she should give him the cold shoulder. That is what a truly outraged woman would do.

"I'll be back in a trice," he said.

She watched him head toward the musicians who sat upon a raised dais at the end of the room.

Go, Mary. Go now.

But a part of her was too greedy to leave. She'd always wanted to dance at a ball. Devil take it, tonight she would.

"We're in luck," he said a few moments later. "Apparently this is not as backward a place as I feared."

As if listening for those very words, the lead violinist plucked the opening chords. Alex held out his hand. She stared at it for a moment.

Don't, don't, don't.

She took it. Lord help her, she couldn't seem to stop herself.

The dress Mary wore, the beautiful gown the earl had brought to her to wear and that had made her gasp at the beauty of it, rustled, the golden threads catching the glow of the candles that hung in wall sconces around the room. Granted, when she curtsied to him, she feared her feet might not last, but Mary didn't care. This was her one dance. Her one and only chance at feeling, for once, like a lady. Her one chance at seeing what it was like on the other side.

He pulled her to him, and Mary's heart sped faster, though in anticipation of the dance or at the contact of their bodies, she couldn't be sure.

"Breathe easy, my lady. I shall not let you stumble."

And for just a moment, just the tiniest fraction of a heartbeat, she really did feel like a lady. Perhaps it was the dress. Perhaps it was the way people stared. But suddenly she felt like the most beautiful, perfect, well-bred lady in the room.

No one else took the floor. Gowns rustled as ladies stepped back, some taking their seats. Candles flickered as a breeze swept through. Men watched from the sidelines.

"Perhaps they don't know the steps?" Alex conjectured.

Mary doubted it. Rather, she had a feeling they wanted to watch a lord dance with his lady.

His lady.

And, oh, how she wished. Aye, for though he'd insulted her greatly by offering to make her his mistress, though he angered her by ordering her about, Mary couldn't deny there was a large part of her that wished to be his lady in the truest sense of the word.

Aye, and a daft, silly fool I am for wanting it.

She was. She knew it, but that didn't make her feel any different. All her life she'd wondered what it'd be like to be on the other side. To be wealthy and pampered and—lord, she couldn't believe she was admitting this—*loved.* And while she knew his lordship didn't love her, he had always been kind . . . always kind. And tonight he'd been man enough to admit he'd been wrong in asking her to become his mistress. She'd never met a man who could admit he was wrong.

So as he lifted her left hand, as he stared down into her starstruck eyes, she allowed herself that fantasy, too. (Why the blazes not? This was her fantasy, after all.) She pretended they were man and wife. That he loved her. That he'd inherited his dukedom. That she was the Duchess of Wainridge. That all the people who looked on were their guests at a party held in her honor. Aye, she'd invited them in celebration of an award she had been given for charity work— No, no. She was trying to open an orphanage and this was a charity event to raise funds. Wait, she hated children. Very well, it was a poorhouse she were wanting to open—

"Follow my lead."

His words brought her back to the present. She met his enigmatic gaze just as they took their first step. Pain shot up her leg, making her gasp.

"Is it too much?" he asked, halting the slow turn he'd been guiding her through.

Lord, she thought as she stared up at him, if she weren't so well grounded, she'd be half in love with him for sure . . . just because he looked down at her so caringly. It made her toes squeeze together.

"I feel as fine as a sixpence."

She didn't, but he didn't need to know that. No, indeed, this was likely the only time she'd ever dance in her life. She would let nothing spoil it.

So she closed her eyes, letting him slowly turn her again, letting her body drift closer—or did he pull her closer?—and then closer still. Letting her mind and her body surrender to the magic, the near fairy-tale quality of being held in his arms. Of dancing with a marquis.

"You look beautiful."

She opened her eyes. "I know."

A sharp huff of laughter escaped him, but she ignored it, closing her eyes again, letting her thoughts be swept away by the majesty of the music.

"That dress fits you perfectly."

She'd been in the midst of imagining herself wearing a coronet, and Mary felt a wee bit irked by his interruption.

"One would think it made for you."

She opened an eye. That was all she spared him. One. "Your cousin said it belonged to a friend." The eye snapped closed.

"Oh, I'm sure it does."

She opened both eyes then, lifting her brows to boot. "M'lord, if you're thinking I don't know it belongs to one of his fancy pieces, you're mistaken. Even *I* know it's cut too low and too tight to be considered proper."

Surprise stretched his brows. Well, time he realized she wasn't a complete fool.

Then those brows drifted down. "On you it looks magnificent."

Well, maybe she *was* a fool, for her heart pitter-pattered as hard as a senile old sailor's. "Aye, though I'd wager you'd rather see me *out* of it."

Did he stumble? She thought he might have.

"Or was it another man who asked me to be his mistress last eve?" she asked.

"It was me. And as I said earlier, I am sorry for it."

"Are you, m'lord," she asked. "Are you indeed?"

He answered right away with a directness she could not deny. "Yes," he said, his gaze unwavering as he looked into her eyes. "I am sorry, Mary, for I realize a woman such as yourself has too much pride to become a man's plaything. You have the most amazing ability to take care of yourself. Indeed, you are a rare gem amongst females and I'm sorry that I offended you."

And lord help her, she felt something inside her shift and tilt like glass in a kaleidoscope. And from nowhere came the thought that she truly liked this man. Liked that he accepted his faults, oftentimes apologizing for them. She liked the way that he sometimes coddled her. Lord, that he'd tried to carry her in his arms even when it became patently obvious that he lacked the strength to do so. But most of all, she liked the way he fought his desire for her, never pressing himself upon her, never making crass comments, just telling her he desired her in that forthright way of his, and then offering her the only solution to the problem he could think of.

" 'Tis all right, my lord," she said, seeing the genuine relief that filled his eyes. "And I thank you for understanding why I said no, and for not pressing the matter."

He nodded his head, saying, "Friends?"

Oh, God, she didn't want to be his friend, she suddenly realized, she wanted to be so much more than that.

"Friends," she said over a lump in her throat because she couldn't escape the truth:

I could fall in love with him.

She stiffened.

Oh, aye, Mary. You could.

"Does your foot pain you again?" he asked.

Good lord.

She was half in love with him already.

Chapter Eighteen

Something had changed. Something barely there but obvious enough for Alex to see. She still danced with him. He still held her, but she was no longer there.

What? *Demme!* What? He'd sensed her softening. Sensed her acceptance of him. Felt that she might, indeed, be coming to forgive him.

He tried to draw her nearer. She resisted. He wondered what the devil to do.

And then, all too quickly, the dance ended. Applause erupted from the crowd. Alex looked up, surprised to realize that they had, indeed, been the only ones on the floor.

She pulled away.

"Is it your feet?" he asked again.

She pushed through bodies, moving at a pace that made Alex suspect it was not at all her feet that bothered her, but something in her mind. Damnation, but he almost had to run to catch up. What the devil?

"Mary," he said when she reached the same seat she'd vacated earlier. "If you are in pain, you have only to say. I would be happy to escort you home."

She wouldn't meet his eyes, and that, more than anything, worried Alex. Mary was, always, direct and to the point. She never hid her head or gave a man anything less than the truth. It was a trait he esteemed the most about her.

"I should like to go home."

And her voice sounded different, too. Or perhaps she was just mimicking her betters. Ballocks, but he wished he could see into her mind.

"I'll call for the carriage."

People stared at him as he turned away, Alex tempted to tell the whole room to go to the devil. Hadn't they ever seen a lord before? Well, of course they had. His cousin. Yet they kept bowing and nodding as if he were the king of England.

You are heir to a dukedom, Alex, and they are not likely to meet someone of your rank ever again.

And, indeed, it was true, though Alex heartily appreciated the way Mary treated him as opposed to the way this crowd reacted. At least she reacted to his person rather than his title.

In due course the carriage was brought around, a groomsman with a torch running in front of it to light the choppy ground. Alex turned back to the assembly room, reluctant to fetch Mary, reluctant because he wanted to spend more time with her, wanted to converse with her, to forget for a night that their worlds were so far apart. Alas, it wasn't meant to be. He turned, shrugging into his cousin's borrowed gray great cloak, his cravat getting in the way of the catch. It took him a moment to realize the reason why he had such a hard time was because his hands shook.

Devil take it, his hands shook.

He straightened, taking a deep breath before going inside. She was right where he left her, staring at the ground, no one daring to approach her, Alex wishing someone would. He would do anything to see her smile again.

In due course her own cloak was fetched, another castoff from his cousin's mistress, no doubt. Spotted ermine framed the hood, the white fur making her look like a fairy princess.

They stepped onto the stone that led down to the waiting carriage. And like magic, the moon slid through a break in the clouds. They both halted, both looked up as one.

"It stopped raining," she observed.

Ah. Words. "Indeed."

"We should be able to return to your father's on the morrow."

Return? Tomorrow? He didn't want to think about that.

"Mary, I—" What?

She turned to look at him, and Alex knew he would never forget the sight of her in that moonlight, the tip of her nose and cheeks and chin illuminated by the light. Her hair peeked out a bit from the edge of the hood, her green eyes looking the color of jade as they stared up with him in . . . what? Was it fear? Sadness? *Desire*?

She lifted a brow, waiting for him to finish.

"Nothing."

She turned, saying, "Mud," as she stared down at the sodden ground.

And Alex felt the most ridiculous urge to take off his greatcoat and lay it down. And why not? It was, after all, his cousin's. Serve him a well-deserved lesson—

Mary leapt.

It was the only way to describe it. She flew through the air like a witch without a broom. Alex's jaw dropped at the sight. Even the footman yelped, then just as quickly said, "Well done, ma'am," as she landed inside. When finished, she peeked around the edge of the door frame as if to say, "Well, hurry up then."

Alex glanced at the footman. The man lifted a brow.

Alex leapt, too, only he knew immediately he wasn't going to make it, even tried to compensate for it by twisting about, which only made it worse, for he ended up a half-foot short of his mark and face down.

"Doop," he thought he heard the footman say, but it might have been *damn*, for Alex's ears were suddenly clogged with mud, as were his nostrils, mouth and eyes.

"Good lord."

That he recognized as Mary's voice, masculine hands reaching down to help lift him up.

He was stuck in the mud.

No exaggeration about it. Bloody stuck in the mud like a rock in sand. He couldn't move, hands having to jerk him free, Alex by turns seeing mud, the servant's face, then mud again.

"Good lord," he thought he heard Mary repeat, and he wasn't sure (his ears were still a bit clogged) but he thought he heard laughter soot the edges of her words.

He tried to see, but the bloody mud kept smearing his vision. He tried to wipe it away, only made it worse, for his hands were covered. "I don't suppose you have a rag, my good man," he said to the hovering groomsman.

Something white and vaguely resembling a square was waved in front of him. Ah. A handkerchief. "Thank you."

His eyes were cleaned first, which enabled him to see Mary staring down at him from the carriage. His ears were next, thus allowing him to hear a slight huffing sound that signaled laughter and that the torch above him hissed and sizzled. He wiped his face last, air catching the wetness and turning his skin cold. When he'd finished, he handed the muddy handkerchief back to the groom who held it out before him like it stank.

"Give me your direction and I'll buy you a new one," Alex said.

"I work for the earl, m'lord. No need to pay a thing."

"I insist, my good man."

The groom seemed to wilt. Alex realized after a moment that he'd doubled over in laughter, his knees bending as he squatted near the ground. It was as if he couldn't take it anymore and unable to hold his chuckles back a second longer, he just collapsed. The coachman on the box began to howl, too, then every other person within sight.

A week ago Alex might have been furious that they dared laugh in his face.

A week ago he might have insisted his cousin fire the lot . . . well, those that worked for him.

A week ago he hadn't been kidnapped, arrested and sprung by a woman who'd confounded, amused and flabbergasted him in return . . . a woman he'd wounded by asking her to become his mistress, a woman, he realized, whose laughter he'd wanted very badly to hear, for he suspected Mary Callahan needed laughter in her life.

"I would not laugh if I were you," he pretended outrage for Mary. "For 'tis *you* all who shall have to put up with my sodden presence."

The wheezing inside the carriage had settled into low chuckles now. He took a step, almost lost his shoes to the sucking mud, but managed to slog his way to the carriage door. He looked inside.

The carriage lantern hanging next to the driver's seat

illuminated her perfectly. There were tears in her eyes, though they were, of course, tears of amusement, and he could swear it was a kind of worry and a sadness, but he must be mistaken, though there could be no doubt about the smile on her lips. Her mouth—that adorable, sassy mouth—grinned widely, her lovely teeth flashing as she tried to contain herself.

"Oh, my lord," she said. "If you only knew how much I needed that laugh."

And then her eyes grew sad again—yes, it was definitely sadness he saw as her laughter slowly faded. Why was she sad? And what would it take to make the laughter return? Straightening, he undid his greatcoat, the fabric so heavy with water and mud, he almost felt lighter when he handed it to the waiting groom.

"Do something with this," he said, using the carriage frame to pull himself inside. When he settled himself opposite her, he began to undo his jacket. Well, Rein's jacket, not that his cousin would likely want it back.

"What are you doing?" she asked.

"Relieving myself of a wet jacket."

She seemed to freeze—odd, that—for she seemed to pale a bit, too.

"Really, m'lord, is that necessary?"

He drew himself up. "Yes, it's necessary. I'm as wet as a goose and smell like one, too." He finished removing his jacket, handing it, too, to the waiting groom, then his waistcoat. And when he finished, he realized she was back to avoiding his gaze again, and it was then that he had the revelation.

He leaned back against the seat, reeling with it. Then slowly, keeping his gaze firmly fixed upon her, he began to undo his shirt.

"What are you doing?" she asked, her expression turning horrified.

"Why, I'm removing my shirt."

"But that, that's—"

"Unseemly?" And he took great pride in, for once, finishing a sentence for *her.*

"Well, yes."

Slowly, feeling rather naughty and not at all very gentlemanlike, he continued to undo the buttons. She turned her head to the side. Wouldn't even peek at him.

Hah, he wanted to cry. *Hah, hah, hah.* He knew it. He just knew it.

She found him attractive, so much so that she didn't want him to be undressed and be near her.

If Alex had been a peacock, he would have fanned his tail feathers. He was, alas, a man, and so he settled for having some very manly thoughts, even though he told himself he'd best not let the knowledge go to his head, for he would never be uncouth enough to press his advantage now that she'd refused his advances.

"Here's a cloth for you, m'lord," said the groom, handing one inside.

"Ah, thank you," he said, feeling rather smug. By God, her attraction to him made him feel good.

And then he caught a glimpse of her nipples. Her *hard* nipples, the cloak she wore covering just the edge of her breasts, the thin fabric of her dress revealing two taut peaks. Cold? Beneath that cloak? Having come from inside the assembly room?

He didn't think so, but just to test his theory, he said, "Did I get it all?"

She wouldn't look at him, and one thing Alex knew about Mary Callahan: she wasn't shy. It wasn't maidenly affront that caused her to avert her gaze. It wasn't embarrassment, not when he'd seen her in next to nothing—bother that—absolutely nothing. She just plain lacked the courage to turn to him.

"Here, m'lord." And bless the groom's heart, he handed in a rug. Alex almost smiled, thanking the man, then wrapped it around him.

"Well?" he asked when he was covered from the waist up. "Did I get it all?"

Finally, she looked at him, and finally, he saw the answer in her eyes.

No fear. No embarrassment. Just a hurried glance that spoke volumes, even though all she said was one word: "Yes."

"Will that bc all, m'lord?" thc scrvant askcd.

Alex turned to the man, nodding, suddenly wanting to be alone with her more than he'd wanted anything in his life. "Yes. And my thanks, sir. I shall commend you to my cousin the earl."

The man pulled his forelock, a countrified show of respect that always made Alex wince, then closed the door.

Darkness enveloped them. Through the glass in the door they could see the torch being carried away, the lantern near the coachman's box taking over.

Alex began to remove his shoes.

"What are you doing?"

He paused, looked into her wide-eyed gaze. "Removing my shoes. The wetness is making my feet cold."

Did he see her swallow? Could she be that affected?

She could. Indeed, if she felt half of what he felt for her, she would be on the verge of losing control, and

Alex, who prided himself on his measured, well-ordered life, suddenly wanted to chuck it all. He wanted to lose control. With her. Now. Tonight. Alas, his scruples wouldn't let him.

He slowly removed his shoes. She looked away again. The carriage began to move off, lurching suddenly as if the wheels had been stuck and the horses forced to pull hard.

He didn't do it on purpose, truth be told, he was hardly thinking straight when it happened. Alex was forced to steady himself thanks to that lurch, forced to reach out a hand, a hand that landed on her knee.

She gasped.

He froze.

And then they lunged at each other. Lord, like two half-crazed individuals, they went at it. A part of Alex registered this, just as a part of him registered that it was *she* kissing *him*. *Her* pressing those soft, pliant lips against *his*. *She* who was assaulting *him*, attacking his lips in the same, forthright manner she applied to everything else in life.

And god help him, he couldn't resist.

Chapter Nineteen

Don't stop, Mary begged with her lips. *Just kiss me.*

And his lips answered her pleas, kissing her in a way at once commanding and yet gentle. That left her anxious and yet wanting. That made her forget the truth that had penetrated when he'd been dancing with her.

She would have to leave him.

And then he pressed her into her seat, Mary's hands coming up against his naked chest. Her mind registered the way his hair felt beneath her hands; the wiry texture of it, the hard ridges of his muscles. Her fingers slid up to his shoulder, marveling at how his skin could be so soft, yet his body so hard, the cord along his shoulders a ridge that made her realize he was no weak-muscled lord.

And then his own hands began to explore. They found the tightness of her nipples, a tautness that had blossomed at the sight of his naked chest. She bent to his will, lifting herself for his hand's eager exploration, crying out when he moved his mouth to the spot that his fingers had just teased.

"Mary," she thought she heard him whisper. "We shouldn't—"

Shouldn't what?

"But—" he abruptly kissed her again, then pulled away. "I—" Back to kissing her again, and pulling back again. "Can't. Seem. To. Stop."

"Bugger this," she said, holding his head at her breasts because, blast it, she wanted him to kiss her there, wanted to feel his wet, hot mouth working her nipple. Wanted him to touch her, to know her, to do things to her. Lord, if he only knew how much.

And he must have gotten the message for he opened his mouth, half-biting the sensitive tip of first one breast, then the other, the heat of his mouth prickling the tip of nipple even more. But he wasn't satisfied with kissing fabric. No, he pulled the edge of her dress down. And then his tongue fluttered at the tip. Mary pulsed everywhere, but most especially between her legs. She watched him turn the tip into a hard nub. Watched as he lapped at her next, then—oh heavens—suckled her.

And yet, it wasn't enough.

She wanted more. Needed to feel more, and the craving came from that most private part of her. She pushed against him, thought she heard him moan, felt that need she'd only ever felt in her dreams begin to build.

Please, she silently begged him with her eyes. *Please, give it to me, whatever* it *is.*

His hand trailed down her belly, headed for that part of her that wanted to be touched. And for a fleeting moment the memory returned of other men trying to touch her there, of how she'd fought against them.

"Mary," she heard him say.

And she realized then that she'd stilled for that moment, and that he'd sensed it and had stopped, his expression one of question as he looked at her.

But the heat between her legs raged, her body demanding she finish whatever it was she started. Nay, not demanded, begged.

"Touch me, Alex," she said. "Touch me and show me that it will be all right."

He blinked at her then, his expression undergoing a change. The hardness in his eyes faded, was replaced by a tender desire she'd never seen on a man's face before.

"Tell me where you want to be touched, Mary, and I shall. Tell me when to stop, and I shall. Command me as if 'tis I who am your servant, for tonight I am all that and more."

She searched his eyes, no, his soul, Mary's mind seeming to touch it for one brief moment.

"Kiss me, m'lord," she said.

He slowly lifted himself, though the carriage made it difficult for it lurched and shook about them. Or mayhap 'twas her that shook? Mayhap, it was all in her mind? She only knew that Alex rose to kiss her and when he did, she felt everything within her still and then scatter like fall leaves before an October breeze.

And then their lips met, only this time 'twas a tender kiss, a gentle, soft and achingly beautiful kiss. Mary felt tears rise.

Slowly, almost as if he didn't want to startle her, his hands rose again, only this time they bypassed her breasts, though she arched into him in anticipation of it. This time he touched her jaw, framing it with both hands, gently, oh so gently, asking her to open for him.

Could she? Did she dare let him kiss her so intimately? What would happen if she did?

She opened for him. His tongue slipped inside her mouth, the warm heat of it a masculine invasion she'd never felt before. She almost withdrew, for the shock of it made her stiffen, but then she got her first taste of him, so spicy and different from her own. And then she got her first touch of him, his pliant tongue stroking her own. Then she almost lost him, that same tongue withdrawing so quickly, she moaned in protest.

Alex must have heard, for he gave it back to her again. And again. And again, until she was dizzy with the way that sweet stroking made her feel.

How long they kissed like that, Mary didn't know, but though her body craved the return of his tongue over and over again, her body also craved something else, something that mirrored the movement of his tongue. Aye, she wanted him inside her, that she knew, for she hadn't worked amongst men and horses not to know how a male and female joined.

But he seemed determined to kiss her all night and so she reached up and grabbed one of his hands, and even his fingers felt harder than her own. Aye, all of him felt harder than her, most especially that place pressing against her thighs.

Lower and lower she guided his hand, his mouth still covering her, their breaths still mingled as one. Her hand brushed his hardness, and she thought she heard him groan. And then she pressed his hand into her, placed it on that spot that had begun to tingle and moisten and burn.

He drew back, murmuring, "Mary," against her lips.

"Please," she answered back.

His lips returned, and with it, his hand, his wide palm pushing into her.

Oh, but he knew how to touch her, for his fingers probed the fabric of her dress, found her nub and pressed into it.

"Alex," she heard herself moan, the muscles in her back flexing, her hips lifting, every sinewy cord in her body tensing to the point that it almost seemed to hurt. No. Not hurt. It felt . . . she threw her head back. It felt so marvelously wonderful, so different from her vague and nebulous dreams it was like looking into a mirror after a fog had been wiped clean. Lord, she thought, straining against his hand. Lord, lord, lord. She wanted . . . she wanted.

What? she almost cried. What the blazes was it?

She'd begun to pant with the strain of that want, that craving to have him finish whatever it was he started. And then he was moving her hand, moving it to the hard length of him tucked down the left side of his leg. He pressed her fingers against him, showed her how to stroke him, and then he lifted her into his arms. And touching him like that, controlling him, aye, making him moan was almost as powerful as the feel of him touching her.

And then she was spinning, spinning, or maybe it was him spinning because all of a sudden she was beneath him on the seat he'd just vacated, his body covering her own. His hands seemed to be everywhere, but most especially beneath her cloak, on her breasts. No, wait, between her legs. God help her, she never wanted him to stop touching her between her legs.

She touched him, too, his hands leaving her again to go to the waistline of his trousers. It gave her pause, the cessation in his assault. She recovered herself momentarily, her heart beating so rapidly she felt it might be close to harm. He stood over her—or as near as he could beneath the roofline of the coach—the carriage lantern swinging about, the cabin swaying. His eyes stared at her so intensely, so heatedly and so unwaveringly, Mary couldn't look away.

And then that look changed. *Say the word*, he silently seemed to say. *Say the word and I'll stop.*

But heaven help her, she didn't want him to stop. Having committed to the course, she would ride the tide all the way.

He nodded. Or perhaps it was the movement of the coach, but suddenly his shoulders tensed, his arms moved around the front of him, the hands that had left her in such a state undoing first one catch, then the other, the flap of his breech, dropping on one side and then the other. His arm muscles flexed, his own nipples turned hard, the light sprinkling of hair on his skin a perfect T across his chest, fading as it went lower, then resuming again in a dark tumble just below his belly.

His breech dropped.

Mary's gaze fell with it only to catch on his shaft, the soft pink of his flesh startling her, as did his size.

"It's—" She swallowed. He lifted a brow. "Bigger than I expected."

He laughed, the sound filling her soul with a winged joy. But then his eyes grew serious, the lids floating down and turning the irises almost black. "Touch me, Mary Callahan. Touch me and feel how much I desire you."

The coach swayed, rounding a bend, but Mary hardly noticed. Oddly enough, just staring at his appendage made the heat between her legs blaze all over again. Like a burning log stabbed by a poker, she began to glow and burn.

"Touch it," he urged.

She reached out hesitantly, her hand moving with the motion of the carriage. He seemed to flex toward her, his lids lowering as her hand hovered.

"Please, Mary," and his tone was a plea.

She touched him.

He gasped, his hips arching toward hers, bringing him closer to her, Mary's fingers gliding along the soft edge of him. He gasped again. She touched him with her fingertips once more.

"Yes," he said. "Yes, Mary, just like that."

Soft, he was. So soft. And yet hard. She ran her finger up and down that hardness, thinking she'd done this to him, that she made him grow hard, made him moan in pleasure. He might be heir to a dukedom, but right now he was all man. *Her* man. Hers to command, hers to rule, hers for tonight.

Only tonight.

The coach lurched even more, Alex having to put out a hand to stop himself from falling on to her. But it was only the sudden loss of vibration, the instant stillness that made her realize they'd done more than round a corner.

"Alex?"

But Alex needed no warning, for he'd already reached down, already pulled up his breeches.

The coachman opened the door just as the fabric cleared Alex's hips, and it was obvious the driver could see what Alex'd done through the carriage window.

But if she had any doubts, they vanished the moment the coachman said, "I see the breeches were muddy too, m'lord."

Chapter Twenty

Embarrassing. Humiliating, Mary thought, closing her bedroom door behind her. It was bad enough the upper servants thought of her as a tart, but now the outside staff would too.

And Alex . . .

She closed her eyes. Alex would follow.

Though he'd given her a polite goodnight below, though he'd bowed over her hand with that ridiculous blanket around his shoulders, she knew he would follow.

The question was, would she let him in?

She crossed her room, shivering. She'd removed the borrowed cloak downstairs, handing it off to a servant just like a toff. Someone had started a fire and for that Mary was grateful, though she supposed the staff was forced to treat her like a proper guest, no matter that it chaffed.

And now the marquis would come to her. Now he would ask to finish what they started in the carriage. The question was, would she let him? Would it be so terrible to have him for a night? Just one night, for as certain as the sun would rise, she knew she'd have to leave him on the morrow. She cared for him. Lord, after tonight, she might more than care for him, and that she couldn't have, for with the caring would come the desire to stay with him.

Ach, Mary, and would that be such a terrible thing?

She closed her eyes, the orange glow from the fire penetrating her lids, the heat from the fire gently nudging her face.

Would it be so bad? she asked herself again.

Fancy clothes? A carriage? Money? She'd be a gentleman's fancy piece. And not just any gentleman, but a marquis, heir to a dukedom, very nearly a prince. And if she could keep his attention long enough, bind her to him in a way that she knew a woman could do, it could last a very long, long time—

She shook her head, surprised at the keening desire that filled, the ache that almost hurt to give in to the urge. But she couldn't. Just couldn't.

But she could have tonight. Aye, just the night.

But why not more?

Because she couldn't, she argued with herself. Always she'd prided herself of the way she controlled her destiny. Aye, those fancy women might hiss at her as she performed. They might call her by rude names, but Mary knew that when the sun went down, she would still be Mary Brown Callahan, seaman's daughter. Not lord so-and-so's mistress.

Ach, but she would love . . .

Something fell down her cheek. Mary was disgusted to realize it was another soddin' tear. And she knew why she cried, too, she knew it was because a part of her wished, lord how it wished, she was a different sort of woman—

Someone touched her shoulder.

Mary jumped.

Alex stepped in front of her, near enough to touch,

close enough to kiss, though how he'd sneaked up on her, she had no idea.

"Why do you cry, Mary Callahan?"

Because I think I'm falling in love with you, she silently answered as she stared up at him mutely. *Because I'm going to have to leave you.*

She closed her eyes again. Bowed her head.

But then he touched her. He lifted her chin just as he had before, the tender gesture making her heart melt. And just the soft touch of his finger against her cheek started the burning. Just the look in his eyes increased the craving. Aye, she wanted this man, if only for a night.

Only a night.

She opened her eyes, reaching up to take his hand, his fingers so much larger than her own. So much harder, too.

"Have you changed your mind?" he asked. "For if you have, I will—"

"Shhh," she said, placing her other hand against his lips, his breath whispering across her fingers, his mouth warm beneath her hand. "Shhh," she warned again, her hand having begun to shake. "Don't say a word, m'lord. Just kiss me."

"Mary," she thought she heard him whisper.

"That's a word—"

He kissed her, pulling her against him, his lips insisting she open. And she did, the flood of feeling that entered her soul returning with a force that made it near impossible to breathe. She wanted him. Aye, how she wanted him. And she would take him. There would be no looking back once the deed was done. Aye, except, perhaps, to revel in the memory of it.

His tongue flicked into her mouth. She gave him her

own tongue, kissing him in a way that sent her blood thrusting through her veins, that made her whole body tighten in response. His hand reached between them, cupping her breasts and her mind screamed the word, *Yes.* Her body told him, *Take me.*

Or perhaps she'd said the words aloud, for suddenly he was looking down at her again, his eyes staring at her with such fierceness, she felt her breasts tighten like a night-blooming flower kissed by the sun.

He grabbed her by the hand, leading her toward the bed and Mary knew the moment had come to make up her mind.

What mind? I lost it the moment we first touched.

He turned her, made her face him and look into his eyes. "Mary—"

"Would you quit talkin', m'lord?"

She thought she saw him smile, but she couldn't be certain for he was kissing her again, aye, that and pulling her down on the bed next to him. And Mary went willingly because she wanted him in the same way he wanted her. She let him undo the catches on her dress because she craved his touch just as he craved hers. She let him slip her gown and chemise off, then watched as he undressed himself, too, because when it came down to it, they were equals, she and he. They weren't lord and servant. They were two beings that wanted to be one, and for her, that meant whatever the consequences.

"Would you like a cover?"

Her gaze roved over him. "It'd be a crime to cover you, m'lord."

"I meant *you*," he said.

"I know," she answered back, for she lay naked, completely and utterly naked beneath him.

He gave a bark of laughter, his naked body glowing in the firelight, his hair loose around his shoulders though she had no recollection of him freeing the strands. That his desire had returned there could be little doubt, his manhood jutting out from between his legs. Yet he didn't seem ashamed. And it occurred to her then that he might feel the same as she. Their nakedness might be a powerful excitement that a part of Mary wished would last forever, the other part wanting satiation in whatever way he would give it to her immediately.

"You make me laugh, Mary Callahan." He began to lower himself. "You make me smile." His body covered her own, his flesh as hot as a burst of steam. "You make me burn for you in a way I never thought possible to burn for a woman."

He half covered her, his lips now inches away.

"Take me, m'lord. Take me now, for I don't want to wait."

She thought he'd kiss her again, right then, but to her surprise, he held back. "Oh, no, my dear, for I've longed for this night too often to rush it."

"Rush it."

He laughed again, his breath wafting over her ear and the nape of her neck.

"No, my dear, for I am determined to give you a pleasure unlike any you've ever had. I'm determined to savor you in the same way I would savor a fine wine. I am determined to make this an evening you and I will never forget, starting now."

She almost told him that this was her first time. That, miraculously, she'd managed to keep her virtue through all the strife of her early life. But to do so would reveal her lack of a husband, and that she couldn't do.

The thought made her somber, and then he covered her fully, and that made her forget her past, made her focus on tonight. Lord, the feel of him against her made her a wee bit mad. He kissed her breasts, and then it returned, that wonderful feeling only he'd ever aroused. Back arching, she clutched at his head, holding his head there for she didn't want him getting any ideas about stopping.

Then he moved lower.

"What are you—"

"Shh," he warned, kissing her belly. She jumped, her body jolting, her limbs buzzing like she touched a piece of metal that was electrically charged by static. Her legs jerked apart. And she wasn't too ashamed to admit that she wanted—oh, lord she wanted—his mouth. There. Yes, there.

She dug her hands into the covers.

"Alex," she moaned.

He left her for a moment. She looked down. He looked up, his intense blue eyes just visible between the apex of her thighs. And then she felt the warm, moist slide of his tongue.

"Bloody hell," she moaned. "I can't believe—"

He licked her again. Modesty made her want to clench her thighs together. Wanton desire made her open even more. And then she simply surrendered, her whole body going lax as she gave in to the feel of him lapping at her there, stroking her there, aye, suckling there. The musky smell of herself wafted up. She groaned at the forbidden smell. And then she began to tighten where he kissed, her muscles seeming to close in on themselves. Such an odd pressure, it was, one that seemed to grow in on itself in pulses and spasms—

He stopped.

She jerked her head up. "What are you doing?"

He looked up from between her legs with a wicked smile.

"For the love of God, don't stop."

Did he chuckle? Lord, she didn't know, she was too busy throwing her head back in disappointment, for he didn't resume that tortuous assault. No, he began to move up her body again.

"Don't," she moaned again. "Keep doing what you were doing."

"I'm not going to stop. I'm going to do this—" His finger entered her.

It made her cry out. Not in pain. Not in shock. But in a jolt of pleasure that made her back arch.

"Because I'm going to do this." He withdrew the finger.

She let loose another moan.

"And this." He entered her again.

Only this time she'd caught on. This time she flexed and arched as she lifted her hips in anticipation. This time she bore down on that finger, clenching it inside her.

"That's it," he said, and now his thumb worked the nub of her woman's mound.

"Alex, if you don't finish this I shall bash you—"

He kissed her again, and the salty taste of herself on him sent her over the edge.

"Alex—"

And off she went, the back of her shoulders coming off the bed as she threw her head back, her hair covering her eyes. Everything pushed outward in a release that made the rush of performing in front of a crowd seem dismal by comparison. Moisture slicked her thighs as a pleasure so incredible, so unexpected, forced the nub between her woman's lips to contract in pleasure. And through it all, he held himself against her, even thrust his finger one last time. It felt like soaring through the air. Like what she'd always imagined flying would be like. She skimmed over the tops of trees on a wave of pleasure. Was thrust on high by an updraft, then down, then back up again. And as she slowly, ever so slowly returned to earth, Mary discovered what it meant to be pleasured. Oh, aye, 'twas a pleasure unlike any she'd had before.

Her body sank onto her coverlet.

Awareness began to return.

"Did you enjoy that?"

She opened eyes she hadn't even known she'd closed, the self-satisfied expression on his face causing her to say, "You know I did, you scurvy knave."

To which he smiled and said, "Excellent, then let us do it again."

Again? Was it possible? Dare she hope?

He moved between her legs, his shaft finding her opening.

Oh, aye. 'Twas possible. As he slid inside her, she knew anything was possible, for this was a different feeling from before. And though she expected it to hurt—lord, what virgin hadn't been told it would hurt like the very devil?—it didn't. He slid right into her, buried himself to the hilt, and as he did, he grazed across an area deep inside that made her jerk.

"Alex?" she questioned, for the feeling was different from before, and yet the same.

"Let it happen again," she heard him say. "Let it come again."

And as he stroked her, his eyes staring into her own in a way that made her feel oddly owned by him, and yet not, she felt it begin to build again. Every time he stroked that place, that center of her being, she jerked and moaned.

His eyes grew glazed, and she had no doubt that her eyes looked the same. Suddenly, the need to give him pleasure became an obsession, a need that fueled her own passion in a way that near consumed her. She tightened around him.

"Mary," he moaned.

Her ankles wrapped around the back of his legs, everything within Mary clenching and squeezing as she fought to give him a release while at the same time gaining her own.

His head dropped next to her ear, as if he couldn't stand to hold it up any longer. "Lord," he huffed. "Lord, lord, lord," he repeated, moving in and out of her. His breathing came faster and faster. Mary's breathing matched. Thrust for thrust, they met each other. Sigh to sigh. Mingled breath to mingled breath. And she was there, almost there, Mary's body coiling in that now familiar way. Oh, aye—lord bless him—he was doing it again.

"Alex," she answered back.

"You're so tight," he panted. "So bloody tight. I need to pull out."

"No." she cried. Just make it happen. Now.

And then he seemed to give up. He pushed inside her and when he did, this time it was different from the first. This time he was inside her, aye, joined with her in a way that made her feel something so sweet, so gentle, and yet so wonderful, it made a liquid warmth spread throughout her body.

They stilled, both of them locked together in a moment

of time that Mary promised she'd never forget. And then slowly, gently, he began to move again, shifted himself so he could look in her eyes.

"You're crying," he said softly.

"Am I?" she sniffed.

"You are."

"Must be something in me eye."

He smiled, gently, as if he understood. And that look, that one look alone, made Mary feel more vulnerable and more cherished than she had in all her days on earth. She felt tears rise again, wishing for just a moment that things were different. Alas, they weren't. She had him for now, but she'd have to give him up on the morrow.

Part Three

What is your fortune, my pretty maid?
My face is my fortune, sir, she said.

Then I can't marry you, my pretty maid
Nobody asked you, sir, she said.

William Pryce,
1790

Chapter Twenty-One

She woke alone the next morning, the haze of pleasure and contentment that had shrouded her sleep evaporating as quickly as summer dew.

Morning had come.

Like the princess without a shoe, the night had passed.

She sat up in bed, sad, contemplative and a whole host of other emotions she couldn't, nay, didn't want to sort out. She had thought one night would be enough; only now did she realize it would never be enough.

In a daze, she got out of bed, pulling on her dressing robe. The door opened. Mary turned. Alex stood there, a tray of food in his hands.

Food? He'd brought her food?

"What are you doing out of bed?"

"I thought I'd get dressed," she said in a voice almost hoarse with tears.

He'd brought her food. No one had ever brought her food before.

He smiled in a way she'd never seen before, either. 'Twas a boyish grin, almost like that of the young grooms just starting out at the circus, and who didn't know that performing day in and day out would eventually take its toll on them. "Did you miss me?"

"No," she said, even as her heart whispered, "Yes."

"I brought you food as I didn't think you'd like a servant stumbling upon us in bed."

The heavenly smell of eggs and ham wafted from beneath silver covers to fill the air with memories of Christmas morn. Being poor, ham had been a luxury Mary'd only been able to indulge in once a year, and lately not at all. And yet Mary couldn't have eaten that ham if it'd been the last morsel of food on earth.

"How are you feeling?" he asked as he went to a small side table placed beneath one of the tall windows. He'd already dressed in his cousin's castoffs, this time a dark blue jacket that did lovely things to his eyes.

"Sore," she finally answered.

She thought she saw his lips compress a bit, almost like he bit back a frown of concern, then he took a seat, the windows beyond revealing a sky so blue and sparkling clean, it looked like an artist's canvas.

"What is it?" Alex asked.

Her head snapped up, surprised that he could so easily read her thoughts. "Why nothing, m'lord."

He didn't appear to believe her, not at first, at least, but he didn't push the matter. She fixed her gaze on the silver cover striped with vertical bars of light that he lifted, exposing a porcelain plate with peacocks decorating the edge of it.

One tiny poached egg stared back at her like a yellow bull's eye, an equally small piece of ham next to it.

"What is the matter?" he asked, and, yes, that was very definitely concern she saw in his eyes. "I admit, I only know how to poach an egg and fry up ham, but I cooked it myself, though it was a battle to get Cook to agree. However, if you want something else, you have only to ask."

He'd cooked?

For her?

Mary stared at him in shock, and then just as suddenly looked away, feeling . . . feeling. Oh, lord, she was about to cry again.

"No thank you, my lord. This will suit me fine."

He looked at her with so much concern, the persistent scratching at her heart turned into a downright thumping.

He cared.

Morning light illuminated a reality she wasn't at all sure she wanted to face.

She felt her hand clench around a fork.

I think I love you.

"You look serious all of a sudden."

Forcing herself to straighten, to give him a cocky smile, she said, "Do I?" covering her tears by blinking and stabbing her fork into her food at the same time.

'ere now, Mary girl. Buck up. You knew what you were getting yourself into.

Had she? Had she really? And blimey, for a woman who hadn't cried above three times afore meeting his lordship, she'd turned into a bleedin' watering pot since.

"Mary?" he said, reaching across the table, and enfolding her cold hand in his. "Whatever is the matter?"

The experience of having to force a bright smile for an audience through all the bruises, all the bumps, all the pains, stood her in good stead then, though until that moment she'd never realized an aching heart could hurt as bad as a fall.

"Why nothing, my lord. I'm right as rain, I am."

His eyes darted from one of her eyes to the other, as if searching each one for an elusive truth.

"You're lying."

Well, of course she was. But there wasn't a blimin' blazes thing he could do about it.

"I'm thinking," she said.

"About what?"

About how hard it's going to be to leave you. "This and that," she said instead.

"What?" he persisted.

Bloody hell! Couldn't he tell she didn't want to talk?

He lifted a brow.

Apparently not.

"I was wondering if I should invite my father to our wedding."

His whole face went slack a moment before his eyes widened.

And now that she'd said the words which were half jest, half serious, she added, "And if your father and my father will get along."

He'd gone as stiff as carriage straps. And she knew then that her silly imagination had gotten bosky on her, because as she watched the way he reacted, as she watched the horrified discomfort grow in his eyes, she realized that once again she'd sold herself on a fairy tale baggage of goods.

God help her, a part of her had hoped . . .

What? That'd you'd be so good in bed he'd offer ta wed you? Are you daft, woman?

She blinked, relieved when no tears fell. "Of course, if you'd rather keep the ceremony small—"

"Mary," he said urgently, his hand squeezing hers gently. Lord, she'd forgotten he held it. "We can't—"

She watched as words were rolled through his mind and then were obviously discarded. And all the while she concentrated on breathing slowly in and out so as not to pant, on keeping her composure, even as she waited for him to say the words she told herself to expect.

"You must understand," he finally said. "Marriage between the two of us would be—" He struggled for words again.

"Heavenly," she finished for him, adding a breathy sigh for good measure.

Aye, and it would, not that I'll ever be knowing.

"I was going to say—"

"Wonderful?" she provided, because heaven help her, she needed to make him squirm, wanted to make him wiggle like a carp on dry land. Make him feel, for just a smidgen of a second, the misery she felt in her heart.

"Impossible," he finally managed to say.

She drew herself up, pasted a look of hurt and surprise and distress—all the things she actually felt, but that she'd die before admitting to him that she really felt—on her face, her poor, bruised heart rejoicing at the look of horror mixed with discomfort that spread through his eyes.

"Not wed me? But I thought—" She acted wounded. Aye, and it was easier than she would have thought. "I assumed that after last eve—"

She stared at him as if she'd grown speechless with shock.

"Mary," he said, letting go of her hand to stand. When she realized he meant to come around to take her in his arms, she stopped him with a hand.

"Ach. Go on with you, my lord. I was only funning."

And it near killed her, but she forced a laugh, a high pitched, *Aren't I a bonny one?* laugh that all but killed her to press out of her lungs. And if he'd listened closely, he might have heard the brittle edge to it. But, like most men, he didn't want to look too deep. If he'd opened his eyes along with his heart, he might have seen more than a laughing woman.

"Sit down," she ordered with a nonchalant wave of her hand. "I know you've no intention of marrying the likes of me."

And you do *know that, don't you, Mary girl?*

Don't you?

"Thank the lord," he said, the words like a foot stamping up and down on her heart. "For a moment I thought—"

"You'd bedded a fool?" she finished for him.

But he had bedded a fool, she admitted. *He had. He had. He had.* Because, devil take it, she'd sell her soul to wed such a man. Such an honorable, kind and *noble* man.

Ach, one that wants you to be his mistress.

Aye, but being angry with him for that would be like being angry at a priest for asking if she wanted to be a nun. His desire to make her his mistress wasn't so much an insult, but rather the result of a being born to a class of men that classified women into two categories: those that were blue-blooded enough to wed, and those that weren't. He had said it best when describing his childhood: It simply *was.*

"Something like that," he said, smiling at her.

And though it felt like it broke her face to do so, she smiled back. Aye, that smile might be a bit misty, but she hoped he attributed it to her laughter.

"Now, as far as the arrangements I should like to make for you . . ."

She let him drone on and on and on about a house in the city, an allowance, clothes; all the things that Mary had always longed for, but that she'd never, ever have if it meant working on her back.

And when he asked if she liked the arrangements, if she thought she could live with them in that self-satisfied way men had when they thought they offered a woman the world, but instead offered them a slab of coal, she looked him right in the eye and said, "No."

To give him credit, it took him a moment to assimilate her answer. "I beg your pardon?"

She gave him a tight smile. "I said no."

He blinked.

"I told you before, Alex, that I'll not be your mistress. Nothing has changed. Nothing at all."

"But last night—"

"Was lovely. Wonderful, even, but meant for my pleasure, nothing more."

She looked down at her plate, picking up her fork again and nonchalantly taking a bite. Of course, she had to work to steady her hands. Had to force herself to breathe. To keep a slight smile on her face as she chewed and chewed and chewed, realizing too late that her mouth was so dry, she couldn't swallow.

"You cannot be serious."

And that angered her enough to force the food down in a gulp. It truly did. Why the blazes should a man get upset when a woman did to him what a man more often did to a woman? "Indeed, I am, my lord."

"But I thought—"

"That I would allow you liberties with my body simply because I am not good enough to wed?"

"No, no—"

"Then what, my lord? What did you think?"

"To be honest, Mary, I didn't think about anything

other than making love to you. And this morning—" He paused for a moment. "This morning I sought only to assure you that last night was no passing fancy on my part."

And she realized then, that in his own way, he was only trying to be kind. She stared at him, so many emotions—love, sorrow, pain—holding her silent as she fought for words to say. And yet one thought floated to the top, a bobbing apple she could not ignore.

She would have to leave today. Immediately. For the truth of the matter was, it would break her heart to stay longer. Her throat tightened as a boulder-sized lump of silent sobs filled it.

"Alex, I—"

"There you are."

They both jumped. Alex was the first to look away, the first to say, "Rein. What the blazes are you doing here?"

And Mary was almost glad for the interruption.

"I'm delivering this." Rein said, holding out a letter. "It was forwarded from Wainridge for Mary, along with a message from the duke, Alex, saying that he's glad you are well."

Mary looked at Rein, the letter he held sending off a warning bell so loud, she hardly registered that Gabby was well.

"Thank you," she said as he came forward, and she recognized the penmanship on the front. John Lasker. The note must be from her father.

She took it from Rein's outstretched hand. "You're looking well this morning, Mrs. Callahan. Did you pass a pleasant evening?"

"Rein," Alex shot, giving his cousin a horrified stare.

But Mary paid him little heed. She was too busy staring at the letter.

"Would you like some privacy to read?" Alex asked.

"No, I—" And something gave within Mary, something dark and heavy and that produced another lump in her throat. "Alex, I'd like to talk to you." She glanced at Rein. "Alone."

"That good in bed, was he?"

"Rein," Alex cried again.

Mary ignored the two, holding Alex's gaze. Her heart began to beat as it did just before a performance. And, indeed, this would be a performance, the hardest of her life. She had to pry her gaze away from his, had to swallow once before she said to Rein, "Please, my lord."

Rein's brow lifted up, the other followed a second later. "Like that, is it? Hmm. I might have known. Very well, I shall leave you be. For a moment."

And with a small bow and a sardonic look that promised many more crass comments, he left the room. Alex said, "You look rather dire."

Her body felt cold, then flushed, her stomach tightened like a half hitch knot. "Alex, we need to talk."

That seemed to catch his attention. She saw the way his lids lowered quickly before he said, "Yes, we do, Mary, for I'll not accept no for an answer."

"Not about that. About something else."

"Something else?"

She turned, trying to put a distance between them, for she feared if he came too near she'd never say what needed to be said. But Lord help her, she felt no better when she faced him again. It made it no easier to look him in the eye, take a deep breath and say, "I'm leaving."

Chapter Twenty-Two

"You're *what*?"

Mary told herself to stand firm, to not be swayed by the look of surprise followed by disbelief that filled his face.

"Leaving, Alex."

"The devil you say."

"I'm sorry, Alex. I know you expected to change my mind about becoming your mistress, but that I shall never do. Thus, I'm leaving."

He crossed to her, Mary silently begging him not to touch her. But he did, the center of her chest instantly aching when he placed a hand against her cheek. "You don't have to become my mistress in the truest sense of the word. I'll forgo setting you up in a house if that makes you feel better. However you'd like it to work, that is what we shall do. We could be happy together, you and I, happy with as little or as much time as you'd like to spend with me."

God, it was as if he sought to intentionally hurt her. "Happy, Alex? With a woman who's lied to you?"

She could see she had his attention now and so she forged on, her hands clenching the cotton fabric of her robe as she forced herself to say. "I'm not really a nurse, though I suspect you've gleaned that already." She looked at him expectantly, and when he said nothing, she added, "I'm a performer with the Royal Circus."

He looked confused for a moment. "The Royal Circus?"

"Aye. In London."

And at last he seemed to understand. His body shifted to its full height.

This is where it begins, Mary realized. Here was where the look in his eyes changed from one of fondness to loathing. She steeled herself for it, but it didn't help to say the words. "However, before joining the circus, I lived in a coastal town, one I'm sure you've heard of. Hollowbrook."

She saw his eyes narrow then, saw the look in them change to one of horror. "The smuggling town?"

"Aye, the smuggling town, one whose free trade operations are run by my father." She braced her feet as if facing a storm. "Tobias Brown."

And there it was, the look she'd dreaded, the one she'd known would come. Abhorrence, the revulsion he felt at being delivered such news there for all the world to see. "Do I take you to mean you're related to Tobias Brown?"

She nodded, facing him as if she didn't care what he thought of her. God willing, one day she might believe that. "He sent me to spy on you, Alex, though I'd no intention of ever doing so. I even sent him a letter when I accepted the position of Gabby's nurse telling him to go to the devil. I thought that would be the end of it. I thought he'd leave you alone, only he must have grown desperate for he kidnapped you . . ."

"Good God."

"I rescued you because I felt responsible, and because

I couldn't let him harm you. Even then I'd begun to care for you."

"Care for me?" he gasped. "You profess to care for me when you entered my house under false pretenses?"

"I knew you would react this way," she said. "I knew it even as I toyed with the idea of not telling you, but I felt you should know the truth before I leave."

"How noble of you, my dear."

She felt her jaw tighten, felt the ache behind her eyes that signaled tears. "And that," she said softly, "is exactly what I knew you'd say, too."

He said nothing. And, God help her, a part of her wished he would—oh, how she wished he would say something, *anything*, that would make the leaving of him easier to bear.

"You lied to me, Mary."

"No," she said quickly. "Not lied, just omitted certain facts about my life."

But it was as if she hadn't spoken. "I cannot tolerate liars." He turned, crossed to the window.

"Alex," she said, a part of her wanting to comfort him even as a part of her felt bitterly disappointed that he reacted in such a way. Her upper lip began to tremble. She sucked it between her teeth. Of course she hadn't expected instant forgiveness, but she'd thought—

What? That he'd welcome the news you were the daughter of an enemy?

She shook her head as if the question had been asked aloud. No, no. She hadn't expected that. But she had expected him to realize she was nothing like her father. Only he hadn't. In the end, all he saw was poor Mary Brown Callahan, smuggler's daughter. And that hurt. Lord, how it stung.

"Alex, please," she heard herself say again, her mind screaming at her to keep quiet. To let him be hurt by her news as she was hurt by his reaction to it. "I know you're upset—"

He whirled on her. "Upset? How could you possibly know how upset I am? I told myself that you were different from other women." He laughed bitterly. "Only never did I realize just exactly how different. Good lord, not only are you an actress, but you're a smuggler's daughter. How ironic."

"I'm not an actress. I ride horses."

She saw his eyes widen, knew the exact moment he realized who she was.

"You're Artemis," he said.

She nodded.

"You're the woman who rides horses astride."

She nodded again. "Yes, Alex, I am. I changed my name to Callahan when I began to perform, and then later the manager of the circus thought I needed something more mysterious. But Artemis is not who I really am. I'm not vulgar. I don't show off my legs to titillate men. I do it because I love the horses—"

"You've been courted by the Prince."

She almost laughed. She couldn't help it. "A lie, one generated by the press."

"How reassuring to know the presses find you newsworthy."

And they did. It was why she knew becoming his mistress would never do. Well, one of the many reasons why.

"And so now you understand why I must leave."

Say, it, a part of her cried. *Say it.*

Don't leave.

I understand.

We can work it out.

I forgive you.

Alas, all he said was, "To be perfectly honest, Mary, I don't know what to think."

But Mary knew that to be a lie. He was wondering how he could have so misjudged her. How he could have become involved with a woman who had deceived him. Alex walked the path of the straight and narrow, never having had to understand that some people didn't have that choice.

She lifted her chin. "Now you see why I must leave?" Ridiculous thing to say, of course he knew.

But I don't want to leave. God, I don't.

He met her gaze, his expression grim, his eyes expressionless, everything about him so controlled it was like the first day they'd met. "Indeed, I do."

Indeed, I do. It felt like he stepped on her heart with the balls of his feet. "I see."

He merely stared at her, putting his hands behind his back as if he faced her across a desk again.

She straightened her shoulders, her face as controlled as his. At least, she tried to make it as controlled, but the corner of her mouth twitched as she fought to control tears. Her eyes burned and her voice quivered as she said, "Then I bid you goodbye, George Alexander Essex Drummond. I . . . I wish you well."

Chapter Twenty-Three

And just like that, it was over.

Mary prided herself on the fact that she didn't cry as she left the earl's estate. Why should she cry when all she'd done was rid herself of a great baboon of a man who held himself in such high esteem, no one could possibly live up to his expectations? She shouldn't be upset. She should rejoice that she'd gotten away.

That was what she told herself.

For as the miles between her and Rein's estate slipped by—the carriage Alex's cousin had lent her for the trip as beautiful and elegant as any she'd fantasized about riding in—she found it harder and harder to maintain control. At first it was a vague burning in her stomach. Then it transformed into an ache in her heart. Next her throat began to tighten, so much so that she found herself swallowing more and more. Only that didn't work, either, for the more she swallowed, the more her eyes seemed to water until she found her nails digging into the fancy dress Lady Dalton hadn't wanted back.

He'd let her leave.

Well, of course he did, Mary girl. What did you expect him to do when you told him the truth? Kiss you in forgiveness like the bloody King?

No, but she had expected him to understand, at least

partly. But he hadn't. He'd been quick to agree that she should leave, never once telling her that he cared too much to let her go.

And that was when she lost control, when the tears finally erupted, though she tried, lord how she tried, to keep them in. But she couldn't, water squirting from her eyes like she was a leaky spigot. She cried at his lack of understanding. She cried at the way he'd looked at her when she'd told him the truth. But most of all, she cried because she felt as if she'd lost a friend.

"So you let her leave?"

Alex didn't want to hear the words. Indeed, he'd incarcerated himself in the only room he knew Rein avoided like the plague: the library.

"Odd, for I thought there was a connection between the two of you. Or rather, that you'd connected last eve, although seeing her in her room this morning reminds me that you two did, indeed, connect, in one way at least."

"Rein, go away—"

"Come back another day," Rein finished for him. "But I shan't do that. Not until you tell me what delicious event transpired that made her leave in a huff of tears and that has you in such a quagmire of self-pity."

"She was crying? And I do not pity myself."

"She looked about to cry, and, yes, you are pitying yourself. Why else would you be closed up in this hideous room?" He shivered as if he stood amongst live gargoyles, taking a seat opposite Alex, who'd settled himself in one of two chairs placed before a cozy fire. It wasn't yet noon, and it was a sunny day outside, but it had turned blustery, damnation, nearly as cold as his soul.

A draft kept coming down the chimney. It blew on the flames, smothering them for a moment before sending them to new heights.

"So tell me, coz, what did you do to break her heart? And might I say, congratulations. I always knew you had it in you to be a true cousin of mine, though I'd begun of late to worry that your affinity for sailing might have something to do with those boys who climb the rigging."

Alex didn't deign to reply. He had no patience for such a conversation. The last thing he wanted to do was talk about Mary.

"Come, come. I'm all agog."

Alex remained silent.

"Did she tell you she is Artemis?"

Alex jerked. "You knew that?"

"Of course. The moment she jumped upon my stallion. Only one female in all of London could have done such a thing. And in a night shift, no less. I knew right then and there that I wanted her to ride me, too. Alas," he sighed. "You claimed her first."

"Why didn't you tell me?"

He shrugged. "I found it amusing to hold my tongue."

Alex looked away. If he hadn't, he might have found himself lunging at Rein and planting him a facer.

"Did you ask her to become your mistress? Because if you didn't, old man, I'll be sorely disappointed in you. I confess myself wildly jealous that you bedded her. Was she any good? I bet she could squeeze the juice—"

"Rein," Alex shot again. "You never know when enough is enough. I swear, you are like my father more and more."

"Much to his delight," Rein said with a smile so

charming, Alex didn't know whether to be insulted or furious.

"And you never did answer my question. Did you ask her to be your mistress? Is that why she left? Did she turn into a mass of maidenly affront? I've heard she's a cold baggage of goods. A number of my friends have approached her for protection, but she wanted nothing to do with them. Rumor has it that she's still a virgin, though I suppose I can now dispel *that* particular notion—"

"Rein, if you do not cease, you will find yourself on the floor with the imprint of my fist on your chin."

"Hit me?" Rein said with a look of affront. "Over a woman? Do not be absurd."

Good lord, what had he ever done to be born into such a family, though he supposed his cousin had no notion as to how far he'd sunk into depravity.

"Why did she leave?" Rein asked yet again.

"It was her choice."

"Are you daft? You *let* her leave? I know above twenty men who would pay her hundreds of pounds—bugger it—who have offered to pay a thousand pounds for one night. And you—" He shook his head. "You, the biggest prig of a man who ever walked the earth, manage to bed the chit only to let her walk away."

Had her favors truly been that sought after? And had she truly turned them all down? Could she have been a virgin? She hadn't bled, but that happened upon occasion.

"Why did she leave?"

"You're not going to leave me be, are you?"

Rein shook his head.

Alex almost got up to leave, but he would only be

hounded until the ends of the earth. "She is the daughter of a bitter enemy."

At last Rein's face lost some of its disgust. "Well, now, *that* I understand."

"Do you? How wonderful. That means the world to me."

"Humph. Sarcasm. From you. I never thought I'd see the day."

"Bugger off, Rein."

"And a curse. Lord, your time with the woman has done you good. Who would have thought a kidnapping, a cross-country trek, and an incarceration would have turned you into a human being? Of course, she rescued you from all that. Not to mention the way she walked all that way on bruised and bloody feet, but I suppose that's a trivial matter."

"Rein, what is your point?"

And for the first time, Rein's expression lost its rakish charm. It startled Alex, the way his face underwent such a dramatic change. For the first time Alex could remember, Rein looked at him with an intelligence and seriousness in his green eyes that made Alex sit up and take notice.

"You are a fool, Alex. A bloody fool. For the first time in your life a woman comes along who shakes you out of your well-ordered world. Who forces you to realize what a stuffed shirt you've become. Who makes you feel, for the first time since I've known you, love. Aye, love, so don't get that offended look upon your face. And after all that, you let her go."

"Of course I let her go. What was I supposed to do? Set her up in a house? Buy her jewels? Take her to the opera?" But that was exactly what he'd offered. *Before.*

"Why not? Who cares who her father is? Who cares that she lied about her vocation? She never lied to you about anything else, did she?"

"I've no idea."

But he had a feeling he did.

"Go to her, Alex," Rein said.

"I will not."

"Why not?"

"Because I cannot." He stood, his legs carrying him to the fireplace, though he had no conscious thought of wanting to go there. "What would my superiors say if I became involved with the daughter of an infamous and wanted smuggler?"

"Who says they have to know?"

"They would find out. Artemis is too well known for it not to be reported by the presses. And then all it would take was for someone to do a bit more digging, to find out she is the daughter of Tobias Brown—"

"And that matters to you?"

Alex whirled to his cousin. "I have worked years, Rein, *years,* to erase the taint of the Wainridge name. You've no idea what it was like growing up with the snickers and snide remarks. I've had to bc above reproach. Spotless in my conduct. And then Mary Callahan comes along." He turned back to the fireplace.

"You're wrong, Alex, for I do, indeed, know what it's like. Though I'm not the Wainridge heir, nor even a Drummond by name, I *am* related to the Drummond clan. Only *unlike* you, I never took people's opinions of me to heart."

"Indeed, you did not," Alex said, deciding that if the gloves were off, he'd give his cousin a few truths. "You went the opposite way. You live your life running from one debacle to the next. Oh, yes, I've heard the tales. I know you've a reputation my father would be proud of. But someday, Rein . . . I pray someday soon, you shall have a rude awakening, for someday you will be faced with a decision like mine: Reputation? Or ruin?"

"And that is where you err, my friend," Rein said, "for she would not have ruined you."

"No, but she would have cast a shadow upon my name, one that might have spread to Gabby."

"Gabby? What figures Gabby in all of this?"

"She is my daughter. My hope is to secure a respectable marriage for her. Granted, she is my by-blow, but she is being raised like a lady. She need only have her father comport himself like a gentleman to secure a match that, while not entirely appropriate for a true lady, will see her well settled with a man who will take care of her."

"God, you're such a prig."

"I beg your pardon."

"You're so full of self-importance I can scarce stomach you."

"I am not arrogant, merely logical."

"Then swallow this bit of logic. She is not your daughter."

They were sparring so fiercely and quickly, Alex didn't immediately take in the words.

"Aye, it's true, though I can see you're having a hard time believing it. But rest assured, I do not lie. She was left on your father's doorstep eight years ago."

"What the devil are you talking about?"

Rein smiled tightly before saying, "He didn't know what to do with her, so he came to me. We discussed it and decided you would make the best father of all the males in the family."

Alex still didn't absorb the words.

"So before you go spouting nonsense of being a good father, think about the fact that you're raising your father's by-blow, instead."

"You're lying," Alex said. "You must be. My father would never do something so shabby. And you . . . not even you could condone it."

"No?" Rein asked. "Then speak to your father yourself. He will tell you the same as I. We toyed with the idea of putting her in a home, but when it came down to do the business, neither of us had the stomach for it."

"A home?"

"She is a bastard, Alex, a little girl born out of wedlock, one who would have likely ended up in a home if her mother hadn't left her at Wainridge. But in the end, we didn't care. She is a Drummond. Your father may be a rogue, but he is not without heart. He gave her to you to raise because he cared too much to raise her himself."

"She's not my daughter." For the first time Alex understood what it felt like to be numb with shock. His limbs quite literally went numb.

"I didn't tell you so that you would disown her. That I would not allow."

"Disown her? Do not be absurd."

Rein nodded. "Good, I only meant to show you what a house of cards you stand on. You shouldn't live your life like you're a bloody saint. Live for the now, Alex. *Carpe diem.*"

"Seize the day? You've taken that saying to the extreme, have you not, Rein? You try to seize every *female* something every day."

"I give up," Rein said, standing. "You're a fool, Alex, one who will one day live to regret your arrogant ways. I had hopes that Mary might get you to open up. To relax a bit. And for a moment, you did. But now you're so caught up in reputation and society's regard that you've forgotten what it's like to truly *live*. I pity you. I truly do."

"Spare me your pity, Rein, for I do not regret my decision to let Mary Callahan go."

"Then you're a bigger fool than I thought. *Non est ad astra mollis e terris via.*"

"I beg your pardon?"

"Look it up, Alex. Lord knows, you'll have the time."

It wasn't until a long while later that Mary remembered the letter, and even then, she reached half blindly into her pocket to pull it out. She had to blink a few times to focus, the words black smudges before her teary eyes.

My dear Mary,

I bid you ill news.

Your father has been arrested. He was taken two days ago when word reached him of Warrick's failed kidnapping, his lordship's escape, I fear, something your father reasoned you were involved with.

I won't lecture you on how siding with his lordship made your father feel, instead I will tell you that upon hearing that news, your father went mad. He rode straight for the Custom House in Exeter, attacking it with a fish pole. They arrested him, Mary, and will undoubtedly send him off to the hulks, for as you know, they've been looking for a reason to incarcerate him. They have one now.

I thought you should know.

Yours,

John Lasker

Mary stared at that letter until her vision whitened and her eyes burned. Only when the carriage lurched did she finally look away.

He would be sent to the hulks.

Well, she always knew the blighter would come to a nasty end, she thought, wiping at her cheeks with her palm and then swiping the dampness on the skirt of her dress.

He would be sent to the hulks where he would likely die of gaol fever.

Who bloody cared? Certainly her brothers might. But she didn't.

It is because you betrayed him that they arrested him.

She covered her ears with her hands, the letter she clutched crinkling. She didn't care. If she hadn't done what she'd done, something else would have caused her father's demise. Look at the lengths he'd gone to in recent weeks to gain revenge. He'd gone mad, he had. That wasn't *her* fault.

She threw the letter on the floor, slamming her back against the cushioned seat as she crossed her arms in front of her.

Ignore the letter, she firmly told herself. *Go back to Wainridge and collect Abu, say goodbye to the whelp, then go back to your life.*

They were going to send her father to the hulks.

Oh, drat it all, who bloody cared? She had just lost the man she loved.

By your own deceit.

All right, yes, she had kept a few things from Alex, but she'd never anticipated coming to care for him.

Falling in love with him.

She closed her eyes and tried to think of something

else, but her thoughts kept running between Alex and her father, only to settle once again on her father. For there was one thing she couldn't escape, no matter how hard she tried. Her father may have treated her ill, he may have ignored her for the past few years, but he was still her father.

Bloody, damn, bleedin' hell.

She was going to try and get him out.

Chapter Twenty-Four

Rein laughed out loud when he read Mary's express later that afternoon. Who would have thought little Mary Brown Callahan would re-enter his life not five hours after she'd left it? Not that he'd ever intended to let her go. No, indeed, she was too interesting to do that. But this was, however, his first official damsel in distress letter.

He looked up from the missive, his lips pursing as he thought it over. He could have fun with this letter, if he were so inclined. Of course, he would likely infuriate his priggish cousin no end.

"Wentworth," he called to his butler. "Bring me ink and paper."

And later still, a missive was received by the marquis of Warrick (though it was a great deal later because it took Rein some time to come up with what to say).

My son, the letter read.

I was on my way to Sherborne with Gabby when she fell quite suddenly ill. I implore you to come to us as soon as possible as she is calling for you in her delirium.

Yours,

Wainridge

Of course, the missive was tersely worded because Rein had feared too many letters would give his forgery away, though if he'd known what a panic it would raise within his cousin, he might have used even fewer words.

"When did this arrive?" Alex asked.

"Just now, m'lord. The man what brought it has instructions to take you to your father."

It was all Alex needed to hear. Leaving a note for Rein explaining that he was on his way to Gabby's bedside, Alex left the moment transportation could be arranged. There was no hesitation on his part. Indeed, upon re-reading the note his concern was so great—his guilt at being away from her even greater—that it banished a fear he'd had that the news she was not his daughter might taint his relationship with her. Indeed, it did quite the contrary, for with nobody but his father, or God forbid, Rein to care for her, Alex felt all the more determined to see to her well-being.

And upstairs, from his spacious suite, Rein watched as his cousin all but leapt into the coach, a wicked smile coming to his lips and a deep chuckle entering his throat.

"Good luck, my cousin. I fear you will need it."

So it was that Mary found herself waiting at an inn for a person she was not expecting: Rein. Of course, if she'd had any inclination of the trick about to be played, she would have booked passage to France and never returned to England (after collecting Abu, of course). Alas, what she did instead was pace the spacious private room she'd secured, her thoughts running between her father and Alex.

So when she heard a masculine voice cry out, "Gabby," and then felt a gust of air that signaled the opening of the door, at first she thought it all part of a weird delusion brought on by the emotional state of her mind.

She turned, thinking she must have misheard, for that couldn't be—

Alex skidded to a halt just on the other side of the door, the black jacket he wore undone in the front, his white cravat loosely tied, his buff breeches stained with mud as if he'd tramped through puddles in a great hurry.

"What the blazes are *you* doing here?"

"What the blazes are *you* doing here?" she shot right back.

"Looking for my daughter."

"Your daughter? Why the blazes would she be here?"

His lids lowered, a fire coming to his eyes that might have worried Mary if she had reason to be concerned. "What the devil have you done with her?"

Odd how a woman could go from licking her wounds to blistering anger in the space of a few hours. For as Mary stared at Alex, she no longer felt hurt; instead she felt rage.

"What do you mean what have *I* done with her. What have *you* done with her, my lord? Have you left her again? That's what you always do to the women in your life, isn't it?"

He took a step toward her, his face looking just as livid as her own must be. "This is no time for games, Mrs. Callahan. I want to know where Gabby is, and I want to know now."

"Mrs. Callahan is it now? What happened to, 'Mary, oh, Mary'." She mimicked his sounds of pleasure.

That was when he closed the distance between them and grabbed her by the shoulders. "If you've harmed her,

I swear I will not rest until you and those in league with you pay. Now. Tell. Me. Where. She. Is."

Mary realized then that something was terribly amiss. Well, she'd actually gleaned that the moment he'd walked into the room, but she had the advantage of knowing she'd summoned Rein.

"Alex, there is nothing wrong with Gabby. I would wager she is at the ducal estate as we speak, driving your father batty."

He stared at her as if having trouble absorbing her words. And, indeed, he likely was.

And then the door closed behind him. Both he and Mary turned, the sound of a key in the lock unmistakable. They both stiffened. And then from the floor came the sound of something being shoved beneath the door. A letter, Mary realized.

Curse that Rein Drummond's head.

"What the devil is going on?" Alex cried.

"I've a feeling, my lord, you'll find your answer there." She pointed to the missive.

He shot her a look before letting her go, her shoulders where he'd touched stinging from the contact. He crossed to the door and scooped up the letter, but he didn't open it immediately. No. He tried the door first. As she suspected, it was locked. He whirled toward her, ripping at the paper as he did so.

"Read it out loud, if you please."

To which Alex shot her a frown, scanning the lines silently, his eyes growing wider and wider above the edge of the paper, the lower half of his face obscured by the parchment.

"Out loud, please," Mary reiterated.

He must have needed to do so because he never even looked up as he read:

My dear cousin,

By now you have gleaned a trick has been played upon you. Indeed, I find myself laughing most uproariously as I envision the look upon your face.

Here Alex looked up. Mary shook her head and rolled her eyes. Alex frowned, returned his attention to the letter.

It seems, dear cousin, that since you will not seize the day yourself, I will have to seize it for you.

Thus, I have instructed my coachman to give the innkeeper an ungodly sum of money to have you and Mary locked in the same room together. Do not think the innkeeper can be bribed, for my coachman has assured him that whatever you offer to pay, I will double when I arrive one hour hence. And don't think to try and escape through the room's one window, for I happen to know that it is wedged shut (a story which I shall regale you with later).

I find myself horribly amused to think of you and Mary locked up tight, though I do worry about those attacks you suffer ever since I locked you in that broom closet as a lad. Who would have thought such a thing would scar you for life? Hence I shall only lock you in for one hour, after which time I shall let you out. If you have not resolved things with the charming Mary by then, please reassure her that I will help her with her little problem in Exeter.

Make good use of the time, dear cousin. Remember: Non est ad astra mollis e terris via—

"There is no easy way from Earth to the stars."

Shock flung Alex's head up. "You know Latin?"

Her expression clearly said *sod off*, just as her lips said, "Of course I know Latin. I was taught to read by a Catholic priest. I had no *choice* but to learn Latin."

It took a moment for her words to sink in, and Rein's letter. "This can not be happening."

"I assure you, my lord, it is."

He looked up again. She wore that dratted gown, the one that was too big for her and made her look like a waif. Her hair lay piled atop her head in an elegant way. In fact, she looked very lovely and far too tempting to suit his peace of mind, despite the overlarge dress.

"What is this 'little problem' in Exeter?"

She lifted her chin in that indomitable way of hers, crossing her arms for good measure. "That, sir, is none of your concern."

"Tell me."

"No."

"I have a right to know by what foul means Rein brought you and me together."

"Believe me, my lord, I've no desire to be here any more than you."

"What help?"

Her arms fell back to her sides. "Oh, very well, if you must know, my father has been incarcerated. I'd asked Rein for help in freeing him during what must have been one of my more delusional moments."

"Why did you not ask me?"

She snorted. "Oh, that is rich. I'm supposed to ask *you*, a man what thinks me a lying trollop, for help?"

But Alex knew she was no trollop. Deep down inside, he knew, for he'd reasoned at some point in the past hour that she could have used the attraction he felt for her to her advantage, and yet she hadn't. Indeed, she could have let him be kidnapped, and yet she hadn't. Could have let him rot in gaol. And yet she hadn't. Could have asked for his help in exchange for sexual favors, and yet she hadn't. As a point of fact, she'd behaved with far more honor and integrity than most men he knew.

"Did you truly send your father that letter telling him you refused to spy on me?"

She looked surprised by the question, then suspicious. "Aye."

"Why?"

"Because, devil take it, I'm not a deceitful person. Greedy, yes. But not deceitful."

Suddenly he felt as tightly drawn as a bowstring behind an arrow. His eyes locked with hers as he asked, "And what were you going to promise Rein in exchange for his 'help'?"

She flicked her hair. "Wouldn't you like to bleedin' know?"

"Yes, Mary, I would. For if it was your services as his *paramour*, you need not go that far."

"And what makes you think I would have offered myself to your cousin?"

"Weren't you?"

She placed her hands on her hips, clucking her tongue, and Alex knew he was in trouble. "That's the problem with you, Alexander Drummond. You think the worst of me time and again. But did you ever think that perhaps I never meant things to go as far as they did with you? That I'd convinced myself to leave the next day while we were at that ball? But then we kissed and it changed everything, for I realized then that I cared for you, and that I didn't want my first time to be with some bumbling fool of a man who wouldn't know what hole to stick his pizzle in. And that I thought of you as a friend, someone who I could trust enough to touch me in a way no man has ever touched me before? That a part of me felt betrayed when I woke up to find you gone the next morn, only to all but melt when I realized you'd brought me food to break my fast."

He saw her eyes begin to redden. Saw the way she inhaled deeply to stifle tears, and now that he looked at her a bit more closely, he realized that her face bore the remnants of those tears: red-rimmed eyes, lips and cheeks flushed.

She'd been crying. Sobbing, if he didn't miss his guess. Over him.

Him.

"And then, later," she said, "when Rein interrupted us, I realized that as a friend I owed you the truth. Only you didn't act like a friend at all. You thought the worst of me. That hurt more than a stab to my heart. That you could not see what type of person I was, despite the difference in our social station, well, I realized then that you were not the person I thought you to be either."

She clenched her hands. "So I tell myself that I shouldn't be surprised that you think me so cheap I'd offer to lie with your cousin as payment for my father. But, damn you, I'm not that sort of person, and I never will be, because I flatly refuse to end up like my mother."

"Your mother?"

With a lift of her chin she said, "She's not dead. Her name is Christina Calloway, the actress, only you might know her as the Duke of Clarence's mistress instead."

Good god.

"I see you recognize the name. Then you'll likely believe me when I tell you she left us when I was five. Just like that." She snapped her fingers. "Wanted to go off and become famous. Sometimes I find it ironic that I've followed so closely in her footsteps, though I took a private vow never to end up on me back like she did." She shook her head. "Only look at what happened. Look at the way I went and fell for you. Oh, aye, Alex, don't look so shocked. I fell for you. Fell for the way you tip my chin up whenever I'm sad. Fell for the way you hold me while I cry. But most of all, I fell for the way you cared for me . . . or used to care for me prior to you branding me a whore."

"I never said you were a—"

She held up a hand. "No, Alex, you did, if not by using the actual name than by insinuation. And it hurt, Alex. Lord, how that hurts."

"Mary, I—"

"No," she almost shouted. "You come striding in here and your first reaction when you see me isn't gladness, it's suspicion that I've done something with your daughter."

He flinched at that.

"How many more times will that happen? How many more times will you leap to the conclusion that I'm a smuggler's daughter first and therefore not to be trusted? When will you learn to trust me?"

"I *do* trust you."

"Do you, Alex. Do you really?"

But he couldn't answer.

"Mary," he tried again.

"No, Alex. Not one more word. I curse your cousin for bringing us back together again when I steeled my heart against you. Having you here in front of me, wanting to touch you, to love you . . . and yet knowing that too much lies between us for there ever to be peace is a worse heartache than the one before."

He took a step toward her. She spun away, retreated near the door, held a hand out. "Do not, Alex."

And all Alex did was stand there because he knew if he were honest with himself, there was nothing much left to say.

"Goodbye, Alex," she told him for the second time, and, he feared, the last.

"Where are you going?"

"Your cousin's a fool if he thinks he can lock *me* in a room."

He saw her reach up, pull something from her upswept locks—a hairpin—then kneel in front of the door. To his absolute and utter shock, he heard the lock click open.

She stood, straightened her shoulders. "I didn't spend six years working alongside Marlo the Magician not to pick up a thing or two." Then she turned toward him, pausing there by the door for a moment, her eyes darting around his face. "Goodbye, my lord."

Chapter Twenty-Five

She left with Rein a half-hour later.

Not him, though he would have helped her if she'd but asked; he owed her that much, but Rein, a man who would sooner seduce a woman rather than give her aid. Rein who couldn't be in a woman's company above five minutes without making some kind of flirtatious remark. Who would not, Alex admitted, help Mary without demanding some kind of payment in return.

Well, she would learn soon enough that he would have been the lesser of two evils.

"Where do I hire a horse?" he asked the innkeeper right after she left.

"At the stable, my lord."

Stables. Of course. Bloody hell, he wasn't thinking straight. He turned on his heel, heading toward the Tudor-style barn without a backward glance. It felt as cold as an icebox outside, the air slapping color into his cheeks. Fortunately, the sky was clear, one of those days where the only clouds were thin strips of white, but it didn't matter for the ground was a sodden mess, Alex accepting the fact that his ride would be a rough one.

"I need a horse," he told the stableman, and as he said the words, something hit him, something nebulous and half-reasoned out, but there nonetheless.

He'd behaved like a cad.

No, he'd behaved as he ought, he told himself. She'd betrayed him.

And you betrayed her *when you asked her to become your mistress.*

He stood in the freezing cold, waiting, and as he did so he couldn't help but think that other than omitting certain facts about her life, she had behaved with a great deal of honor and courage, while he . . . he had behaved exactly as his father by bedding and then discarding her.

"Out o' the way," someone yelled.

The words interrupted his musings, Alex jumping out of the way just in time. Something big and black flew by. A horse, he realized, one that spun and snorted and made Alex wonder if perhaps a coach might be a better mode of transportation.

He almost told the groom to bring him another mount, but as he stared at that horse, something that could only be called shame filled him.

He had behaved as his father.

Damnation. He should go after her.

But Alex hadn't taken into account that hired cattle were ofttimes the worst cattle. The horse he rode was no exception. Any half-fledged hope of catching Rein and Mary was banished within the first half-hour. And though he tried to hire something faster on his way to Exeter, it was not to be.

So it was that he arrived hours after Rein, Alex heading straight to Exeter gaol only to spy—much to his shock—Rein's carriage parked out front. Alex hurried then, only when he looked between the parted royal blue curtains that covered the dirty glass there was Rein, but no Mary.

Alex knew then. He knew that he'd missed her, and the keening disappointment he felt was so great, Alex could only stop and stare at the sleeping Rein. Finally, he dismounted, Rein's tiger jumping down from the back of the coach to open the door. His cousin's snore could likely be heard across the Channel.

"Rein," Alex called.

Rein startled, his snore hitching in his throat and turning into a startled gulp. He blinked a few times, his green eyes coming to focus on Alex. "Coz," he cried as if delighted to see him, his upper body straightening. "You *did* follow. How delightful. I told Mary you would, but she didn't believe me."

"Where is she?"

Rein smiled that sublime smile of his. "Gone. As is Tobias Brown."

"Bastard."

"Why are you insulting me? *You* were the one that refused to help her."

"*She* refused *me*."

"In more ways than one," Rein said with a smug smile.

Alex nearly turned away in frustration, but he only got halfway before swinging back again. "How long ago did she leave?"

His cousin shrugged. "Minutes, hours, days. I confess myself a bit groggy from sleep." He faked a yawn, stretched like a lazy cat.

Alex almost jerked Rein out of the carriage and tossed him onto the ground. He would have done so, too, if such an act wouldn't reduce him to his cousin's level. Very well, he'd just have to ride after her again.

"Where are you going?" Rein asked as he led his horse away.

Alex didn't respond.

"If you're going after her, I'm afraid I must insist that you don't."

Whipping around to face his cousin, Alex snapped, "And I'm afraid you have no control over my actions."

"No, but I can tell you that Mary doesn't want to see you again."

Odd how the words took Alex by surprise. He'd known she was angry with him, certainly, but to never want to see him again?

Rein's expression took on a seriousness Alex had only ever seen once before. "She did, indeed, fall in love with you, Alex. She told me so herself, but I suspect she told you, too. But that is not why she doesn't want to see you again. Indeed, I find myself thinking she is truly the most noble creature I've ever met."

"What did she say?"

And then his cousin's eyes took on a sadness, indeed, a sympathy Alex would never have expected. "She told me she doesn't want you to come after her. That she is furious with you, which, if you knew anything at all about women would scare you half to death. She also mentioned that even if she could forgive you, and she is certain she cannot, that you would likely keep her behind closed doors just to avoid the shame such a union would cause you."

"She said that I would be ashamed of her?"

"She did."

Alex simply stared at his cousin as he replayed the words. "Wherever did she get such an idea?"

"From you, of course. Oh, I'm certain you did not say so directly, but you are such a confounded prig, Alex, what else is she supposed to think? However, as odd as it may seem, I will have to side with you. I may be a rake. I may be a scoundrel, but even I would be hard pressed to tell you that all will be well. As you know, such alliances are frowned on by society."

"Alliance? What alliance? You make it sound as if I shall wed her."

"Will you not, Alex? Isn't that exactly what you want to do?" Rein asked, his voice low.

Marriage. He couldn't marry her. Ridiculous. Far-fetched.

Tempting.

"I find myself almost feeling sorry for you, Alex, for I realize quite suddenly that you're not such a prig after all. Beneath that stuffy exterior lies a man of great conscience. I admire that about you, almost wish I had the same type of heart." He smiled. "Almost."

He loved her. Good lord, somewhere along the way he'd fallen in love with her.

"Give her up, Alex. Do as she asks, if not for your sake than for her own. Only think what the *ton* will do to her. She will not bear it well."

"She would bear it like a queen," Alex said, and he knew he was right. "She would tell them all to go to the devil and she would mean every word."

"Alex, she does not want to see you again. Accept that fact and go on with your life. Forget about Mary."

And for the first time in a long, long while, Alex felt tears in his eyes. "I don't think I can."

"You love her that much?"

And there was no sense in denying it anymore. "I do, Rein. She is the most amazing female. All her life she's had to deal with one setback after another, and yet she has persevered. Triumphed even. How can I possibly turn my back on a woman who deserves a happily ever after? How?"

Rein held his gaze, neither of them blinking. And then his cousin slowly lowered his lids, slowly shook his head as he said, "You know, I was truly hoping you'd say that."

Chapter Twenty-Six

Mary told herself that she'd made the right decision. And though on some level she believed she had indeed done the right thing, it made it no easier to bear. She told herself she should be proud of herself. A union with Alex would have only ended up in heartache and pain. If he didn't want to admit that, she could. And had.

And so she traveled by post chaise, the rickety and crowded coach a far cry from the ones their lordships owned. And as she did she tried to buoy her spirits by recounting how much coin the earl had given her. Quite a bit of it, actually. And though Mary had been tempted to throw it back in his face, she was not that proud. Silly for falling in love with a marquis, yes, but not proud.

Only the one task remained, that of fetching Abu. And though she dreaded going back to Wainridge, she couldn't leave her one friend in the world behind.

Hours later her heart beat hard against the wall of her chest as the ducal estate approached. It looked a grand sight different what with the fields and the lake and such awash in pristine sunlight. The water became a looking glass for the cerulean sky above, the swans floated across the surface with elegantly arched necks and V-shaped wakes. What had looked gray and dull in rain now glowed gold and bright: the large granite blocks that made up the walls, the windows, even the wood frames that held that glass. And to all of it she must say goodbye.

"I've come to collect my things," she said to the gray-haired housekeeper. "Specifically my monkey."

Mary had expected the woman to treat her with the same cold disdain as she had upon their first meeting. Instead she said almost cordially, "Is that little imp yours then?" her stern face looking almost pretty. "Lord above, we wondered where he'd come from." And then she stepped aside. "Gabby is playing with him in her room."

Mary's legs felt like blocks of stone all of a sudden. "Has she befriended him then?"

"She has."

"Ballocks."

"Indeed," she said, though Mary had expected a look of censure, she was surprised to see, instead, a look of compassion. "Leaving then, are you?"

"I am."

"I see."

And Mary had a feeling she did, all too clearly.

She found Gabby exactly where the housekeeper had claimed she'd be, Mary's knocking on the door answered by a sweet-sounding voice that completely belied the contrary nature of the child within.

She pushed on the door, Gabby sitting at a table with a doll and a miniature, blue-floral tea set laid out for two. "You," she pronounced in a long, drawn out way that made it clear she didn't mean the word as a greeting. "I was hoping the kidnappers might keep *you.*"

Ach, but she made it difficult to love her, she truly did. It fair boggled Mary's mind that a child could look so adorable in her gray and white play frock and her tumbled locks gathered at the top of her head and tied with a big blue ribbon, and yet speak with a forked tongue. Boggled the mind.

And then Mary's heart lifted as a familiar, joyful screech filled the air. She spun toward the giant bed that Gabby must surely get lost in. Abu's pink face contorted into a smile as he galloped toward her on two feet and two hands.

"Henry," Gabby cried at the same time Mary said, "Abu, you little wretch. Did you miss me?"

And lord help her as the monkey leapt into her arms, Mary almost broke down. As it was, it took a monumental effort to dam the moisture that gathered in the corners of her eyes. The monkey clicked and chatted, Mary inhaling his unique monkey scent, her throat tightening until it was all she could do to breathe.

"He's yours," she heard Gabby say in an accusatory voice.

Mary had to clench tight for a few moments while she gained control, had to swallow past the catches in her breath brought on by the lump of emotions lodged in her throat. Had to steel herself before she lifted her face and said, "Aye."

"You can't have him back."

And at that moment Mary came close to crying again, for the look on the child's face, the arrogance and disdain brought to mind Alex.

"I'm sorry, whelp. I really am."

"You can't have him," she said again, the little girl slowly standing.

And what made it all the more worse for Mary was that she knew how the child felt, for even though Gabby hadn't had Abu for the years that Mary had had Admiral, in a child's mind days were nearly as long as weeks.

"Gabby, please, don't make this more difficult—"

"Where's my father?"

"Not here."

She saw another kind of disappointment enter the girl's eyes, and Mary swore in that moment that if Alex didn't start spending more time with the child, she would hunt him down and kill him. Well, at least maim him.

"He's coming soon," she reassured. "I left ahead of him."

"Well, when he arrives I shall have *him* tell you to give Henry over."

"I'm afraid he won't."

"Yes, he will."

Ach, moppet, if only you knew how much I sympathize. If only you knew.

Mary moved, Abu shifting to her shoulder in that familiar way of his. She didn't stop until she stood before the girl, kneeling down to be at eye level. She wanted to touch the girl's hand, but knew Gabby wouldn't allow it. Instead she contented herself with staring into familiar blue eyes. Alex's eyes. The pang of her loss washed over her anew.

"Gabby, I know you don't like me. Lord knows, I've no real reason to like you, but you might be surprised to learn that I do. I really do."

That seemed to freeze the little girl, her gaze going into an unblinking stare.

"My father didn't want to be near me, either," Mary admitted.

She knew Gabby tried not to show a reaction, but she couldn't stop the tell-tale widening of her eyes.

"Aye, I know that's what you think your father does. Stays away because he doesn't want to be near you. I felt the same thing myself when I was younger, but I can tell you that in your father's case it isn't true. To him duty is everything. His position with the Crown is of utmost importance. If anything ever caused him to lose that respect—"

Like her.

It would destroy him.

She couldn't go on for a moment, Mary having to almost pant to contain her tears. "So," she finally continued, "if he leaves you alone it's not because he doesn't like you or love you or want to be with you. It's because he feels duty bound to do so. He loves you, Gabby. Very much. I know this because all he could think about when we were in danger was returning to you. He loves you, whelp, as much as Abu loves me."

The little girl blinked. But not by word or deed did Mary know if she understood, or even cared to understand.

"Abu is like *my* child. I love him very much, and that sort of bond never goes away. Not for your father and certainly not for Abu and me."

And something about those words gave Mary pause for a moment.

"His name is Abu?"

"Yes. After the monkey in Arabian Nights."

Gabby rolled her eyes. "It's a silly name."

"Do you think so? I've always liked it."

"It's silly."

"Well, it was the name he had when he was given to me, half starved and afraid of his own shadow, which is not good when one lives with a circus."

"You lived with a circus?" Finally there was a glimmer of interest in Gabby's eyes.

"Aye," Mary said hoarsely. "And I'm returning to it today."

"You're leaving?" And bless her heart, the child looked momentarily overjoyed.

"I am. But your father knows where to find me should you wish to visit us."

"It's Abu who I'd want to see."

"Of course."

And though Mary expected more protests, Gabby surprised her by sticking her chin up and clenching her hands at her sides. "You will take good care of him."

It was an order. So like her father she was. Mary almost smiled. "I will."

And the sight of the little girl's sudden tears made Mary's heart break in two.

"Goodbye . . . Abu," she said softly.

The monkey chattered at the child excitedly, turning to face the girl.

"Goodbye, Gabby," Mary said.

She expected the child to ignore her, but she surprised her again by nodding. It was only a nod, but it was progress.

Ach, Mary, as if you need to be worryin' about that now.

Lips pressed together to stop their trembling, Mary turned, slowly leaving the room. Only when the door closed did Mary hear a sound. It was muffled, but unmistakable.

In-drawn breaths, big ones. The child cried, though she tried to contain her tears.

And lord help her, Mary cried, too.

* * *

Oddly enough, however, it was Gabby's courage in letting Abu go that gave Mary strength in the coming days. Yet though she steeled herself against the pain, she couldn't stop the thoughts. Each day she found herself remembering things, silly things, like the way his feet had felt against her legs when they'd lain in bed together. The way he had of looking at her as if he couldn't quite believe she'd said what she'd said. The way he'd tried so hard to control his anger at that magistrate.

The memories drove her mad.

She threw herself into her work, taking risks that even her fellow performers winced at. The crowds loved it, and Mary was unable to stop herself from searching the audience each and every day for the one face she both wanted and didn't want to see.

He never came.

That was the worst of it, for each time her performance was over, her eyes grew hot from the tears that came to her eyes. Ach, she knew she were a daft-witted fool for crying over the cull, but words were like those candy drops they sold at the show, filling only for a time.

But Mary Callahan hadn't survived ten years in London without having a fall or two. And though it was near impossible to do, Mary did what she always did; she focused on her riding, something that was easy to do, for every hostess in London seemed to be holding a party in honor of Princess Charlotte's wedding to Prince Leopold. Their troupe had been asked to play numerous private parties, and Mary welcomed the extra blunt for she'd become more determined than ever to buy her own string of horses and set out on her own. And though she told herself that performing in front of a bunch of bleedin' nabobs was the last thing she wanted to do, Mary refused to let her affair with Alex ruin her life.

So why, then, did her heart leap when she was told she had someone waiting for her after one of her performances? Why did she feel like running toward the small tent set up for performers to change in? Why did her hands shake when she pulled aside the curtain, her breath held as a man turned toward her.

"Father?"

And, indeed, Tobias Brown stood in the corner of the tent, looking frail and . . . old, far older than he actually was. The sun and the sea had chiseled away at his skin until all that remained were lines and wrinkles. He seemed shorter than she remembered, too, the hulking shoulders she used to marvel at when he was younger now nothing more than protruding bone.

"Aye, it's me," he said, shifting from one foot to another as he eyed her in that odd way of his—as if he couldn't believe he'd sired her. And perhaps he couldn't. "I see life's treating you well."

She huffed. "As if you care what my life is like."

He actually looked a bit chagrined at that.

"Come here to ask me another favor, have you? I should have thought you'd learned your lesson by now."

"Ach, Mary lass, no need to get hostility-like. It's me what should be mad at you after what you done."

"What I done? You're lucky I didn't let you rot in that gaol."

"Nothing wrong with being in college."

"They might have hung you for what you did to Alex."

"Alex is it now?"

"Get out," she said. *And quickly*, she silently added,

because she didn't think she could stomach the sight of yet another man who'd betrayed her for much longer.

"No."

"Leave, father. I've nothing more to say to you."

"Not until I speak my piece."

"Then speak it already."

He frowned, looking uncomfortable. "Truth be told, I didn't want to come here, but John Lasker made me come. Said I owed it to you."

"Owed me what?"

And suddenly he looked about as comfortable as a man trying to balance atop a floating barrel.

"This isn't easy."

Mary waited, crossing her arms for good measure.

"Mary," he said at last. "Your mother didn't completely abandon ye. She sent letters, a slew of them, ones asking how ye were and if ye wanted to meet her."

Mary felt her mouth drop open.

"'Tis true."

She had survived nasty tumbles off horses, had conquered London despite her sex and her age, barely found the strength to get up every morning after the pain of losing Alex. This made her feel pain again, only for an altogether different reason.

"I've been wanting to tell you for years, except I didn't know how to do it. And then later, when you ran away, I told myself you didn't deserve to know. I was so bent up with me anger I didn't see straight. And then you betrayed me. Truth be told, you're the last person I expected to bribe me out of college. But you did. John says that's proof that you care."

She almost told him she didn't. Almost lied to him out of spite, but Mary wasn't that hard.

"Is that all?"

"Aye."

She opened the flap of the tent, wanting him to leave.

"I'm sorry, Mary girl," her father said, and he actually sounded like he meant it. "And I'm sorry for what I did to old Admiral all those years ago, too. It were a rotten thing to do, and not a day goes by that I don't regret it."

He stood before her, the proud and callous man Mary remembered suddenly staring at her with tears in his eyes. And of all the silly things, she felt tears of her own.

"I accept your apology, Father."

Neither one of them made a move. Truth be told, it would take years for that to happen.

"Well, then. I'll be going. But afore I do, I want to tell you how proud I am of you, Mary. The way you ride them horses, it's somethin' ta see."

"You've seen me ride?"

"Aye. I've watched your performance every night this week."

She stiffened.

"Knew you didn't see me. I'll wager there was only one face you were looking for in that crowd."

She wondered how he knew, but she supposed it didn't matter. But something held her back, some brutal bond of honesty that had suddenly sprung between them.

"And as to that I'll say nothin' more than he doesn't deserve you, Mary lass. Not if he doesn't see what a bonny woman he's given up."

It grew hard to swallow. Lawks, hard, even, to see, for her tears were born of a pain that her father—a man who Mary would have sworn despised her up until a few moments ago—could say such a thing, while Alex . . . well, Alex couldn't.

* * *

Oddly enough, her father's visit didn't make things easier on her. If anything, it made things harder. She fluctuated between despising Alex for having so little faith in her and wanting to see him so much it hurt.

So it was that three mornings later she found herself on the way to another party, only this time it was a villa perched on the edge of Regent's Park, proclaiming the owner to be of phenomenal wealth if the size of the place and the seclusion from other homes in the area was any indication. Three stories tall it was, with large windows that reflected the surrounding park, a home as majestic as its owner, no doubt. Bloody hell.

"It belongs to the Duke of Wainridge," Samuel, the circus's manager, told her, obviously following her gaze.

Mary turned toward the man. "The who?"

"Duke of Wainridge. You know, Wicked Wainridge. Surely you've heard of him before? I'll wager all of London has heard of him and his ancestors."

"Dear God."

"Don't worry none, luv. He's promised to be on his best behavior."

Mary just stared in horror until suddenly, abruptly, hysterical laughter welled up within her. But just as quickly, she straightened. "Did the duke come to you to schedule the event?"

"The duke's steward did, aye, but he said the duke had a particular desire to see you perform. Isn't that somethin', Mary? You've come to the attention of a duke."

She'd begun to shake, her anger and resentment making it hard to breathe. Hateful man. How could he be so cruel? How? She should leave. Thwart him. And Alex, too, if he was in on his father's plans. And how could he not be? She felt her eyes begin to burn. How could he not be?

"Go on out behind the carriages, lass, and get ready. I'll call you when 'tis time."

Mary almost told him no. Almost told him she couldn't perform. But as she looked up at the house Alex's father owned, she realized she was made of sterner stuff. She may not have been noble born, but she had the iron will of the nobility. Aye, and the pride. Try to put her in her place, would they? She would just see about that.

"Lord, would you look at all them swells," said the groom a half-hour later as he peeked out of a crack between the carriages they'd lined up to shield them from the guests' view. "Never imagined they lived so grand. Would you look at the fancy lace at the table. My mam would give her left bubby for just a tiny scrap of it."

"Hush," she said, brushing at her jewel-encrusted white tunic. For as she listened to the groom drone on, she realized she'd deluded herself. Grandly, spectacularly deluded herself, for when she'd taken a peek at all those swells a few moments ago, when she'd watched them glitter and glow like a gaudy chandelier, it had made her want to cry out.

That was Alex's life out there. A life she'd never share with him.

She tilted her head back, closed her eyes. She couldn't do it. She just couldn't.

"Get ready, get ready," Samuel said, coming around the back of a carriage. "They're gathering."

Mary stared blindly at the manager, her body frozen as indecision felt like ballast to her legs. Funny, for she'd never thought of herself as a coward. And yet here she was ready to slink away like a beaten puppy.

"Mary?"

She tilted up her chin. Damn him. Damn them all. She would do it, she would show him that she was no hound kicked by his master's toe.

"I'll be there in a moment, Samuel," she said.

With a broad smile, the manager left, Mary herself going to where the horses were tied up behind the carriages. There were six chestnut geldings, each wearing sparkling white tack with a dandy white feather stuck in their bridles. They lifted their heads as she approached. In a daze, she checked the surcingle buckled around the lead horse's girth, untied him from the rope tether, swung up on his back.

She could do this.

They'd arranged a ring out of hay bales beyond the carriages, Mary waiting what seemed an eternity for Samuel's signal, and when it came, even then she hesitated. But with a lift of her head and a proud stretch of her body, she kicked her horse forward and blindly headed toward the ring. She waited until two strides away before standing atop the horse's back. The wind whistled in her ears, the familiar rhythm of the horse cantering beneath her still sore feet helping to steady her. And it was then, and only then, that she looked up.

Alex stood in the center of the ring.

Shock made her knees lock, made her wobble. Her horse felt the change, thought she meant to stop.

He did.

She didn't.

Mary flew through the air, her body instinctively curling itself into a ball. She'd fallen off a thousand times, sometimes badly, other times, like this time, with a grace that almost made it look planned.

She landed right at Alex's feet, blast it all.

"Mary," he said, squatting down next to her. "Are you hurt?"

She glared up at him, biting back the urge to cluck her tongue. "What the bleedin' blazes do *you* care?"

Funny, but her words made him smile. "Ahh, Mary my love, how I missed your saucy tongue."

My love? The beard splitter. The Abraham cove. She wasn't his love. "Burn in hell."

He laughed then. "Still as saucy as ever."

"I'll give you some sauce, you—"

"Shhh," he said, placing his finger against her lips. "For once in your life, be silent Mary, while a man tells you what is in his heart."

And lord help her, something in the way he looked at her, in the way he seemed to still, to contemplate something very serious indeed, made her hold her tongue.

But despite the silence, he didn't say anything immediately. "I've been practicing this moment for nearly a week and damned if I know what to say." And then he scratched at his arm and Mary realized he was nervous. *Nervous.*

She looked into his eyes, the expression in the blue depths as deep as the ocean his eyes reminded her of. And when he reached out and gently swiped away a lock of her hair, Mary's heart leapt.

"I love you, Mary Brown Callahan."

Oh, God. She must be dreaming.

"If anything, my time away from you to set this all up has made me realize just exactly how much."

"Alex—"

"Shh," he said. "Don't talk. Listen. If I don't get this over with I'm afraid the itching will drive me mad."

And so she held still, even as a part of her thought she must surely be dreaming.

"You think I don't trust you, Mary, but I do. Even when you told me who you really were, I had to fight the urge to go to you, to tell you that it would be all right. A part of me couldn't believe that I would bend my principles so much, but I realized later that it was because despite what you'd done, I knew you to be a good person. An amazing person, really, one I was fortunate to get to know."

She was crying silently now, tears running down the side of her face. He saw them, wiped them away tenderly. "And so the question became how to convince *you* to trust *me*. No," he shook his head slightly. "That's not right. The question became how to convince you that if it comes down to a choice between you and my career, I choose you. If it comes down to a choice between you and my reputation, I choose you. If it comes down to being disowned by my father, I would still choose you. You see, nothing matters but you. Nothing. And so Rein and I concocted a scheme. We would invite half the *ton*, including the prince. Yes, dear Mary, the Prince of Wales is over there, waiting to meet you, for he has great sympathy for our plight having been forbidden to marry for love. As such he has pledged his support. But even if he hadn't done that, even if he'd laughed me out of Windsor, it wouldn't have mattered, as long as I had you."

"Oh, Alex."

And now he tipped her chin up as he had so many times before. "So I'm going to ask you to stay with me, Mary. Not as my mistress, but as my marchioness—"

"Alex," and the name was almost a sob.

"It will not be easy," he said. "Even now, today, you might get cut by those who think themselves above you. We may never be accepted into polite society, something that might be for the better, now that I think upon it."

She smiled.

He smiled, too, and then he kissed her, the two of them still kneeling on the ground, though it felt like Mary flew. She heard people gasp, but he didn't seem to care. He broke it off only when he wanted to, she had a feeling. Only when he judged the time right to say, "Stand up, please."

Stand up?

"Alex—"

"I can't propose to you on the ground now, can I?"

Oh, lord. He really meant to go through with it. He truly did.

And will you accept his challenge, Mary? Will you face those silly nabobs and thumb your nose at them?

Her answer was to stand, ignoring the minor twinges associated with her fall. She stood as a marquis, a peer of the realm, heir to a bleedin' dukedom, stayed on the ground, positioned himself so that he knelt on one knee, reached into his pocket and said, "Mary Elizabeth Brown Callahan. Will you do me the honor—the very great honor—of becoming my marchioness? Of filling my life with laughter and saucy comments. Of forever speaking your mind. Of forever being"—and for the first time she saw tears in his eyes—"my friend?"

Oh, she thought. *Oh, oh, oh.*

"Yes, Alex," she said with a voice choked by tears. "Yes, oh yes."

He stood abruptly, pulling her up against him and into

his arms. And it was then, and only then, that Mary finally understood that it was for real. She was not hallucinating as the result of an injury. She was not lying on the ground, unconscious, likely with a silly smile on her face. Alex's smell, touch and presence was all too real.

"Alex," she murmured against his lapel, and his arms tightened around her as if he were afraid she might gallop away. But she was a long, long way from doing that.

All too soon he pulled back, wiping tears away from his own eyes with his thumb as he turned and led her out of the ring and toward the *ton.* She recognized Rein, who smiled at her mischievously, and Alex's father, who, of all things, silently applauded. The rest stared at her with various degrees of shock and outrage. More than one glanced in the direction of a man Mary knew was the Prince of Wales. Lord, he looked just like the drawings she'd seen of him in print-shop windows: plump with puffy cheeks.

Her theory was confirmed when Alex stopped before him, bowing deeply before saying, "Your highness, may I present my fiancée, Miss Mary Brown?"

There were startled murmurings from the crowd. Mary waited for cries of "Scandalous," and "Outrageous," cries she'd heard once before at Rein's home. But, oddly enough, nothing happened. Indeed, every member of the *ton* looked at the prince, a prince who came forward and said, "Indeed you may, Warrick. Indeed you may."

And as if in a dream, Mary saw the expression on people's faces change. It amazed her how it happened, for one minute they were staring at her and Alex in horror, the next they were . . . smiling?

"Curtsy, Mary," she heard Alex say under his breath.

Yes, of course. And this time as she bent her knee, the

slits on her glittering skirts spreading as she clutched them in her left hand and sank to the ground, she took great care in how she did it. It was a perfect curtsy. Elegant. Graceful, with just the right angle to her head. When she stood again, Alex stared down at her proudly, just before he pulled her into his arms again. And before she could say a word, he kissed her, and the last of her doubts slipped way on the gossamer wings of love. It was real. She was loved. By a lord.

What a curious, crazy, wonderful world.

Epilogue

"That's it," Mary's breathless voice urged. "That's it, Alex. Harder. Harder."

Alex gritted his teeth, doing as she asked, his brow beaded in sweat as he sought to please her.

"There," she said on a sigh. "There. Don't move. Shift to the right a bit. There. There."

Insatiable wench. She never let up. He would die of exhaustion by the time he was fifty-five.

"Here it comes, Alex. Don't stop."

Stop? How could he bloody stop?

"Three, two, one . . ."

And now she was counting. Good lord.

"Hang on."

And then he was sailing . . . flying through the air just as she was, their horses landing almost in unison.

She gave out a laugh of exhalation, Alex glancing over, and for a moment, he nearly forgot to hang on. This, he decided on his own sigh, this was the reason why he tortured himself on a daily basis learning how to ride Sailor. She was delightful in her exuberance. Magnificent in her joy. Lovely in her high spirits, her cheeks glowing a heightened red, her hair tucked up under a jaunty cap. Piles of that hair had still come loose, the result of her impatience to be off and riding and having to wear a riding habit in order to do so.

"Hurrah," she commended, her patina-green eyes highlighted by the copper color of her jacket as she drew her horse down to a trot and then a walk. Alex did the same. "Well done, my lord. Sailor took that magnificently. I don't believe I've ever seen anything as glorious as you and Sailor sailing over that fence."

Alex had. Lord, he had. Right now. She took his breath away, literally, for the way his chest tightened had nothing to do with riding his horse and everything to do with her.

She turned to him, obviously expecting a comment back, and when all he did was stare, she lifted an auburn brow. "What the blazes are you staring at?"

"You."

The other brow lifted, and then her whole face softened as she tipped her head back and laughed. "I thought I had mud on the tip of my nose."

He shook his head. "If you did, it would do nothing to detract from your beauty."

"Ach, go on with you," she said on a laugh. "I'm a mess, I am, and I suspect your pretty words have more to do with wanting to get under my skirts than my being in good looks this morn."

This time it was his turn to laugh, the sound of it causing nearby crickets to go silent. It had dawned a perfect day, yellow-green patches of grass where the sun trickled through the trees sometimes rising with a ghostly steam at the sun's startling touch. It had rained last evening, their horse's hooves squishing the moisture from the ground in rhythmic steps.

"I assure you, my dear," he said. "I have no such designs on your virtue."

"What a corker."

And in a move that would have done Mary's fellow performers proud, Alex jumped down while his horse still moved. Sailor jerked his head up as he did so, almost as if to say, "Again?" And, indeed, Alex often dismounted in this spot, often looked up at Mary as he did now. Often held out his arms and said, "Care to wap with me, my dear?"

A giggle escaped her. "Hmm," she said. "I'm not at all sure I should. I hear the future Duke of Wainridge is rather wicked."

It was his turn to chuckle. "And I hear the future Duchess of Wainridge has something of a reputation herself."

"And what reputation would that be?"

She slid down into his arms, Alex saying tenderly, "That she's an irrepressible hoyden. That she says and does the most outlandish things." He softened his gaze. "That everyone loves her—even her stepdaughter—despite rumors that the two of them despise one another."

She reached up and touched his cheek in a gesture both familiar and poignant for the memories it evoked. "It has not been easy."

"No," he said. "But I knew it would all work out in the end. Society has grown to accept and love you." He kissed her lightly, drew back. "Gabby, too, for she needed someone like you, though I can well understand why she would put you off wanting a child."

"I never said I didn't want a child," she said, placing a finger against her lip. "I said just not right now."

And something in her eyes, something in the way she

looked at him above the shadow of her lashes made him murmur, "What are you trying to say?"

The finger traced a pattern around his lips, then around again. "I'm saying that perhaps, just perhaps, you might be able to change my mind about producing an heir."

His heart stalled like a bird on a current of air. "Mary, are you certain?"

She nodded.

"But what made you change your mind?"

She smiled softly. "A number of things. Being reunited with my mother and realizing how much she loved me. Well, all of us, and how sad it was that in the end, she ended up with none of us by her side. Visiting with my father to try and resolve things and realizing that in his own way, he loved his children, too. Even me. But most of all, being with you."

He lifted a brow. "Being with me?"

"Aye, my love, for watching you with Gabby, seeing how wonderful you are, makes me realize that even if I end up as poor a mother as my own, our children will always, *always* have their father to love them, too."

And above them, a breeze stirred, fluttering leaves to the point that they sounded like a waterfall. A squirrel chattered near them. Insects zipped by them on wings pushed by a wind. Alex noticed none of it. Indeed, all he could do was cup his wife's face, slowly bend down, murmuring just before he kissed her, "Well, if you insist . . ."

But it wasn't nine months later, nor even ten, nor even eleven months later that the sound of Alex's heir rang through Warrick Hall. Alas, the creation of a child took longer than Alex and Mary had expected, much to their delight.

And so it was that the newest heir to the Duke of Wainridge was born, and, indeed, when the Marquis of Warrick pulled back his swaddling (because one must always see for oneself that one's child is, indeed, a boy), he verified that everything was as it should be.

And when the aforementioned marquis ascended to the title of duke many years later, he went down in history not as a tempter of innocents, not as a Wicked Wainridge, but rather, as one who had been himself . . . *tempted.*

Author's Note

The real mistress of the Duke of Clarence was, indeed, an actress. Her name was Dora Jordan, and like my heroine's mother, she bore the duke children, ten of them to be exact. She was also involved before she met the duke, bearing her former lover four children. Alas, she died alone and penniless in France, discarded by the love of her life after he bowed to pressure from his family.

The first equestrian performances were put on by Philip Astley and his wife "Petsy" sometime around 1766. In 1782 Charles Hughes opened a rival establishment which he called the "Royal Circus," which is the first use of the word in that context. The acts were much the same as they are today with juggling, tightrope dancing and, of course, trick-riding.

I hope you enjoyed Alex and Mary's story. As always, my goal is to bring you wacky, zany stories that make you laugh out loud and (hopefully) sigh at the end.

Blessings,
Pamela

About the Author

Bestselling author Pamela Britton blames her zany sense of humor and wacky story ideas on the amount of Fruity Pebbles she consumes. Not wanting to actually have to work for a living, Pamela has enjoyed a variety of odd careers such as modeling, working for race teams—including NASCAR's Winston Cup—and drawing horses for a living.

Over the years, Pamela's novels have garnered numerous awards, including a nomination for Best First Historical Romance by *Romantic Times* Magazine and Best Paranormal Romance by *Affaire de Coeur* Magazine. Pamela's second book, *Enchanted by Your Kisses*, was an Amazon.com bestseller resulting in Pamela having to choose between writing full-time or selling insurance. Difficult decision.

When not imbibing Fruity Pebble milk, Pamela enjoys showing her horse, Peasy, and cheering on her professional rodeo cowboy husband, Michael. The two live on their West Coast ranch (aka: Noah's Ark) along with their daughter, Codi, and a very loud, very obnoxious African Grey Parrot prone to telling her to "Shut up!"

Please visit her at her Web site at: *www.pamelabritton.com* or write to her at: c/o Pamela Britton, P.O. Box 1281, Anderson, CA 96007.

More

Pamela Britton!

Please turn the page

for a preview of

SCANDAL

available in

July 2004.

Prologue

It all began over a dog. Silly as it may seem, the day Charles Reinleigh Drummond Montgomery, sixth earl of Sherborne, flattened the duke of Wroxly's terrier was a dark day indeed.

Never mind that the dog had often been likened to a canine cannibal. And that it had bitten no fewer than ten and five children. And that in recent months a bounty had been placed upon its head: ten shillings (the result of a collection Wroxly Park's staff had gathered) to whoever disposed of the carnivorous pooch. None of that mattered for the dog was loved by the duke, so much so that Rein, who had no preference either way, felt very bad indeed when the thump turned out to be . . . well, not a thump.

"What have you done?" the duke asked as Rein lay the precious Pookey before him.

Rein, who was to think later that he'd never seen a man turn so instantly pale, said, "He ran in front of my phaeton, Uncle." Actually, Rein was reasonably certain the dog's proximity to his carriage had been *no* coincidence, but he kept such theories to himself.

"You ran him over?"

"Actually, it was more of a glancing blow. Very quick, I assur—"

"You ran *over* him," the duke raged, his eyes turning as red as that little speck one saw in the corner of a bovine's eye.

"I'm sorry, Uncle." And Rein truly was, for he was not without compassion. Truth be told, he had rather a fondness for animals, even those that enjoyed the taste of human flesh, like Pookey.

But the duke was pointing to the door now, his finger stabbing the air with so much force, his whole arm vibrated. "Get out."

"Now, Uncle—"

"I refuse to tolerate your presence for a second more," he said with a veritable waterfall of saliva. "You charge from one scandal to another. Indeed, look at you now, a bruise around your eye—"

"It was an accident."

"Long have I considered *you* an accident."

"I say, *that's* rather harsh."

"You are a blight on our family tree. Placing an advertisement offering Windsor Castle for lease," the duke raged.

"You heard about that?" asked Rein, wiping at his cheek.

"Suspending a carriage from Windsor Bridge," his uncle went on, ignoring him.

An engineering marvel, not that Rein had done the mathematical calculations.

"Creating fake stones and tossing them upon your

professor as he walked into Eton's school yard thereby giving him a fit of apoplexy—"

"I never meant to actually *harm* the man—"

"And then getting not only yourself, but my *Freddie* thrown out of Eton, and that after being expelled from Oxford because of that incident with the barmaid—"

"Yes, but that was *years* ago—"

"And then to come here and do—" his uncle's eyes caught on the dog, his expression turning to one of grief. "—this to my precious Pookey."

Which made Rein feel as vile as the wet bottom of a bag filled with rotted apples. "Uncle, I truly am sor—"

"No," the duke shot, "No. I will not listen to another word of your excuses. For eighteen years I have tolerated your presence, but no more. From here on out you shall never set foot at Wroxly Park again."

"But I—"

"Out," the duke roared like a Shakespearean actor. "Out, I say,"

Damned spot, Rein silently added. But he didn't chide the old man for stealing the great player's lines. No. Instead he bowed and exited the scene.

And there it might have ended, but for one thing: Years later Rein became the duke's heir.

About the same time Rein was banished forever more from Wroxly Park, eleven-year-old Anna Brooks was trying very hard to understand where she fit into the world. Born to a captain in the King's Navy, and a gently bred but impoverished seamstress, she was not exactly poor, not exactly orphaned (her mother and father were alive, but often sailed together), but rather the girl in the village whom everyone knew would become a governess, or a missionary, or *something* that involved Anna supporting herself in some humdrum way.

This was a source of constant irritation for Anna who'd been taught by her mother that a woman's life could be far from humdrum. Why, she could even captain a ship (which her mother did upon occasion, when her father's superiors weren't looking). So when she overheard Lavinia Herbert say to Elliot Spencer, a boy whom Anna had developed a *tendre* for, that Anna would do well to enter a convent so that she could begin her life's work early, Anna was outraged. Work in a convent, indeed. She was destined for a far greater purpose in life than tending the gardens at Our Lady of the Fountains Convent. Unlike Lavinia, Anna had a brain.

And so she came up with a plan, and a rather good one at that, she thought. Working day and night she began to construct her greatest creation, something that would prove her brilliance: a ship (though it was more the size of a row boat), for Anna was something of an inventor. But this ship would be lighter, faster and more maneuverable than other ships.

Alas, it didn't turn out quite that way.

Oh, she built the ship. It just looked rather, well, odd. First, it was shaped rather queer; like a fish caught in the throes of a death arc. And the main mast tipped to port. And her sail. Well, Anna was quite convinced window coverings were not meant for sails, even if they did look unique what with the pattern of roses printed upon them.

Still, on the day of the race Anna optimistically stood by her 'boat', she was proud. The thing did, indeed, float, even if it was in the way that flotsam often clotted together on a stagnant lake.

The people of Porthollow, bless their hearts, were not cruel enough to laugh when they saw her creation repining on the sand. Indeed, they called out good luck to each other and smooth sailing as the racers stood by in preparation to launch on that sunny and clear day. Elliot, that youthful object of her secret fantasies, however, suffered no such compassion, Elliot being a boy, and everyone knew how unfeeling a male child could be.

"You'll sink within ten seconds," he predicted from his position next to her.

"I will not," Anna said, fussing with her cloak nervously.

"You will."

But Anna had taken her boat out last eve and so she knew she was relatively safe. Thus, she decided not to argue the point. Instead she flicked her cloak off her shoulders in the manner of a great Naval captain, gave Elliot an arch look, and shoved off.

Things didn't work out quite the way she'd planned.

One, the boat she'd spent so many hours crafting had gotten wet (as boats were supposed to do), the result being that the wood was now water-saturated, thus making it more heavy and the boat—much to Anna's dismay—no longer buoyant.

Two, the pegs she had pounded in to secure the timbers had swelled and worked loose during the night, the result being that the moment she shoved off, she heard a rather startling couple of *pops* followed by an ominous *twang*.

"Hell's bells," she used her father's favorite curse.

She glanced up at Elliot, who had launched his sleek little sloop next to her.

He smirked from his hunched position beneath the main sail.

She closed her eyes.

He started counting.

She was up to her knees at five.

Eight saw her to her waist.

Nine put her up to her shoulders.

And ten? Well, ten was garbled by the water in her ears.

Anna decided she would allow herself to drown.

Alas, Elliot would not let her.

He dived in, coming to her rescue like one of the Titans protecting his ladylove. Anna's keen intellect suddenly reasoned that this was a much better way of gaining his attention, so she held her breath, feeling strong, manly arms swoop her up and pull her to the surface.

"Anna Brooks," he gasped as they surfaced, "you are the veriest fool I've ever seen."

Anna didn't care. Oh, she just didn't care. The feel of Elliot's arms around her. The touch of his body against hers. The scent of his salt-laden coat . . . it made her head swim. She would, she decided as Elliot carried her toward the shore, her 'ship', his sloop, and the concerned cries of the crowd forgotten, remember the moment for as long as she lived.

And, indeed, a half-hour later as she made her way home, wet, embarrassed, bemused, and yet never defeated, Anna did relive the moment. Again and again and again. Elliot had rescued her. He had held her close and—well—while he hadn't kissed her, he might have if she'd played her part a bit better. Things couldn't have gone better.

Hmm. She frowned as she walked up the middle of the lane, perhaps they could have, for she'd have liked to have sailed into the bay next to him, but she hadn't taken into account the weight of the wood once wet, a lapse on her part. And those pegs. She should have compensated for the swelling. For half a heartbeat her mind spun with a mathematical calculation, one that compensated for the weight of the wood and the amount of swelling and the pressure such swelling would cause, Elliot momentarily forgotten, but only a short moment, for a voice penetrated her musings.

"Oh, miss," Anna heard someone say.

Anna hated being interrupted when she was in the middle of a calculation. It was the same feeling she got when she was interrupted reading a book. *Pop.* Out of the story. She looked up, surprised to see Sarah, the maid of all work her parents employed, standing off to the right of the road.

"Been waiting for you, I have."

"Sarah, why are you not in town for the May Day celebrations?"

And for a moment the pretty little maid couldn't speak she was so overcome by emotion.

And Anna knew. She just knew in the way that people know when someone is coming up behind you. The way a person knows bad news is on the horizon by the way a body shivers with cold. The way one senses something ominous has happened, though not exactly how, or what, only that it has happened.

"It is my parents, is it not?"

The maid nodded, her eyes filling with fresh tears.

"I'm so sorry, Miss. So sorry. Their ship went down two weeks ago."

Two weeks ago?

Anna closed her eyes, a pressure building behind them. She tried not to cry. Lord, wasn't that silly? She tried not to cry so Sarah would not feel bad. But she couldn't stop the tears. A grief filled her such as she'd never known before, and would likely never feel again. One so instant and so all encompassing she could only find the strength to utter one word, "No," in a small little voice.

Mama.

Papa.

Gone.

Though Anna was only eleven, though she'd yet to experience life and all its pains and sorrows, she was bright enough and astute enough to realize the blow she'd just been dealt was one that would change her life forever. That nothing, absolutely nothing, would ever be the same again.

And, indeed, it never was.

* * *

Many years later, long after a heartbroken little girl went off to live in London, the poor duke of Wroxly was told that Rein Montgomery was now his heir.

"My heir?" the duke roared.

"Yes, your grace." The man swallowed, watching as the duke's face reddened past his gray hairline.

"Impossible," and his green eyes all but snapped the word at him.

"I'm afraid not."

"I will not allow it."

"You have no choice."

"We could kill him." The duke affirmed, his jowls quivering like a chicken's wattle as he bobbed his head. "Kill him as he killed my Freddie." He nodded for emphasis, the ducal hair, which had never been very prevalent, shaken into streamers that stuck out in the manner of porcupine quills.

"Your grace," the solicitor felt the need to point out. "Your son died in a duel—"

"He would never have involved himself with that woman if his cousin Rein had not expressed interest in her himself."

"Yes, but the fact remains that your son involved himself with a married woman, one whose husband felt understandably cuckolded when your son—"

"My son would never have done something so dishonorable if not for Rein Montgomery," the duke said, his voice rising in volume until he doubled over in a fit of coughing, a cough that had gotten worse since his son's death. When he regained himself, he straightened, saying in a low voice, "I will not have that—" The duke swallowed. "I will not have that wastrel, that instigator, that *killer* inherit my lands, not while my poor Freddie lies in the ground."

At that moment, the solicitor felt almost sorry for the duke, only the glimmer of madness he saw in his grace's eyes caused that pity to turn to concern.

"Something must be done," the duke said.

And, indeed, something was.

Two years later the former earl of Sherborne sat before the duke of Wroxly's solicitor to hear the reading of a Will that promised to make him rich beyond belief. Alas, he didn't want to appear too anxious and so he studied his nails (and admitted he needed a new manicure), barely able to contain himself as he waited for the solicitor to get to the good part, the part where his uncle left him everything.

"As to my heir, Charles Reinleigh Drummond Montgomery—"

At last. Rein perked up.

"—I leave nothing."

Rein blinked. Blinked again. Then said in a low voice, "I beg your pardon?"

"I can, of course," the solicitor read on, "do nothing about those lands that are entailed, however, the rest of my estate—those properties that produce the Wroxly wealth—those I leave in trust—"

In trust?

"Until such a day as a new heir is born, or the title

passes on. Those lands will then revert to the rightful heir, unless—"

And Rein knew he wouldn't like what came next. His hands clutched the arms of the red chair he sat in, his cheek twitching in a spasm he clenched it so hard.

"Unless the current Duke of Wroxly can prove his worth—"

What the blazes did *that* mean?

"—by living on his own for one month's time without aid from friends or family, and without telling a single soul of his plight, and by leaving to do so immediately so as not to alert those friends and family, and so that he is unable to stash certain funds to help him through the process."

Stash funds? What the *blazes* was the solicitor talking about?

"If, and only if," the solicitor read on, "the new Duke of Wroxly succeeds in this endeavor, will he be allowed to inherit the properties mentioned above."

"What the blazes *is* this?" Rein could contain himself no more.

The solicitor looked up, lowering the paper he'd been reading from to a position right above his well-polished cherry desk, the reflection of his nearly bald head a near mirror image on the desk's surface.

"This," the solicitor explained, the glass in his spectacles turning almost white with a glare, "is what the duke came up with to test you."

"Test me?"

The solicitor nodded. "You, your grace, shall live on you own for one month's time without aid from friends or family or servants, and without using a penny of your own wealth, nor telling anyone who you are. You must live by your wits and your wits alone, and if you do not—" The little man tapped the edges of the will on his desk. "—you won't get a farthing from those properties not entailed. In short, your grace, if you fail in this challenge, you will be destroyed both financially and personally."

And all Rein did was stare, his hands fingers clenching tighter and tighter until the fabric caught under his nails.

"Bastard," he hissed.

THE EDITOR'S DIARY

Dear Reader,

Telling the truth isn't easy, but sometimes keeping a secret is even harder. And the consequences can have devastating and sometimes naughty effects, as both Mary Callahan and Lily Holt have discovered in our Warner Forever titles this January.

Amanda Quick says, "**Pamela Britton** writes the kind of wonderfully romantic, sexy, witty historical romances that readers dream of discovering when they go into a bookstore." Well, fear not—your dreams are about to come true with her newest book, **TEMPTED**. Alexander Drumming is certainly no innocent. With a rather colorful reputation behind him as a rake of the highest order, he has vowed to give up his wicked ways. But now he needs a woman—an amazing woman to tame his little hellcat of a daughter. Spirited and intelligent, Mary Callahan is the perfect nursemaid. But her luscious lips and mysterious, bedroom eyes look more like trouble than salvation to Alexander. For Mary is hiding a secret and soon these two people will find themselves on the brink of scandal and will learn the risks of mixing danger and desire . . .

Moving from naughty seductions in Regency England to a childhood sweetheart reunion, we offer **Susan Crandall's THE ROAD HOME**. Karen Robards calls Susan Crandall "an up-and-coming star" and she couldn't be more right. Desperate to make a new start, Lily Holt reluctantly moves back home to Indiana with her teenaged son. But they've barely unpacked their bags when he gets into trouble again. Hoping that a job at the local marina will straighten him out, Lily is shocked to learn his boss is Clay Winters, the man who broke her heart fourteen years ago. Common sense begs her to stay away, but she simply can't resist the broad-shouldered man who can still make her feel like no one else can. Her body aches for him, as it did all those years ago. But as explosive secrets come to light, will he break her heart a second time or help her heal it?

To find out more about Warner Forever, these January titles, and the authors, visit us at www.warnerforever.com.

With warmest wishes,

Karen Kosztolnyik

Karen Kosztolnyik, Senior Editor

P.S. Valentine's Day is coming up so celebrate it with a handful of chocolates and these two Warner Forever titles, guaranteed to make your heart skip a beat. Karen Rose pens a bone-chilling romantic suspense about a serial killer preying on teenaged girls and the widowed cop and his teenaged son's schoolteacher who vow to bring him to justice in **HAVE YOU SEEN HER?**; and Kimberly Raye delivers the funny and sexy story of a woman who trades lessons in the art of sexual fulfillment for a handsome NASCAR driver's insight into the male mind in **KISS ME ONCE, KISS ME TWICE**.